PASS INTERFERENCE

GODS OF THE GRIDIRON: BOOK 3

SHANNA SWENSON

PASS INTERFERENCE
Shanna Swenson

PASS INTERFERENCE is an original work of fiction. Names, characters, places, organizations and incidents either are the product of the author's imagination or are used fictitiously. Any resemblance to actual persons, living or dead, events, businesses, companies, or locales is entirely coincidental.

Copyright © 2020 by Shanna Swenson

Paperback ISBN: 978-1-7329626-7-5

www.shannaswenson.com

For permission requests, write to the author at shannaswen@gmail.com

Edited by Jennifer Soucy

ebook design by: OliviaProDesign

Gods of the Gridiron logo designed by:
Books and Moods Designs

For my baby sister, Katie
*There is **no one** like a sister*
And I thank God everyday that you are mine

POSEIDON- GOD OF THE SEAS

"Hear, Poseidon, ruler of the sea profound, whose liquid grasp begirds the solid ground; who, at the bottom of the stormy main, dark and deep-bosomed holdest they watery reign. Thy awful hand the brazen trident bears, and sea's utmost bound thy will reveres."

—*Orphic Hymn 17 to Poseidon (trans. Taylor) (Greek hymns C3rd B.C. to 2nd A.D.)*

FOREWORD

This book is a fun twist on the classic poor girl meets prince story we've all come to know and love, *Cinderella*.

Paxton Guthrie was inspired by the swoony linebacker, Clay Matthews, formerly #52 for the Packers—We miss you, Matthews!

He's big, blond, and crushes QBs like nobody else...

PROLOGUE

Paxton "Poseidon" Guthrie laughed and patted his teammate's shoulder as they entered the doors of the exclusive gentlemen's club, *RISE*.

It was one of the classiest, most luxurious strip clubs he'd ever been in, and he'd frequented many in his twenty-five years on the planet. Brilliant Chandeliers cascaded from the ceiling and the curtains were gold and black; even the poles were shimmering, along with the masked dancers. Damn, so this was what $5,000 a year membership bought a man, huh?

Quillan Layton seemed to be just as impressed as he smirked over at Pax, his thick brows rising.

It was Monday night, practically their "Friday." They'd been watching game film all day and got out of meetings by four. It had been Pax's idea for a night on the town and who could pass up an opportunity to come to one of the most infamous gentlemen's clubs in Atlanta? Especially when Quil had an invite he'd never cashed in. Plus, he owed Pax big time for the charity event he was doing come Friday night, all because Quil had pussied out on Madi.

They were escorted by one of the hostesses to a table closest to the center stage where a woman in a deep purple and silver wig and matching mask danced on the pole. She had a great body from what he could see. It was covered in thin lace that matched the rest of her "costume." She winked at Quil, and Pax rolled his eyes.

Quil had that broody, broken hero look—the one the ladies just swooned over. Tall, dark, and handsome—or so they'd said. Pax was a sandy blond, blue-eyed California boy with a gold tan and a build as solid as a Ford F-150. He could lift tires as big as Quil without straining. He was a linebacker who crushed quarterbacks for a living. Pax was...*totally* getting passed up by the hot stripper for Quil.

"Dude, what the fuck!" Paxton mumbled under his breath. "Every damn time."

Funny thing was, Quil wasn't even interested...or so it always seemed. And Pax could understand. Quillan's wife died last year and he was now raising a six-year-old little girl alone thanks to her drug addiction.

"Uh, no thank you," Quil answered as the stripper whispered into his ear, running her hand along his jaw then down his chest to his ink-sleeved forearm.

Pax was close enough to hear her say, "Don't worry, stud. I'm clean."

It wouldn't have mattered if she was clean and housed a platinum-coated pussy, Quil wasn't gonna touch a stripper. He hadn't thus far anyway. What made this one any different?

Pax noted her body was covered in tattoos: various flowers, hearts, a pirate, a skull. Her porcelain skin was a paradox of seamless designs running from the wrist of her left arm, diagonally across her back and down her entire right leg. Her nose was pierced with a sexy little diamond that emphasized her button nose and her eyes were big and doe-like, lashes thick.

"C'mon over here and sit on Poseidon's lap, angel. I'll let you release the Kraken if you're a good girl."

She smirked at the challenge before her, turning her attention back to Quil. She moved into his lap, much to his dismay it would seem. She tilted her head quizzically and studied him as if he had a hidden road map in his eyes.

"If he's Poseidon then who are you?" she asked Quillan.

"Oh, he's Hades," Pax answered for him, knowing Quil was a man of few words.

"*Hades*, huh?" That seemed to excite her even more. *Well, damn,* Pax thought.

Pax looked over at Quillan as the stripper began to rock her body against him and checked his watch. He'd give the girl another three minutes before Quil told her to am-scray in typical Hades fashion. The TE didn't mind watching, but he didn't want to participate—not usually, anyway.

As Pax waited, a shot girl came by and took his drink order. Quil ordered a tonic on ice. Just a tonic.

Damn, looks like I'm drinking by myself too, Pax scowled to himself. Pax didn't drink often, but he was craving hard liquor tonight. He was anxious, dreading the shit-show to come—a shit-show his CEO had got him into. He was certain his date on Friday night wouldn't be quite as sexy as the chick seated on his buddy's lap.

"You don't like me, do you, god of darkness?" The exotic—in more ways than one—dancer asked Quil.

She didn't know that Quil wasn't one for small talk. Until one got to know him, he didn't have much to say. Quil was philosophical after all; he got that from both his Spanish and Native American roots.

"Perhaps a kiss will change your mind." She arched a brow.

Before Quillan could protest, the stripper was grabbing his shirt collar and had her tongue down his throat. Pax harrumphed. Damn, what the hell kinda club was this and where was *his* stripper—or was only one assigned per table?

He looked around and motioned to the approaching shooter girl; he thanked her for the drinks and asked for a dance too. She gave him a nod and set their drinks down. Meanwhile, Quil suddenly seemed interested in the stripper now that she'd overpowered him; not that Pax could blame him, she was licking Quil's lips like he was made of chocolate or something. Shit! The lucky S.O.B. And fuck, she had a tongue ring too.

Pax shook his head. *No damn fair.* He was the one who'd wanted to come out tonight and have a good time, but it looked like Quil was the one having the good time.

Quil appeared to come to then, the wicked enchantresses' curse breaking, if only momentarily. He gripped her shoulders and pulled her back some, gaping at her strangely.

"Oh, you suddenly remember you two aren't *alone?* Hi! Yeah, remember me?" Pax smarted, and Quil glanced over at him, looking dazed and confused.

Damn! Again, Pax was blown away. When was the last time he'd been kissed stupid like that? It'd been a long time.

"Yeah, you're buying the drinks too, asshole. I can't believe I'm stuck doing your dirty work Friday night because you aren't man enough to take some stuck-up Atlanta socialite out to dinner. Meanwhile, I'll just sit here and watch you make out with the hot stripper too. Yeah, suck all the fun out of my week, why don't you? Rub it in my face a little more. You're a real dick, you know that?" Pax whined and crossed his arms over his chest.

"Would you excuse us, *señorita?*" Quil gave purple-silver stripper a sweet grin. She leaned into him, sucking his earlobe for a moment before finally hopping off his lap and throwing a business card in her place.

"The name's Obsidian. Give me a call when you're not babysitting 'Whiny' over here, dark god, and I'll give you a *real* show." She blew a kiss to Quil and cocked her head sassily at Pax before turning on her heel and sashaying off.

"Welcome back, earthling," Paxton scoffed as Quil glanced his way, mouth wide in a grin.

"Pax, you're a total buzzkill."

"Me? This was supposed to be *my* night, not yours, damn you!"

"God, you're always only thinking of yourself, *mocoso*." Quil shook his head incredulously.

"*Brat*? Seriously? You wanna go there?"

"Oh, shut up. I got rid of her. Now let's find one for you since you can't have fun without a woman around."

Pax knew he was pouting, but dammit, it wasn't fair. The thoughts of having to go out to dinner with some overstuffed, ugly, rich broad he didn't know just for show was about as appealing as getting a root canal. He realized he'd volunteered and hadn't made a big deal out of it at the time, but Quil had been giving him that puppy dog look and Madi had been so damn persistent; he'd been put into a catch-22.

"I still can't believe I'm doing this for you."

"Oh come off it! You're doing this for the *team*, not just for me."

"Last I remember, *pal*, it was your neck in the noose, not mine."

"Stop acting like you're doing us both a favor here, *amigo*. You don't wanna do it, say the fucking word and I'll—"

"No, I already agreed, and Madi—"

"Then shut the fuck up about it. Go on the damn date, go home, and get over it... *pendejo*."

They sipped their drinks before Quil nudged him and they watched the next masked dancer on stage as she performed in a sexy and gifted way, moving over the pole and floor like she was part of both. These girls weren't just typical strippers; there was advanced choreography to all this. Even the way they walked was different, the songs were different. This club was...well, just different. And in a good way, too.

"I would say 'Gracias,' but you haven't done anything yet," Quil teased him.

"Yeah, yeah! You're just upset that I scared off tongue-ring girl."

"You would be too if she'd kissed *you* like that," Quillan scoffed.

"Is that black heart of yours softening, Hades?" Pax feigned shock.

"You know, Pax, as surprised as you'd be with my answer, there are things about married life that I *do* miss... and not just the sex." Quil leaned back in his chair and looked over at him.

"Yeah, well, you go right ahead, man. I don't want nothing to do with it. Brett and Trav are whipped, like totally and completely, and just wait til those babies get here. It'll be even worse."

Quil snorted. "Oh? You think so, huh? Let me tell you a little secret, *playboy*. When you hold the *niño* that you created in your arms for the first time, there's *nothing* in the world that even comes close. Not even a hot stripper with a tongue ring French-kissing you." Quil sighed heavily. "Remember I told you that!"

The man had to be crazy. As a scantily clad stripper in a red mask walked by and winked, Pax admired her tight body; he knew Quil'd just been too long without a woman.

Nothing beat the single life, nothing beat the quiet, nothing beat the freedom of being "unchained."

And *nothing* would ever lead him to think otherwise!

CHAPTER ONE

"You're a good sport, Pax," the lovely Madison McFadden smiled over at him and kissed his cheek. Madi was the CEO and VP of the team Paxton played for, the Atlanta Gladiators, and she was also his friend, as well as the wife of his QB, the infamous Zeus, Brett "Brickhouse" McFadden.

Paxton "Poseidon" Guthrie had played for the Gladiators for the last three—going on four—years now. He was an outside linebacker and loved his defense, getting to play alongside the legendary cornerback from San Antonio, Lincoln "Lazarus" Porter.

Pax was a California native with a penchant—and reputation—for crushing QBs, as well as being a hippie surfer—which he was cool with because he *was*. His mom was a naturalist and a vegan, and Pax had followed in her footsteps.

Tonight, his reputation would precede him. He'd gotten roped into doing this stupid date to help raise money for the Atlanta Children's Hospital in their annual charity auction. All week, women (and men) were able to donate money and have their names entered for a chance to win the prize. The prize they were auctioning off? A date with Paxton Guthrie. The men got a date with one of the cheerleaders. Not only was Pax single, he was also apparently a hot commodity with the ladies. As they pulled up in the limo, women practically swarmed it.

"Damn, look at all the eligible women of Atlanta. Hell-ooo, ladies," Pax cooed and gazed at the mob of women of various races, sizes, and ages all there to see who the lucky winner for tonight's once-in-a-lifetime happy hour with him.

"Now, Pax. Remember, no sex, no kissing—just good, old-fash-ioned fun. Think of this as pre-pubescent middle school."

"Seriously, Madi? Would I disappoint you? I'll be your golden boy."

Madi's blonde brow went up, not trusting him as far as she could throw him—which wouldn't be far at all. "I know you're young and this lady might—"

"Yes, mom." He rolled his eyes. "C'mon. It's a couple hours. How much trouble could I get into in that time frame? Wait. Don't answer that." Madi looked miffed when he smiled playfully. "Hey, I'm not Travis."

"Travis is a saint now that he's with Skyla. It's not your place to replace his bad boy-ness, just remember that."

"Did you just make up a word?"

"All words are made up," she smirked. "But seriously, you're sexless tonight. Ya got me? The last thing this organization needs is bad publicity or a sexual harassment lawsuit on our hands while we're soaring like we are right now."

"I'm a heavy supporter of women's rights as you *well* know, Mrs. McFadden." He gave her a big boyish grin, and she leaned back in to hug him.

"Thanks for doing this."

"Thank me tomorrow, Mad. Let's go rip this Band-Aid off."

Pax was simply eager to see who his date was, get it over with, and be ready for his game against Tennessee on Sunday night. It was the second weekend in October, and they'd won all four games they'd played thus far—week three had been their bye week. The

Gods of the Gridiron had their eyes on the Super Bowl this year, and they aimed to get there.

He got out of the black limo first, adjusting his turquoise blue Tommy Bahama button-down shirt—the one he'd specifically chosen to highlight his bright blue eyes—and his slacks before turning to the flashing cameras and giving a bright smile. He then turned to assist his boss from the car. She looked stunning as always in a flattering crimson pants suit, perfect for her tall, athletic figure with strappy gold heels that Pax thought were sexy. Her blonde hair was pinned back and her lips painted red to match her outfit. He took her hand and tucked it into his arm as they walked the red carpet to the entrance of the arena.

So many participants had entered, they'd had to change venues, Madi told him earlier. The auction and drive had garnered lots of interest for the hospital and their team, and Pax knew it was because they'd been doing so well this year. And maybe it had to do with him. He'd been compared to Thor all week; he'd take that. Being paralleled to the Australian heartthrob, Chris Hemsworth, was a compliment he'd take over and over again.

Mics were shoved at them, and the crowd roared in the background. Numerous questions were flung their way, and Madi slowed her walk so that Pax could answer a couple. She nudged him with her elbow, as if to say, "Go ahead. We have a minute or so."

"Mr. Guthrie, are you excited about your mystery date tonight?"

"Yes, I am. It's my pleasure to serve our fine city, and if that means taking some time to enjoy the view," he paused and looked over to a sexy little brunette next to the reporter, winking dramatically. She swooned, and the crowd went wild again. "And indulge one of them with my charms, then I'm the man for the job."

Another reporter with a mic and camera man shoved in next to the one Pax was talking to. "So, Poseidon, your fury has only started to be unleashed. You've already gotten three sacks, fifteen tackles, two forced fumbles, and a pass defended this season. What are you hoping to accomplish this weekend in Nashville?"

"Let's just say, I'll be releasing the *Kraken* for sure." He laughed, and Madi tugged on his elbow subtly, signaling for them to continue walking.

They took a few more questions. Madi got a couple in regards to the organization and her husband, including, "Is his bedroom etiquette what's honed Zeus's thunderbolt throwing skills?"

To which she teasingly replied with, "I tell you what: Zeus has never been more accurate."

The crowd loved that one; even Pax was shocked when Madi smirked up at him. *Newlyweds!*

Neither Madi and Brett, nor Travis and Skyla, had gone public with their pregnancies. It was a team secret, and Pax liked being a keeper of ones so big. The ladies wanted to at least get through their first trimesters, for obvious reasons.

The throng of ladies was dense as Madi and Paxton moved into the building and toward the podium set up on a stage. Pax continued to be floored. Where had all these lovely women been hiding? He would be sure to check his Instagram later so he could DM a couple of them who were probably tagging his account with pictures right that moment for future dates. He winked at a gorgeous African goddess to his left and grinned seductively at a redhead to his right.

He sincerely hoped his date wasn't the highly unattractive lady standing a few feet from the podium. If so, he was just gonna have to fake it til he made it—and possibly get drunk to get through this. He would be polite no matter what, he knew, but threw some good vibes up into the universe that the view he'd have all night wouldn't be that of her.

He reminded himself to be cordial, even if his date wasn't the hottest chick in the room. He was a nice guy. He wasn't like Travis. Yeah, Pax was a little cocky—hell, he'd sacked a shit ton of quarterbacks recently and had received the title of Poseidon for God's sake. Of course he was somewhat self-assured; how could he not be? But he was also a lover of nature, the ocean, meditation, and sunsets. He had a more artistic, more romantic side than most of his teammates...or so he thought, anyway. He was more in touch with his feminine side and the guys always made fun of him for eating his "rabbit food" and drinking "fermented shit." He was constantly reminding them that beer and booze were fermented too. But he knew it didn't matter.

Paxton Guthrie was confident in his sexuality and in himself. Their words and badgering didn't bother him. He loved his teammates, and they loved him. And even if he had no intentions of getting married—*ever*—he loved their ladies, too. They were all like family and, since Hunter Thomas had passed, Pax realized just how short life was.

He smiled at Madi as he escorted her up the steps and to the podium. The room was doused in crimson and gold, the Gladiators logo, as well as that of Atlanta Children's Hospital—ACH.

Madi shushed the crowd with her hands and laughed heartily. She was so good with the media and so professional. "Down, girls." That got a laugh out of the camera crew, the organizers, and the crowd. Pax played his part with a shrug. "I want to thank you all for your support of a great cause. You've raised two million dollars in a week. That's a lot of money. All so you can have a chance with the studly Poseidon here." Cheers, applause, and screams echoed in the crowd; it was deafening. Madi shushed them down again with a laugh. "Paxton Guthrie is quite a catch, I have to say." Madi winked over at him, and he dramatically feigned a blush and shyness. "And here in a minute, we're gonna draw the name of the lucky lady who'll get to spend the next two hours with him, have dinner with him at The Palms, and get to know what makes Poseidon salty and sweet," Madi purred. Pax almost rolled his eyes but smiled instead as she made her way back to his side.

"Way to pump me up, boss," he whispered as she pulled him in for a hug.

"You're up, merman."

He kissed her cheek and released her, puffing his chest out as he walked toward the podium.

He grinned to the audience and when he got to the mic, the crowd shelved it immediately. He decided to bring his charm out. "Hello, ladies." Swoons answered him, and he laughed heartily. "Seriously though, I'm floored at the responses this week. I just want to thank you for your charitable donations. I see the women of Atlanta love their Gladiators." Cheers and applause answered him. "And their children's hospital. I'm looking forward to taking the lucky winner out and making her feel like a goddess." Hoots and cat calls. Pax grinned even as Madi warned him with her eyes to "watch it," as he returned to her side.

"Just remember this goddess won't be getting your lips or your manhood tonight," she whispered.

"Yes, ma'am." He mimicked a southern drawl, and Madi rolled her eyes.

The homely woman took the podium, and Pax secretly hoped she wouldn't be part of the drawing. She, too, thanked everyone and began pulling a big box over with the names, assumedly.

When she called out the name, "Rebecca Ryan," Pax held his breath, but no one answered. Ms. Vulture quieted the crowd and said the name again. Nothing. Pax looked around then down at Madison, who shrugged. Again, Rebecca Ryan was called and finally a sheepish little voice returned, "I'm here."

Pax's gaze was drawn to the woman now moving slowly down the red-carpet runner below. She had flawless, porcelain skin, black-framed glasses, and dark ribbons of hair framing a round face. But it was her body that he couldn't take his eyes off of. She was petite but built— like a petite, little brick dollhouse. She had curvy hips and good-sized breasts whose cleavage teased the V-neckline of a black, silk dress that came to her knees. Her legs were lean and muscular, and she wore a pair of fuck-me heels. *Damn! This is my date?*

The ugly woman took Rebecca's hands as she approached and congratulated her. Rebecca's cheeks reddened, and Pax felt somewhat humbled.

She had that whole sexy-librarian-closet-sex-freak vibe going on. Pax was very pleased.

"Well, so far so good, right?" Madi whispered.

"Yeah, *about* that no sex thing?" Pax teased, and Madi elbowed his side again.

"I will chop your man parts off if you even think—"

"Just kidding, mama bear. Relax."

"Mr. Guthrie, would you like to come meet your date for the evening?" Ms. Vulture asked, and Pax nodded eagerly.

"*Would* I? Look at this stunning goddess." He approached and beckoned to Rebecca's hands. She gaped up at him, her lips opening in an O around her lip gloss. He smiled big. "Ladies, I've made her speechless already. It's gonna be a long night." He smirked, and she gulped. Finally, she looked down to his hands, comprehending that he wanted to hold them, and slowly brought them up, placing the small, delicate phalanges in his much, much bigger ones.

Pax felt a little jolt spike through him and heard Rebecca gasp softly. He looked into her eyes.

Wow, they were so green, like the greenest-green, hazel with specks of yellow and gold; deep, guarded, an enigma of secrets he longed to explore.

Soon, he heard laughter, and Ms. Vulture was saying, "Earth." She looked annoyed.

Pax smirked. "I'm now the one speechless," he said to the laughing audience then looked back at Rebecca. "I'm Pax, it's a pleasure."

"Rebecca." She, again, looked like she would die from the mortification. Pax couldn't wait to get her away from the crowd so he could tap into that quiet side and learn more about her.

Vulture lady thanked Rebecca for her donations and handed the mic off to Paxton, who seemed to handle the public much easier than little Ms. Introvert Becca next to him. "Well, I don't know about you guys, but I've got a hot date to go on so thanks for everything and Go Gladiators."

Madi waved them toward her amidst the deafening crowd as mics and cameras were shoved back toward them. Pax's hand settled against Rebecca's smooth, bare back, making his dick jerk to life. *Down boy, you gotta play it soft tonight. No fun for you,* Pax told himself.

Despite what he was telling Quil just Monday night about the ladies, it wasn't entirely true. He'd been having issues lately. Not with women or dates or strip clubs, but getting erections. The last time he'd had sex, like a month ago, he'd only pretended to finish. The hot blonde with fake breasts and long fingernails hadn't been doing it for him, and he just couldn't continue to abide it. He figured he'd just been tired or overworked from practice and stress of the season, Hunter's death, the pressures of life. He'd made up all these excuses for his twenty-five-year-old body to not respond to a beautiful woman, but deep down, he knew he just wasn't impressed with fakeness any longer.

Women had been throwing themselves at him for years, and he'd graciously taken what had been offered—well not *all* that had been offered. But now he was stuck in a rut. He loved women—looking at them, hearing their voices—but he was bored.

And as he looked shy, petite Rebecca over, he quickly saw that there was nothing boring about her. She looked new and fresh; nothing superficial. Light makeup, real boobs, no cosmetic surgical procedures. Just a real, genuine woman... Yeah *not!* She'd donated a huge chunk of money for a date with him—*Damn, Pax, your radar on people* sucks!

Madison turned and smiled at Rebecca, introducing herself as they were ushered to yet another limo sitting out back of the building; she opened the car door. "Madison McFadden, thank you for your support."

"It's an honor, Mrs. McFadden."

Madi just deepened her smile and turned to Pax. "Have fun, you two. Pax, call me later." Paxton opened his palm, signaling for Rebecca to get in first, and she slid in.

"Keep your dick in your pants tonight, Pax. I'm not *fuckin'* kiddin'," Madi whisper-growled in his ear as she kissed his cheek.

Pax's brows went up, Madi wasn't one for swearing, so he knew she was dead serious. If she knew his little problem, she would know there was no need to worry. But he nodded diligently anyway and stepped into the limo to enjoy his hot date for the evening, Rebecca.

CHAPTER TWO

Rebecca Ryan attempted to swallow down her nervousness as dream-boat Paxton Guthrie slid into the limo beside her, and the car began to move. Her sister, Veda, had been the one to encourage this, and now she was sure she would faint as her celebrity crush settled next to her and gave her a big grin.

God, he was even more attractive in person than on the telly—and so much bigger. At six-four, two-sixty, he was a powerhouse—built like a tank. Hell, he ate QBs for breakfast. What had she expected? What she *hadn't* expected was how soft his features were and how beautiful he was without the serious expression he wore on game day; of course she'd seen him smiling during interviews and seen pictures of him out of uniform—more jovial when he wasn't primed to destroy a player. But this—this was even better than what she could've dreamed.

His deep blue eyes assessed her, not as if she were being held helplessly under a microscope, but in a way that had her body tingling. Did he like what he saw? She ran her eyes back over his face, admiring his bone structure. He had the face of a warrior with a strong square jaw and high cheekbones, a long, straight nose that had possibly been broken a time or two. His lips were plump and enticing and his shoulder-length blond hair—usually worn down on game days—was back in a ponytail, making him look regal and from a simpler time. His neck was thick and showed his strength as he swallowed.

"You're quiet even in private," he said with a brief laugh.

"Sorry, I—I'm just star-struck is all."

"Well, I promise I do the same things all people do. I binge-watch Netflix and occasionally eat ice cream when doing so. Oh, and I also play video games."

Rebecca's brows went up in surprise. He seemed like he wouldn't even own a TV. He appeared too primal for life's nonsense, but she reminded herself he wasn't a hero from one of her books or Jamie from *Outlander*, so she came back to reality. "And you like to surf?"

"I do. But I haven't surfed since May when I was back home during the off-season."

Rebecca gave him an understanding smile.

"So you must be a big fan, huh?"

Big fan was an understatement; she was *obsessed* with him. She'd never even watched football until she'd seen him on TV one Sunday last year while Veda was watching a game. He reminded her of Thor and Jamie Fraser rolled into one fine hunk of a man. Her breath had stilled when he'd started talking, his deep voice as smooth as silk. Veda had teased her and said, "Looks like you'll be watching football with me finally, huh?" And Rebecca had, the entire game, looking for Number 52. Boy, was he an impressive specimen of a man when he was on the hunt. She'd been completely entranced—as she was now —by the magnitude of his overwhelming presence.

When Veda had seen the ad earlier this week, she'd pushed Rebecca to donate.

"We don't have that kind of money, Vey!"

"Becca, you don't need tons of money. We'll donate a vast number of pennies, and you'll get an entry for each one."

And so they had; it'd really been a clever idea. Rebecca had begrudgingly taken out one-hundred-dollars from her savings, reminding her twin that amount of money could buy so much, but Veda hadn't taken no for an answer. It was all Becca could afford under the circumstances since she, her mom, and her sister were on a tight budget. It didn't help their cause that Veda was constantly getting fired for her sassy mouth and flippant behavior...as well as her outrageous sense of style.

$100 equated to 10,000 pennies for 10,000 entries, of which Becca was sure was cheating. But apparently, she'd been the only one who'd done so. Much to her shock and amazement, it was completely "within the contest guidelines" and "smart," the lady who'd taken her donation had said. The donation was also for a good cause, and Becca and Veda volunteered weekly at the children's hospital. They'd lost their sister to Non-Hodgkin's lymphoma just as they might lose their mother to the same disease, if these last treatments didn't work.

Rebecca noticed Mr. Drop-Dead-Gorgeous looking at her expectantly, and she blushed, realizing she hadn't answered his question about being a fan. She tended to be spacey at times, her mind going to all kinds of thoughts randomly. "Oh, I apologize. Yes, I am a big fan. I mean, I wasn't until last year. But I've watched you ever since."

"*Me*, huh? And what about the games?" His brows rose, and she could have all out swooned over how sexy he was.

"Pardon?" Rebecca gave him a funny look. What was he asking?

"You said you watch *me*, not my games," he smirked.

"Well, no. I mean, yes. I mean—" *Jesus, Mary and Joseph*, how was she ever going to get through this night? She couldn't even have a conversation with the man without stumbling all over herself. *This was a bad idea*, she told herself for the millionth time.

Paxton gave a robust laugh. "Becca, I'm only kidding. I'm flattered, honestly." His hand came to rest on her own, and her heart literally leapt into her throat. *Great, now I'm gonna choke on my own heart!* "I *can* call you Becca, right?"

She nodded, gulped and stammered with, "Of-of course. Everyone else does."

"I like your dress."

He looked down and so did Becca, feeling completely exposed as her milky-white breasts threatened to spill out of Veda's ridiculously tight V-neck dress. Her thighs were also more uncovered than was typical for her.

She felt completely self-conscious; her fair, almost ghostly, complexion was stark white in comparison to his perfectly sun-kissed skin. She gulped and attempted to readjust the material in a vain effort. Her tits were apparently not gonna be sharing the fabric with the rest of her body. Of *course* he liked the dress!

"What do you do for a living, Rebecca?"

It took her a minute to regain her composure. After all, men didn't usually look at her the way Paxton was right now, and she didn't usually have normal conversations with the ones she'd met in the past. She was a dorky historian who attracted other dorky historians.

"I, uh, I'm a historian and tour guide at the Atlanta Museum of Natural History."

"Oh wow, that's cool. History's fun."

"Fun? History's fascinating, awe-inspiring, and incredibly influential for those that study it. There's much we can learn from it; it foretells the future and forewarns of repetition, if only people would pay more attention. History, from what I've gathered, is cyclical; it tends to come full circle again and again. There's an entire socio-philosophical theory about it and can be traced all the way back to ancient times..."

Becca knew she wasn't the only one to come to such conclusions, but felt her cheeks heat as Pax smirked over at her. She realized she'd lost him somewhere during her socio-philosophic babble. She tended to get tunnel-vision when she spoke of her work.

"Any favorite time frames?" Paxton asked after a moment.

"All of them!" she spat out passionately, getting a hearty chuckle out of Pax. "Sorry, I, uh—"

"No, I asked. Tell me." He adjusted in the seat, turning his body toward hers. She had his full attention now.

Oh lord! The last thing she wanted was to get wrapped up in talking about her career; they'd be in the limo all night while she beguiled him with stories of Sacagawea, the Battle of Gettysburg, and life on the Nile River during the reign of Nefertiti.

Veda's words echoed through Becca's head then, "And don't you *dare* talk history. You'll have him passed out asleep in thirty minutes or less. You're going on a *date*, not narrating a bedtime story!"

"Another time, perhaps." She looked down, fiddling with her hands.

His blond brows arched. *Oh!* Right; there wouldn't be another time.

"I, uh, I love all history honestly—from ancient Egypt to the Wright Brothers. But I'm incredibly awed by the Celts and their traditions and lifestyle. I'm Irish so…" she trailed off. Not like he cared where her ancestors came from.

"That's cool." Ugh, it was the answer most people gave when she got passionate about her own genealogy, too. *Dammit, Becca, you're blowing this!* "Celtic, huh? I can see that in your hair and skin tone… and your emerald-green eyes."

She blushed. If she had to guess his heritage, she would say he had some Dutch in there somewhere or Welsh. That tanned skin…

"I'm not sure of my ancestry." He seemed to answer her unspoken question. "I was adopted."

Rebecca's jaw dropped. She hadn't expected that. Nor that he would admit to it. Was that *public* knowledge?

"You're definitely European, for sure," she quipped, her mind stating the first thing that came to it.

"Or from Antarctica." He looked up thoughtfully, his big palm cupping his perfectly square jaw, and Becca grinned. Paxton laughed and patted her hand. "I'm just messin' around. I've thought about doing that whole DNA ancestry thing. It seems kinda neat."

Becca nodded, afraid to voice anymore thoughts on the matter— afraid to screw this date up any more than she already had. Before she could form another thought, he was asking more questions.

"So what do you do for fun?"

Fun? *What's that,* she started to ask, but decided not to get into talks of her chaotic life. "I don't have much free time."

"Oh? You gotta play as much as you work. Don't you know the quote?"

Her mind was running through all kinds of ideas for how this man might 'play,' but she shoved them out. "I, uh, I like to read, obviously..." *History geek!* "I, too, watch Netflix on occasion, and I can play the flute."

"You know, I never learned an instrument. Embarrassing, right?"

What was embarrassing about that? He was a powerful athlete. He ran after quarterbacks and could stand upright on a surf board; that was a feat unto itself. She had no words. Paxton simply looked down, grinning.

"What do you watch on Netflix? Let me guess... *Lost in Space?*" She frowned. "No? How about *The Witcher?*"

She shook her head. "I loved *Peaky Blinders, Knightfall,* and of course, *Outlander.* I haven't seen the others, but they're in my list." She confessed.

"Should've known. Celtic roots and all." He opened his palms out. "I haven't started *Outlander* yet. But it seems I watch more Netflix than you." He feigned a guilty look, and she giggled. "Oh, wow."

"What?"

"You have the sexiest little laugh."

Her eyes hit his. Had he just called her *sexy?* No, he said her laugh...

"Sorry. I, uh..." He looked away as if he were uncomfortable then looked back at her, quickly shelving it. "You like The Palms?"

"Oh, I-I uh, I've never been."

With the amount of medical bills owed to the hospital for Mam's treatments, Becca barely got by with a weekly grocery budget, let alone eating out. It wasn't a luxury she nor Veda afforded.

"Well, you're in for a treat then."

She felt her cheeks flush, unable to form a response.

"So, if I were to come to The Museum of Natural History, could I get a 'personal' tour?" His grin made her insides flutter, and the look in his eyes gave her the impression that he wanted to tour more than the museum exhibits. All the "personal" things she wanted to do to him, with him... *Focus, Becca! Focus!*

"Uh, of course, I—I could arrange something."

"I'd really like that." His hand moved gently over the back of hers, and she visibly shivered. How could the touch of a man built to destroy be so soft? "Do you have family here?"

Becca nodded, for her lungs were frozen by his touch; unable to draw air in, completely in awe of his beauty.

"That's nice. I wish I did."

"Your mom is back in Hawaii?" Oh good, her voice had been recovered; she wouldn't need to go digging through Lost and Found.

He nodded his head. "Yeah, just moved back from California—Huntington Beach, aka Surf City, USA—where I was raised. My mother was born in Hawaii, but we moved from Oahu to California when I was nine. I was actually born in Cali." He looked down bashfully. "My parents divorced not long after that. My father apparently made a new family in Missouri. I hadn't seen nor heard from him in over a decade, then year before last he attempted to reach out to me. It's true what they say about people coming out of the woodwork when you come into wealth..." Paxton trailed off, and Becca found herself gaping—not only at the sadness of the man before her, but at the awe that he had opened up to her about something so intimate. "Sorry," he quipped with a smirk. "On the next episode of *Lifestyles of the Rich and Famous*, Paxton Guthrie will be talking about his dog, *Ol' Yeller*," Paxton scoffed sarcastically.

"I'm sorry, Paxton," was all Rebecca could say at that moment.

She wouldn't get into her pathetically-sad life with him. He'd end up simply leaving her in the limo and hitching a ride to the nearest bar if she did.

"No, *I'm* sorry. You're just really easy to talk to." His eyes pierced hers again, and she realized she was seeing a side of him that no one else got to. Why was he telling her all this? She'd barely spoken ten words; how was she easy to talk to? She *sucked* at talking to people she didn't know, unless it came to what she was passionate about. Then one couldn't shut her up. "Hey, this is supposed to be fun, right?" That big sexy smile of his came back.

She nodded with a sly smile herself.

The limo came to a halt at that moment—perfect timing—and once again Becca's heart raced. Pax took her hand and assisted her after he'd gotten out of the vehicle.

The Palms was extravagant, even from the outside, and Rebecca couldn't fathom the cost of the food within. A month's worth of groceries would be gone in an instant. Wasteful, that's what it was.

They were immediately sat when Pax came through the door, her arm tucked through his. Rebecca took in the elegant restaurant, boasting gold embellishments, marble-tiled floors, and chandeliers. It smelled of old money and the air seemed stuffy, like she couldn't take a deep breath in.

They were led to a private table set up on the deck overlooking the Chattahoochee River with a big window. *Oh, good*; at least there was that.

Pax helped her to a chair before the maître d' placed a napkin in her lap and handed her a menu. There were no prices listed; that *had* to mean it was astronomical.

Becca smiled over at Pax as he asked her if she was a wine drinker and whether she preferred white or red. She didn't much care since she didn't drink often. Wine was another unaffordable luxury. She chose white, and Pax ordered a bottle of something French she'd probably not be able to repeat if asked.

She browsed the menu, seeing numerous French words that she

was vaguely familiar with. She wouldn't be picky. If he wanted to order for her, that was fine. She was here to see him, not to eat, and didn't even know if she *could* eat as her stomach twisted into knots.

"The ceviche is to die for. Let's have one of those, Sven," Pax stated once the waiter had presented the wine and poured them a glass.

Sven nodded and walked away.

"See anything that strikes your fancy, m'lady?"

Becca couldn't even pronounce half of the menu, but wasn't inclined to admit it. It had been too long since she'd taken Latin, and Irish had obviously come easy; not French. "Any suggestions?"

"The halibut cheeks are exquisite, if you like fish."

"I love fish. A filet works, too." What the heck were halibut cheeks? She'd never had them but bet they were prime dollar. Not like it mattered to *him* though, she remembered. She didn't miss the way Pax wrinkled his nose; she frowned. "You don't like," Becca talked as she read, "Kobe beef?" Oh *shit*! Of course it was a Kobe beef filet! *Never mind, I'll do the halibut*, she thought.

"I'm pescatarian." *Pesce meant fish, right?* "I don't eat poultry or meat."

Becca nodded. How did a man get as big as he was by only eating fish and vegetables? Her curiosity got the better of her. "Do you eat eggs?"

He nodded, "And milk and cheese. Although not much. They're treats."

Then she, personally, *treated* herself a lot.

"I know what you're thinking, but my mom was a vegetarian, and it just stuck with me. I've never even taken a bite of steak or chicken."

Rebecca found herself gaping again. How did one live without sampling the simple, most delicious things in life?

"You keep dropping your jaw like that, Ms. Ryan, and I'll be compelled to stick something unspeakable into that beautiful mouth of yours." His grin was devious, and butterflies filled Rebecca's belly, her lower half tingling. *Good lord!*

Becca hadn't ever had a man speak to her that way and wasn't sure whether to be turned on or appalled. Her sister, on the other hand, would pull him to the closest bathroom and have him make good on that promise; Becca wasn't her sister, though. She immediately closed her mouth and looked down at the pristine white napkin in her lap.

Pax cleared his throat when Sven returned with the ceviche—whatever the heck that was—and Becca chose to stick to fish. She didn't want to repulse him by ordering a steak, although he insisted she get whatever she wanted. All the while, she couldn't get the image of her lips wrapping around his hard member out of her head. Her cheeks pinkened when he brought his wine glass up and toasted her.

"Cheers."

"Slàinte mhaith," Becca answered.

"Here's to history. May we always learn from it and do better in the future."

Becca grinned big at that; she always found herself saying roughly the same statement. "To history. And to you, Mr. Guthrie, and ACH for making a difference."

Pax nodded, and they drank the wine that tasted smoother and more amazing than any she'd ever had; she even moaned as she pulled the glass away. "Wow, that's delicious." And she wasn't much of a wine fan to begin with.

"It's a good year," he stated and motioned to the ceviche. "Try this. You like sushi, right?"

"Are you kidding? I love sushi." But she quickly noted as the flavors of lime, shrimp, fish, cilantro and avocado ran across her tongue, that this was so much better. "Yum."

"Right? It's one of my favorites."

"Mmm, this could turn me pescatarian, for sure."

"Join the club, baby, I'll show you the dark side." He winked, and she tried not to focus too much on the fact that he'd just called her baby. "Just wait until you try this fish coming, I might just make a believer out of you tonight."

His enthusiasm was infectious, and she found herself relaxing with him.

Paxton's broad frame filled his shirt out so nicely, the fabric stretching tight across his massive chest. Blond hair peeked out of the top two buttons of the button-down, tempting her. He'd rolled the sleeves of his blue shirt up and appeared to be comfortable with her, in turn; she couldn't help but notice the hair covering his tanned forearms, bleached white from the sun.

Becca began asking him questions, about the team, about his job, about football, and he answered them in kind as they dined on a salad set before them. He was excited for Sunday's game against the Titans and stated his aspirations for the Super Bowl; she could immediately see he was passionate about his fellow teammates and the sport itself, which excited her too.

"I'll bring you to the complex one day and let you meet the rest of the team, if you want," he said it more as a question, and it made her heart pound in her chest.

"Really? You'd do that?"

"Sure, why not? You're a big fan, right?"

She looked down, embarrassment painting her cheeks at the thoughts of the big Fathead in her room of him in his Poseidon pose, looking all the world like a sexy Greek god. "Well, I'm a big fan of Paxton Guthrie."

He arched a brow. "Mmm, so you've said before. I bet you got a wall of my face in your room, don't cha, sweetness? I'm the last thing you see at night before you go to bed and the first thing you see when your beautiful head rises."

She wouldn't confirm nor deny the allegations; his own head was big enough already. "I'll never tell."

"Then I guess I'll just have to find out for myself then."

The challenge in his eyes was unmistakable, and Becca didn't know how to react. She'd never really been pursued by a man before, save for a professor in college that had turned out to be a creeper and the guy at the museum who'd taken her out for coffee a couple times, always came in for tours but stood in the back now. Again, another creeper. Why did she attract weirdos? *Oh, because I am one.*

Pax cleared his throat again and blushed. "So...you from here, Becca?"

She internally squealed as he continued to call her by her nickname and nodded. "Sorta. I'm a transplant. I'm originally from Ireland, but a Georgia peach now. Since I was eight."

"Mmm, a peach indeed." He winked. She could get used to getting flirted with by this stud; it was as if she were dreaming. "Where do you live?"

"I'm not telling you! You might come stalk me," she teased.

He laughed as she'd hoped he would. "Cautious. I respect that."

"I live in an apartment downtown with my mother and sister," she admitted.

"Three girls under one roof. I bet that gets interesting." His expression was one of surprise.

Indeed, it did. Rebecca nodded. "It's entertaining, to say the least." She shrugged. "What about you?"

"Oh, I have a house not far from here. I just bought it last year. It's swanky. So if you ever need privacy, hit me up. It's more square feet than I'll need in three lifetimes."

She laughed. *Fat chance at that!* She'd never see him again after tonight. They both knew that.

"So, three girls under one roof..." he said again as if that prospect was unbelievable to him.

Rebecca looked down. "Yeah, my mom has lymphoma, and my sister and I take care of her."

"I'm sorry to hear that."

"Thank you. One of us is always there with her. It's usually my sister in the daytime and me at night, due to my work hours. Every time we think she's hurdled the bar, another setback comes along."

He reached his hand out and took hers. "That's tough. I'm sorry."

Tough? He didn't know the meaning of tough. After her young sister's death, chaos had erupted. He only thought *he* was tough. If he had to live a day in her shoes...

Rebecca pulled her hand away and frowned, thinking about how inconsequential her life was to the mighty Poseidon.

Just then their entrees came, and she marveled over the delicacy in front of her. The hearty portion of perfectly pan-seared filet of fish, the al-dente asparagus and couscous, the lemon twist and garnish of parsley. It was too pretty to eat and more expensive than any meal she'd ever had. It seemed so frivolous and profligate, while her mother and sister were probably having Hamburger Helper back home. Why in God's name was she here?

She'd be sure to take a to-go box home so Mam could have a taste of it. But then how tacky would that look to Big Shot Paxton Guthrie? Never mind...

She felt his hand on hers again and looked up into his crystal, sky-blue eyes—eyes holding such beauty, so open. "Did I say something to upset you?" He furrowed his brows.

Becca quickly shook her head and tried to smile, truly grateful for this once-in-a-lifetime opportunity to be here with him in such an opulent setting.

"I gotta ask: what made you enter the raffle for this date? How'd you hear about it?"

Oh great, Pax. Open Pandora's box, why don't ya? she thought but then decided only to give him what he'd asked.

"Oh, my sister and I frequently volunteer at the hospital." That answered the question without bringing up events she'd rather not discuss on a first—and only—date.

"Wow, you're a real humanitarian, Becca. You make me look like Darth Vader over here."

She giggled and got a chin chuck as he smiled at her.

"You like the halibut?" he asked sincerely.

She hadn't even tasted it yet, so she plucked up her fork and dove in. The thick, white fish held its form, akin to a filet of beef, and the flavors caressed her tongue as she bit into the juicy meat, moaning aloud as she savored it. It was literally the *best* thing she'd ever tasted.

"Oh, my God." She moaned again and closed her eyes. *Holy shit!* If this was how the rich lived, she could do this for all eternity. Could food actually make a person have an orgasm? If so, it was happening. It was a food orgasm—a food-gasm.

When she looked up at Pax, the look on his face both frightened and electrified her all at the same time. His blue eyes had become stormy, his jaw clenched, and his brows were drawn in a tight line. His fist tightened on the table, and she saw his Adam's apple bob. He'd become Poseidon, right there at their dinner table, and she suddenly felt an unrelenting desire to beg him—for mercy or rapture she wasn't quite sure.

She watched his chest rise and fall as his breathing accelerated and his eyes continue to drill into her own. Time stood still. The wine was making her head buzz. That was it. That's all this was, a trip for her overstressed mind. She was seeing things—hearing things as he said, "I wonder...is that what you'd sound like with me inside you, sweetness?"

She was dreaming...

She wasn't dreaming as his hand moved up her arm and shoulder, ever so slowly until he touched her jaw. His big hand could have obscured half her face, could smother her. But again, he was so gentle; his touch was having a tumultuous effect on her insides. She watched him lean in, as if in slow motion. His head tilted, his lips opened ever so slowly. She was falling, her eyes closing, her body yielding...

A throat cleared, and they shot apart as if canon fire had blasted between them.

Rebecca held her chest and looked up to see an embarrassed maître d' avoiding their eyes.

"Is everything to your liking, Mr. Guthrie?"

It took Pax a moment to respond as he resettled in the chair and took in a deep breath.

"Everything's exquisite. Thank you so much, Sven. You can bring us a dessert menu here in about ten minutes or so."

And just like that, Becca's bubble burst. He was rushing dinner. There had been no moment between them. And how could there be? He was the "prince," she was the "peasant girl."

She knew good and well how this story *really* ended.

CHAPTER THREE

F*uck! This is so not fair!* Paxton thought as Madi's words kept repeating in the back of his head, but his dick was being completely defiant. There was something about this sexy little historian that had him itching to have her on her back, screaming his name in ecstasy.

Maybe it'd simply been too long for him, maybe it was the wine, or maybe it was that he'd been told he couldn't have her; either way, he wanted her so bad he couldn't sit still.

Her little pink tongue, licking the crème brûlée off her spoon now, had him practically drooling like one of Pavlov's dogs. He couldn't pinpoint it. She wasn't even his type. He liked blondes, he liked wild, adventurous, tall supermodels. Rebecca was... well, she was a historian for one thing who preferred books to jet-skis, piano to rock and roll, and sweaters to bikinis. Not to mention that she was downright edible. Hell, who was he kidding? He'd never been one to discriminate where women were considered and neither had his cock. And this woman oozed a subtle sex appeal that every cell in his body sucked in like it was starved and she was the elixir of life.

"Wow! That was amazing, but now I'm stuffed." Becca sighed and patted her flat belly.

"It's ok to indulge every now and then," He eyed her cunningly.

Something in her eyes told him she hadn't indulged in far too long, and he was picking up on that vibe, his body reading all her signs.

Hell, of course Rebecca hadn't indulged. She lived with two other women—cramped into a tiny apartment, he was sure—and volunteered at the hospital, taking care of her sick mother when she wasn't working. This lady was Mother Theresa reborn. And Pax felt like a dick. This dinner was probably the finest she'd ever had in her life, and here he was sitting "high on the hog" while they struggled. It'd been clear as she dined with him that she wasn't used to the bounty Pax was. And all the while, all he could think about was licking the whipped cream she'd moved off the dessert they'd been sharing from her delectable naked body. He was a sick man and when this was over, he was scheduling an appointment with a psychiatrist.

"Indulgence? Ha," she scoffed, confirming his suspicions.

"You *do* know that lovers and warriors are not bound by the rules of fair play?" Paxton stated, eyebrow cocked. He begged himself to stop flirting with her, even as his body heat rose when her eyes burned into his own. He stared back for the longest time, her features unreadable before she finally looked down.

"Thank you, Paxton. For this. For tonight. It's been unbelievable. Truly."

Oh, God, how I want to make it even more unbelievable for you, you sweet, juicy peach, he thought as his eyes drifted to her breasts.

Stop thinking, he told himself and closed his eyes. Madi would fucking kill him for the things he'd said—and imagined—in the last hour. She was right; this was a sexual harassment lawsuit waiting to happen, and he was gonna get torn a new asshole.

He had to get a grip on himself. He set the wine glass down, threw a few hundred dollar bills down—pulling them from his wallet in a frenzy—and stood.

"Ready?" he asked and tried to calm his nerves.

Paxton took Rebecca's arm in his as they walked through the restaurant, eyes staring them down as they went. Eyes of wonder, eyes of awe, eyes of envy looking at him, looking at her. He kept his head forward and ignored them as usual.

Upon walking outside, they were bombarded with flashing lights and mics thrown into their faces as they practically ran to the limo.

Back in the limo, Paxton sidled up next to her as he pulled the door closed, all too aware of her warmth plastered beside him in the dimly lit seat. He was quiet but for a few moments as they rode back towards the convention center.

"Rebecca, I—"

"Thank you again, Paxton. It was truly amazing." She gave him a stunning smile that ripped into his gut with force.

"You're welcome..." He took her hand in his once more, the pull to do so overpowering. "I really don't want this night to end yet."

As much as he didn't want to admit it, it was true. They both felt it—didn't they?

She looked up into his eyes, surprise residing in the jade green depths. God, he was getting lost in them, so hopelessly lost.

"James," Paxton called to the driver, who quickly opened the separator window, "take us to Centennial Park."

"Straight away, sir," James called back and closed the window.

"Maybe there won't be too many people this time of night. There's a great coffee stand there," Paxton stated, smiling.

Rebecca returned it with a gulp, and Pax prayed he didn't do anything more stupid than what he'd already done with this woman who was so mysteriously intriguing to him.

He had to behave or Madison McFadden, wife to the god-king Zeus, would put his head on a spike out front of the Colosseum to warn others of her wrath.

PAXTON HELD Rebecca close as the Ferris wheel moved up to let yet another passenger on.

"I'm sorry, I didn't realize you were afraid of heights." Paxton sighed, feeling like a real asshole.

"It's ok, really. I've heard the views from here are spectacular." She shuddered as the gondola moved, squeezing her eyes shut.

"That would actually require you to open your eyes, sweetheart." Paxton took her face in his hands. Rebecca opened her eyes and smiled at him.

"I think I have a spectacular enough view just looking at you."

"You flatter me. You are far more beautiful than I could ever be."

"You think so?" She looked surprised. Had no one ever told her how beautiful she was?

"Yes, absolutely."

Rebecca dared to peek out the window of their gondola and whimpered as she looked down at the concrete and people below.

"Becca, don't look down. Just look out. Over there; see the lights?" Pax pointed as his hand pressed against the small of her back. "My uncle and I took a ride on the Ferris wheel in my hometown at the fair one year. I'd never been on one, and he encouraged me to ride it in order to combat my fears. I never wanted to disappoint him so I did. That was the first of many firsts." He laughed, remembering his uncle's patience with the troubled child Paxton had been—stepping in when Pax's dad left.

"Pax?" Rebecca asked patiently, licking her lips eagerly.

"Yeah?"

"Can I ask a favor?" her voice trembled as she turned toward him and bowed her head.

"Sure, sweetness."

She grinned at the nickname he'd abruptly given her. "I know you may not want to. I mean… This night is almost perfect…but it would be even more so…" she trailed off and pulled her lips in. His finger touched her chin, bringing it up so she was forced to look into his eyes.

"I'm listening, baby," he coaxed.

"It—It'd be utterly *perfect* if-if you kissed me," she stated, barely above a whisper.

Pax responded with a short laugh, slightly amused and slightly aroused. *Fuck yeah it would be!* But deep down, he knew how serious Madi had been about him being chaste. What if this was a set up and this woman had been planted to ruin the Gladiators? Not that Paxton even believed in conspiracy theories in the first place, but this could be bad for the team if the media caught wind of it or if this girl ran to the news stations and claimed he'd not only sexually harassed her but also had "sexually assaulted" her too.

But he saw nothing apart from raw need as he looked deeply into her eyes, searching for any sign of deception. She was one of his biggest fans, right? Those sexy lips and that yummy body... He simply couldn't resist any longer.

He leaned into her, her breasts pressing into his chest as one hand went to her face, the other to her waist. Her head angled opposite his, and he slowly lowered his lips to meet hers, pressing them ever so gently to the soft little rosebuds. He delicately moved his mouth over hers and softened his lips, kissing her pliant ones.

Becca moaned quietly as he deepened the kiss, and his tongue grazed her teeth. Her mouth opened for him, and his tongue plunged in, desperately seeking to taste her. Paxton moaned too, loving how sweet and giving she was. She returned his passion, her tongue taking on a rhythm of its own, bringing his sex to life as her arms wrapped around his neck. His desires were cresting, like a writhing wave hurtling swiftly toward the shore. His deprived cock was starving for this sultry brunette who made him want to expose everything she was hiding deep inside. Their kiss was hot and hungry—as hot and hungry as his desire was. Within minutes, their hands were moving over one another, and they were breathless as they spent their pent-up passions.

Paxton's arousal was rapidly becoming a throbbing burden in his pants, and he longed to press his rock-hard erection against her softness. He groaned at the hindrance, moving his face down to her neck, kissing and sucking at the tender flesh of her throat and collar bone. His hands grabbed for those perky breasts of hers, and her pleasure cry awoke something primal within him; he knew he had to have her.

He gripped her hips then and pulled her over the seat and onto his lap—her dress riding up ever so slightly on her thighs. She straddled him, and Pax anticipated showing her the beast she'd incited.

Once he pressed her down onto his erection, she gasped and looked at him in both surprise and lust. Her eyes had changed; they gotten darker somehow. A timid smile crossed her lips as she shyly rocked her hips against his hardness, answering the call of their bodies—a call they were unable to ignore any longer.

"Oh shit, baby…fuck," he groaned and his head flew back as he arched his hips against hers. Her lips fell on his, and she kissed him again. He cupped her face in his hands and took control. His tongue plunged into her mouth once more, possessively and punishingly, sucking and tormenting hers. God, he wanted to be inside her more than he'd ever wanted anything in his life up to now. His heart raced and his breath grew ragged at his plight.

Suddenly, a grave realization came over him, and he stilled their pitching pelvises.

"Paxton, what's wrong?" Rebecca glanced at him then up and out, into the stillness of the glass. Abruptly, they were assaulted by a thousand flashes of lights. She screamed and covered her eyes, temporarily blinded.

"Jesus Christ!" Paxton swore at the paparazzi. His aching sex receded uncomfortably in protest. "Well, so much for discretion." He smiled sadly up at her as she blinked, attempting to bring her sight back.

He helped her off of him and apologized. They readjusted themselves as best they could for two lovebirds caught red-handed, and the door opened.

Paxton sighed internally and anticipated the coming headline all over the news for the following morning: *Paxton Guthrie Sails Sky High on Date with Contest Winner*.

Damn it to Hell, just... Damn!

CHAPTER FOUR

"What the actual *fuck* were you thinking?" Madi sailed into him first thing the next morning when he got to the complex.

Atlanta's Rising Football Star Soars to New Heights on his Charity Date, was the caption on the first newspaper Paxton had thrown at him upon entering her office. It had a very erotic picture of Rebecca atop him, his hand on her breast as they kissed in a passionate embrace.

The next read, *XX-rated Ferris Wheel Ride. Guthrie Caught Thoroughly Enjoying his Date. Being a Fan has its Perks!* He literally cringed, awaiting what new headlines would appear before the day was through.

It'd been all over the internet, Facebook, Instagram, Twitter, and every news station; even ESPN and the NFL network had their opinions on the matter.

"I told you in no uncertain terms to keep your dick in your damn pants..."

"I did," he protested, but she held a hand up.

"Ok—*next* time, I'll draw a picture for you so you get a better idea, since you're apparently an *idiot*." Madi cried and rolled her eyes.

"C'mon, Mad, you don't have to be such a..."

He held his tongue as Zeus's stormy eyes warned him to can it.

"Pax, this is *exactly* what I was talking about when I said that this," Madi pointed to the headline, "wasn't the bad publicity that we needed. The charity event was supposed to make the team look *charitable*. Now you've made yourself out to look like a pompous playboy who took advantage of the situation. I would've expected this from Travis, not you."

Great! Now he was just some testosterone-crazed stereotype.

"So, he'll give a personal apology on behalf of the NFL," Pax's manager said over the speaker phone.

Pax nodded. "And one to Rebecca, too."

"That's not gonna be good enough. How do we know this girl wasn't trying to purposefully sabotage you?" Madi asked.

"Why would she?"

"I dunno, because both you and the team have a lot of *money*," she growled sarcastically.

"C'mon, she's not like that. She..." Pax defended.

"You don't even *know* her. You were with her for two hours. Wake up, Romeo, and stop being so naïve. This is how people get ruined for all they have. This is *supposed* to be our year, Pax."

Madison was so furious with him, and he felt bad, really bad. She stood from her chair and moved to the window to look out it. One hand went to her chin, the other to her growing baby bump, and in that moment, she looked like a fierce mother-warrior taking on the world.

Pax gulped at both the raw emotion oozing from her and the sexuality of the pose. It was ancient, beautiful, and symbolic all at once. Brett saw it too and was immediately drawn to his wife, stepping up behind her and wrapping his arms around her. But the fierce queen, Hera, was as tough as her king—even if not physically; she turned back to Pax to "handle" him.

"I have to suspend you, Pax."

"What? Why?"

"I warned you. Don't you *dare* blame me! It's what the league wants, to teach you a lesson."

"That's bullshit. I'm not a child. I'm a grown-ass man!"

"Exactly. A grown-ass man who made a very poor decision. What you do in the privacy of your home is one thing, out in public is quite another."

Pax huffed and crossed his arms over his chest, moving forward to sit on the edge of the chair. "How long?"

"A couple weeks, at least."

"Seriously? Can't you just fine me or something?"

"Oh, you're getting fined too," she smirked and gave him the once over.

"This is total entrapment. So, I can't kiss who I want, when I want? Isn't this America?"

"You know what? This is *exactly* why you're being suspended. You're acting like a selfish brat! This *isn't* about you! Now, get out of my sight."

"Madi, c'mon. I—"

"Paxton, as bad as this is for you. Imagine what *her* life is gonna be like for weeks to come," Brett stated. "You get to go home and hide behind a gate, watch Netflix, and sleep in. She'll be harassed, ridiculed, maybe even lose her job and guess what? After all that happens, she might just decide in the long run it's worth it to play the victim and come after your money. You might wanna call your lawyer." Zeus's frown tore hard into Paxton's guts. He hated that he'd disappointed his QB, his CEO, his team.

Pax realized that he was being a selfish prick.

He was a selfish *fucking* prick!

REBECCA SIPPED her coffee on Tuesday and stared out at the beautiful October day.

"Look at the bright side," Veda said. "Now you can be with Mam all week." Her tone had changed. Yesterday, she was chomping at the bit for Paxton Guthrie's blood.

"That son of a bitch, I'll fuckin' kill him." Veda growled, her emerald green eyes flaming brightly. *"He's gonna pay."*

"Don't, Veda. Please, just—"

"You lost your job because of him! A job you've loved. A job you'd wanted your whole damn life. And now what?"

Rebecca had shrugged. She had no idea what. All she knew was that she'd been devastated to come in on Monday morning and been asked to clear her things from her desk. When she'd gone to ask why, her boss, Wes Hardin, threw the newspaper down at her.

She needed no other explanation *why* when she saw her provocative pose on top of Pax's lap on the Ferris Wheel gondola.

It had been the single most wonderful, and single most mortifying, moment of her entire life. And now she would pay for it forever; the stain would mark her for life.

She'd been lucky to avoid the media, as she'd been home for two days caring for her mother after her treatment. But Monday, it was as if the entire world had found her following her termination.

They'd been there in front of the museum, shoving mics into her face, cameras flashing all around her. It was the stuff of nightmares as they followed her to her car, and she'd been on the verge of a panic attack.

Veda had been on the hunt then. "We're gonna have to get a lawyer, Bec," she'd insisted.

"Really? And how can we afford one of those?" Becca had rolled her eyes and pointed to the mass of medical bills she was paying online.

"We sue that dickhead."

"What? Why?"

"For defamation of character, for starters. Sexual assault—"

"No! He didn't sexually assault me."

"Umm, did you *not* see the picture on page 5 of this tabloid?" Veda had scoffed and practically thrown it at her.

Becca hadn't needed to see it. She knew what the pose looked like. It looked like he'd been the aggressor. One of his palms was cupping her breast, the other was gripping her hip and butt cheek. She could still remember his masculine smell, the taste of his lips, how aroused she'd been by his hands on her, the growl that rumbled his broad chest. She'd looked down, ashamed at how much she'd wanted him and how she'd thrown her inhibitions to the wind in the throes of a passionate embrace.

"Look, he got a slap on the wrist. Meanwhile, we're sitting here on the verge of eviction. I picked up another shift tonight."

"C'mon, Veda, you said that you were gonna stop working at that place."

"Yeah, I know I did. But I can't. At least not right now, anyway. Besides, you know I don't mind it. *And* it's damn good money. Money that we need right now while you search for another job."

"My reputation is trashed. I'll be lucky if McDonald's will hire me." Becca pouted.

"Come work at *RISE* then."

"No, I-I can't. I don't know how you—" Rebecca didn't finish the statement. They'd had these conversations before, and Veda knew how she felt about stripping.

Veda had always been a "showgirl" though, which was why she was also an NFL cheerleader too. Somehow, she'd found a makeup that covered all her vibrant tattoos and used the clear rings to cover her visible piercings. She wasn't a stickler for rules—in fact, Veda preferred to be a rule breaker—but she did her best to follow them in order to keep the job. The Gladiators cheerleaders weren't as scantily clad as some of the other teams and their rules weren't as strict but still stringent enough for no flexibility. It didn't pay as much money as everyone thought, but it was great for her portfolio; Veda had always wanted to be a model.

"I just wish there was some way for me to recover my job."

"Do what I said and call a lawyer."

Rebecca shook her head in disagreement. Even if she could afford it, she wouldn't do that to Paxton. She'd asked him to kiss her —to make the date perfect—and in those few moments, it had been. Neither of them could've anticipated the sparks that would explode around them when their lips touched, the jolt of electricity that had jarred them, and the alignment that would come.

Oh, what was she saying! Obviously, she'd been the only one to feel it. If he had, he wasn't gonna do a blasted thing about it.

"I'll find a job, sister. Don't discount me. There are other places."

Veda's deep eyes looked into Becca's. "I know how much your career means to you."

"And I know how much yours means to you."

Veda rolled her eyes. "A dream…"

"No, you can be *anything* you want to be."

"Grow up, Bec. This is the real world. You work your ass off then you die. Might as well have a little fun while we're here though, huh? Come to *RISE* with me tonight. I'll introduce you to the owner. She's super chill."

Rebecca wouldn't shed her clothes for money, plus she was a horrible dancer. Until the time came that they were gonna starve, she had to simply maintain her morality; Veda had abandoned hers long ago. One of them had to be able to enter Heaven's gate so that they could rally for the other. They were twins, after all.

"I'll start searching right now. I'll find something good before the day's out, I promise." Becca was glad for the savings they had thanks to Vey's dancing.

"I believe in you, sis. But if you can't find anything because of this fuckhead, I'm calling a lawyer for you. How dare you suffer for him being horny!"

Such was life. Women had been suffering for men's lack of inhibitions for centuries. What made this one any different?

PAX WIPED HIS EYES. He'd started watching *Outlander* two days ago and had gotten hooked thanks to Rebecca. He'd been watching hours of it nonstop—damn Netflix and their automatic six seconds to the next episode BS. It was easy to binge when it was so convenient. Now, he was emotionally destroyed and reeling from this last episode he'd just watched. He sat up and ran his hands over his face.

He'd been stewing since his suspension Saturday and had come home and drank far too much, which he'd regretted come Sunday. He'd watched his team win an impeccable game without him and stewed even more as the gorgeous brunette flashed through his head. She was stunning, porcelain skin, eyes as green as jade, and a sweetness behind her smile that he'd longed to explore. He couldn't forget the taste of that sweetness, the eagerness in her kiss, or the pull of their bodies as he'd grabbed her and sinfully indulged on the sweet lass atop his lap.

Now, he was being punished for it. And his punishment was palpable as he swore at his stupidity.

It wasn't fair. He couldn't have anticipated how amazing their kiss would be. He hadn't meant to let it go that far and never imagined the media— Oh, never mind, of course the media would prey on them; they were the media.

"Dammit!" he growled and grabbed his phone for the first time all day.

A headline caught his attention. *Local Historian Fired for Professional Misconduct.*

"Oh no," Pax mumbled as he began reading about Rebecca's termination for "conduct unbecoming" of a member of the historical society. Sonovabitch! Now, he'd gone and gotten her fired. He felt like a real asshole. He had to make this right. Somehow, he had to make this right.

He immediately moved through his contacts and selected his lawyer, Humphrey Williams. The man answered on the second ring, and Paxton sighed. "Humph, man, I need to run something by you."

He then began to tell him about an outlandish idea.

CHAPTER FIVE

Rebecca walked into the children's hospital, feeling her cheeks flush as she looked down. People whispered, giggled, and ambled about, and she couldn't help but feel that all eyes were on her. She was still mortified to be seen out in public, attempting to fly under the radar. When she hadn't made a public statement, the cameras had begun to disband little by little, but she couldn't stay cooped up in her apartment forever—not with her mother's cancer treatments and her own things to do.

She was still going to maintain her volunteer work while her mother got treatment. After all, the hospitals were side by side, and seeing the children always made her feel better.

Carter came up then and gave her a smile as she checked in at registration.

"Ms. Ryan, you're looking lovely today."

"Oh, thank you, Carter." Carter Burns ran the program she volunteered for. He was handsome enough, boyishly so, but his gray eyes always seemed to unnerve her. There was something about him that gave her and Veda the "creeper" vibe.

"I heard about your misfortunes. I'm so sorry." His hand came to her shoulder and cupped it softly. "How dare that man lay hands on you like that."

Rebecca's cheeks flamed and she looked up. Carter's brows were drawn angrily.

"People with money get away with things they shouldn't."

He stared at her for long moments before the lady at the front issued her a temporary badge for the time she would be there, snapping Carter out of his mood.

He smiled again and took the badge, thanking the lady.

He then motioned for Rebecca to accompany him down the hallway and handed her the badge.

They moved shoulder to shoulder, not in a particular rush, although Becca felt uncomfortable with the closeness and awkward silence as they moved down the hallway.

"Rebecca, I—" Carter began only to stop as Rebecca gasped when a giant frame halted her in her tracks. Her nose brushed a sternum and big arms pulled her against a large chest.

Her breath whooshed out of her as she was squeezed tightly into an embrace.

"There's my gorgeous lass," a familiar deep voice said.

When she was pulled back, Rebecca gaped at the beautiful smiling face of Paxton Guthrie.

"P-Pax!"

"I know I'm late, honey, but I promise, it's for a damn good reason."

Before she could respond, his plump lips were on hers, kissing her softly yet firmly. She stifled a moan and pushed at his chest, confused to Hell and back.

"Sorry, Becca bear, I missed you." He rubbed his nose against her own, and she knew her gawking mouth could've fit a Buick in it. "You left your ring at the house last night. Kinda hard to tell the whole world we're engaged if you don't wear my ring, bunny." He shoved a diamond solitaire onto her left ring finger and pulled her back into his chest. "Just go along with it, I'll explain in a minute," he whispered softly into the ear opposite the side Carter was standing on.

When Pax pulled back, he smiled over at an equally shocked Carter Burns, his hand staying possessively on Becca's back. "Paxton Guthrie. I'm Becca's fiancé."

Carter's grunt of surprise matched Becca's. He gulped and looked down, as if furious for a moment before collecting himself. "Carter Burns. I'm the volunteer program director here at ACH."

"Good to meet ya. I was told you're the man to see about volunteering around here."

Carter again looked taken off guard before nodding.

"Well, I got my badge for the day. Where do I start?"

Rebecca knew she was just as out of sorts, but Pax's pat on her back signaled her forward as Carter led them down the long hall. Pax's hand interlocked with hers, and she felt her entire body tingle at his overwhelming presence. She'd forgotten how huge he was.

Carter led them back to a room, where he began explaining their tasks for the day. They'd be handing out events brochures and coloring pamphlets to the inpatient rooms on the third floor. "You can team up with your *fiancée* here and let her show you the ropes. Welcome, Mr. Guthrie."

Carter huffed off and left them to their own devices. Pax then pulled her into a supply room where Becca's mouth opened once again as he propped himself against the closed door.

He ran a hand through his blond curls and looked back at her with a crooked grin. "Sorry to accost you once again, but I—"

"*Fiancée?* Pax, what is—?"

"Look, it was the only thing I could do to save your reputation—and your job. I'm sorry, by the way, about the Ferris wheel. I—" He looked down before his eyes met hers again and he stepped forward, taking her hands. "When I found out you'd lost your job, I knew that I couldn't just sit by and do nothing, so I took action. We can break up any time you want. Although, the longer we stretch this out, I feel the better it will be for you."

What was he saying? Her mind hadn't gone past the word "Ferris wheel." Of course he'd be sorry about that? It had meant nothing to him and everything to her.

"Becca, say something—please?" he insisted.

"I—" She closed her eyes. "I don't understand."

"I told your boss, and the hospital event coordinators, that I asked you to marry me on the Ferris wheel. Thus our reaction."

"You *what?*" Had she heard him right?

"Yeah, see, we've been dating for some time in private." He made air quotes. "And I arranged the charity raffle date as a means for a romantic engagement for us to go public."

Oh my God! He'd lied to everyone. Holy cac. What happened if they found out the truth?

"I know what you're thinking, Rebecca. But it will be easier than you think. We'll both pick a date that no one can track us to any particular place. We met during the off-season, and you and I hit it off and began a secret relationship; no one will know otherwise, unless we tell them."

Rebecca began to absorb his words. He'd faked an engagement to save face. Somehow, she felt that it wasn't just *her* reputation he'd been trying to salvage. What did this entail for her, being engaged to an NFL star?

"Ok, so what's the plan?" Her pounding heart relinquished as her brain took charge.

"We just make it look legit. I'll need to meet your family, you'll need to meet mine. I'll introduce you to the guys and— What?"

"My job?" she grimaced.

He smiled. "You got it back. You can start back as soon as you want. Your boss was a tough nut to crack, but I think he has a romantic side. I had to do a lot of groveling on that one." He scowled, looking off as if he didn't want to discuss what type of groveling he'd had to do.

She took in a deep breath and turned away from him, in an

attempt to calm her racing mind and heart. He'd gone to her boss. He'd come to the hospital. He'd saved her character!

"Look, I know this is sudden and unexpected," he said as he came up behind her. "I just couldn't, in good conscience, leave you to the dogs, the media, the image I left you with on Friday night." Or the sting that his suspension had left in its wake, she was sure.

"Pax, I...I don't know what to say. Thank you."

"No need to thank me. I wanted to do it. Rebecca, I *am* sorry for all this. Can you forgive me?" He turned her around to look at him, his finger hovering at her chin.

How could she not forgive a gorgeous face like his? With his jaw and cheekbones looking like they'd been carved from marble? Those blue eyes the color of the sky on a cloudless day. Those lips, the bottom one plumper than the top. She was nodding and grinning at him before her brain could form a proper answer.

He pulled her into his embrace, cradling her head against his huge pec as his palm went to her back.

When he pulled back, he gripped her shoulders gently. "Now, *fiancée*, teach me the ropes of volunteer work with these adorable kiddos."

Rebecca smiled and nodded.

They set to work, going room to room. Some of the kids recognized Paxton, others didn't. Some were very sick, while others looked as healthy as horses. Pax treated them all with kindness, eagerness, and concern, which touched Rebecca's heart. He joked with them and made them laugh. He was a big kid, himself, and made her laugh in turn.

When two hours had passed, she gasped as she looked at her watch. "Oh, no."

"What's wrong?" Pax asked and gripped her forearm.

"I have to go get my mam."

"Ok. Can I come too?"

She gulped, unsure how to respond at first. If they were gonna pull this off, he needed to meet her family and very soon.

God help him, though, when he met her sister.

PAXTON SMILED at Rebecca's mother, Kathleen, as she scooped another portion of spaghetti onto his plate. The woman favored Rebecca a great deal, save for she was paler—probably from the cancer treatments.

"Thank you, Mrs. Ryan. It's delicious."

"You're so very welcome, Mr. Guthrie. I'm glad you're enjoying it," she answered with a grin, and Pax's face lit up too.

The apartment they lived in was small compared to his mansion, and he'd been surprised to learn that Rebecca, her mom, and her sister all lived together here.

When Veda, Rebecca's twin, walked into the door, he knew right away the disdain she had for him.

She'd eyed him suspiciously and turned without giving him a handshake or greeting. She'd gripped Rebecca's arm, pulling her to another room where he heard them arguing. When they'd returned, Veda's eyes tore into his like heat-seeking missiles.

He looked at her now, waiting for her to speak for the first time. She'd held her tongue thus far, simply watching and observing him. She was—in appearance—identical to Becca in every way: height, build, and facial features, her eyes as green as Becca's. Her nose and lips were the exact same. But that's where the similarities ended. Veda had lots of tattoos and piercings: a nose ring, tongue ring, and various colorful tattoos covering her arms and her chest. She was also mean-looking, her eyes staying narrowed and her lips pulled taut.

Even now, Veda's brows rose. "Becca, how'd the talk with the *lawyer* go today?"

Becca frowned over at her sister, seeming confused.

"That's right, *Big Shot*, I advised her to sue you for defamation of character and sexual assault. As you can see, not all of us live in the lap of luxury like you do."

Pax looked around the cramped table and felt a kick to his gut.

"Like I told Rebecca, I simply want to clear her name and reputation. We'll be making a public statement tomorrow. She has her job—"

"That doesn't take the stain of the pictures away. People aren't just going to forget it. And I'm certain you're still suspended. Aren't ya...*Poseidon?*"

"As I plan to tell every social media outlet that will listen, I proposed to Rebecca on the Ferris wheel and—"

"That's awfully romantic, surfer boy. But again, not everyone is going to simply overlook what they saw... I'll believe it when I see it on the telly tomorrow and not a minute sooner. Mark my words. If you think you're gonna weasel your way out of clearing this cac completely up, you have another thing coming. My sister here is practically a damn nun; compared to me, she's an angel so I'll warn you not to get on my bad side. If you so much as dream of betraying her trust, I'll cut yer bollocks off and feed them to you through a funnel. You got me?" Veda pointed her butter knife in his direction, the fire in her eyes unmistakable.

"I swear, I would never do anything to hurt Rebecca. It's why I'm here."

"Veda, please dinna threaten our guests," Kathleen cooed as if this were commonplace—Veda pointing a knife at their dinner guests. "Especially at the dinner table. Manners."

Veda put the knife down, but the daggers shooting from her eyes were still just as sharp. Pax looked down.

"Mr. Guthrie, we do appreciate what ye've done thus far. Rebecca loved her job and at least that's been repaired. Once the announcement comes tomorrow, her life will be closer to normal."

"Ha!" Veda laughed around a bite of meatballs. "Her life will *never* be normal again, Mam. Even long after this engagement is over, she'll be hounded by cameras. But I bet lover boy here didn't even bother to consider that, now did he?"

Damn, this chick was ruthless. Untrusting, cutthroat, cynical.

"Vey, please?" Becca whispered and gave her sister a look. "Pax is doing the best he can with an unfortunate situation. I'm not innocent in this either."

"Pax, huh? All comfy cozy, eh? Well, he might have you two snowed, but not me. I see this for exactly what it is and hopefully, the media doesn't pick up the scent too. I can smell bullshit a mile away and this asshole reeks of it." Veda slammed down her fork and stood, throwing her napkin in her chair and huffing off down the back hallway.

Kathleen smiled over at Paxton then, a sad, regretful smile. "You'll have to forgive me eldest daughter. She's always been the feistier of the two and overly protective of her family, ever since her father left us."

Oh, wow! Becca's father had left, too? He hadn't known that.

"It's quite alright. I do understand. But please know that I have no intentions of not making good on my promise. I *will* be there tomorrow. I will make the announcement with you by my side, Rebecca," he nodded to Becca with certainty, "and I will continue to carry this out, for as long as it takes to give you your life back." He tried to push his conviction into both their eyes. "It's the least I can do."

Rebecca and her mother both gave him a big smile then, and the three of them finished their dinner.

Kathleen took the dirty plates away, insisting Becca and Pax needed to get "acquainted" and that she didn't mind cleaning up since Becca had cooked.

Becca led him out of the apartment and down to a little courtyard out back. It overlooked a small pond with a fountain, stone-paved walkways, and benches and was nicely landscaped with green grass, trees, and various flowerbeds and bushes.

"This is nice," Pax stated as he took her hand, and they sat on one of the benches.

"It's where I come to read sometimes when I need a break from Veda and Mam."

"She's hardcore, huh?" It didn't take a rocket scientist to know he was referring to Becca's cynical twin sister.

"Oh, you have *no* idea," she stated truthfully. "She scares me sometimes."

The way she said that made Pax gulp instead of laugh. He hadn't doubted that Veda would make good on her promise to castrate him.

"I really am sorry for all this."

"Don't be. I'm the one who asked you to kiss me."

"And I'm the one who pulled you onto my lap," Pax stated with regret. Although the kiss had been freaking incredible, and he longed to do it again.

"Still, you didn't—"

"I *shouldn't* have."

When their eyes sought one another's, he saw sadness in hers and moved his hand up to her cheek. "I regret ruining your name, Becca, but I don't regret our kiss. You need to know that." Her alabaster cheeks reddened, and she glanced down. Paxton smiled. "Speaking of, maybe we should practice for our announcement tomorrow. The media will expect a display, and we need to make it look like we're a happy couple and all."

Becca licked her lips and the little pink rosebuds shone beneath the flood light above them, beckoning to him. He moved in, without hesitation. He felt her breast against his pec as she leaned into him. His hand moved to cup her face—*God, it was so small in his hand*—and his lips brushed hers. The moan that escaped him was feral and hungry, and he longed to feed that beast with the sweet honey that oozed from every pore of Rebecca Ryan's milky white skin. Her mouth opened to his as he pulled her closer and deepened the kiss.

Her hand moved to his chest, and he was assaulted by waves of rolling desire. She gripped his shirt and moaned in turn, making his dick jump in response. *Holy fuck*, he wanted to feel her, every inch of her, taste her bare flesh, enter her and see if she felt as wonderful as the kisses he'd taken from her thus far had.

His tongue plunged in—since his cock was clothed and couldn't —and he took more, but only what she was giving him, which wasn't enough for his starving lust. He groaned as her tongue stroked across his own, her passion matching his as her hand moved up to cup his face, moving into his mane. "Mmm, Pax," she murmured as she pulled back just enough for a breath, her sultry lips hovering just a hair from his own.

The sounds of footsteps brought him back to reality, and Paxton pulled back to see if they were about to be ambushed by the paparazzi. He breathed a sigh of relief as he saw a jogger running on the path in front of them.

"Damn, Becca… you taste like Heaven, angel."

Becca blushed again and it turned him on like nobody's business. He bet she would be a shy lover and that thought made his cock grow even harder. *What the fuck is wrong with me?* he thought. But knew it was because he'd been with many women over the years that were at the opposite end of the spectrum than Rebecca was: well-experienced, or "loose women" as his uncle would say. He'd never been with anyone as timid as Becca, and the thoughts of possessing a woman as sweet and soft and stunning as Rebecca Ryan made him ravenous.

As her green eyes burned licking, hot desire into him, he tried to calm his pounding heart and aching loins. He barely knew her, and they had to be careful here, especially out in public; they'd both learned the hard way about what being reckless and irresponsible did. Pax looked around, feeling unguarded, and Rebecca frowned.

"Sorry," he said, "I just don't want another camera crew raining on our parade." He cupped her cheek and gave her a reassuring smile. "You're so beautiful, you know that?"

Becca shook her head. "No, Veda's the beautiful one. I'm just plain."

"Yeah, I think I'll pass. She's got serial killer vibes."

Becca gave a hearty laugh, and it was music to his soul; he returned it.

"She's really got a huge heart underneath that tough exterior, I swear."

"Yeah, I bet most can't get past that first layer though."

"She's guarded. After Pa left, she hasn't let anyone close again."

"And what about you?"

"No one has ever wanted to get close to me. I'm intimidating too, but in a different way. I guess I'm too smart or nerdy or…"

"Or *nothing*. You're as inviting as an open book into a fantasy world."

"You read fantasy?" She looked up at him in awe.

"Well, I don't read *much* of anything to be honest. I play *Skyrim* though and I love to watch movies and shows, *Game of Thrones* is one of my faves. Oh, I've been watching *Outlander*, by the way."

"It's great, right?"

"It is. Heartbreaking in parts though, I had to take a break after Episode 15."

"Oh yes. That was rough."

"Randall is like the worst villain *ever*."

Rebecca cringed. "For sure." She turned serious then, her thumb stroking across his cheekbone as she stared back into his eyes, making him shiver. "For what it's worth, Paxton, I sincerely appreciate everything you've done. Maybe one day my sister will be grateful for it too."

"It's alright. I understand her reservations. I would feel the same way. Although, I don't have any siblings to be protective of, myself."

"It has it's pros and cons," Becca smirked, "but I love her so much and having a twin is a rewarding experience. We can read each other sometimes, I swear, and feel the others' hearts."

"So, I've heard. It's quite a phenomenon."

Becca nodded her head in agreement.

"This is nice," Pax stated, rubbing his fingers over Rebecca's forearm and looking at her swollen lips.

"I have to admit, I'm not regretting spending extra time with you. It's a treat."

Pax grinned. "Perks of engagement."

They sat still and quiet for a time, listening to the fountain and the sounds of the October evening. Pax pulled Rebecca into his arms, settling her head in the crook of his shoulder, her side against his chest, his arm draping over her tiny frame. It felt good to have her there propped against him, her warm body intimately pressing into his. Her hair smelled delicious, like lilacs and honey, and her stroking of his arm made him shiver with a million sensations he couldn't describe.

He knew it was getting late when Rebecca yawned.

He smiled. "Well, I'd better go. I'll come get you tomorrow morning. I've called for a press release at nine."

"Thank you again, Pax."

"No thanks necessary. I'm glad it was something I could fix. You should be able to live your life without my fame interfering, and I won't be satisfied until you do."

He walked her to her door and leaned against the jamb as he bid her a goodnight.

"Sleep well, fiancée."

She grinned and leaned into him. Her lips puckered, and he groaned as he took them eagerly, cupping her small face in his hands. He kissed her with a passion that exposed his vulnerability. When he pulled back, he knew this was going to be difficult for him —leaving her.

"See you tomorrow." He winked and moved out of the door frame.

As he got to his car, his heart felt like it might explode.

He had a fake fiancée, he had a fake engagement to pull off, and he had *real* feelings for the historian that he'd had only one date with.

He was in some serious trouble.

CHAPTER SIX

The lights of thousands of cameras flashed all around them as Paxton pulled Rebecca to his side. She could do nothing but smile, abject fear tearing at her tender heart.

He'd just announced their engagement to the media, stating he'd proposed the night of their date in the gondola of the Ferris wheel—thus prompting the reaction of him and his "fiancée." And they bought the hoax, it would seem.

Questions flew all around them:

"How long have you two been together?"

"How long have you known Mr. Guthrie?"

"When do you plan to wed?"

The one Pax responded to was, "So, you *sabotaged* the charity date raffle, Mr. Guthrie?"

"Sabotage is a strong word. No, I did no such thing. I set it up with the organizer to select Rebecca's name from the box. After all, you can't really go out on a date with someone else when you already *have* a serious girlfriend. Well, not if you wanna keep said girlfriend." Pax chuckled and gave that charming smile that the cameras couldn't seem to get enough of. He rocked Rebecca against his side and kissed the top of her head. "ACH was very generous to hide my secret well. Rebecca here had no idea. I was trying to do something incredibly romantic, but it seemed to only backfire in our faces."

"And why would you need to keep your relationship a *secret*, Paxton?" A blonde reporter in a vibrant red dress, matching lips, and heels asked.

Oh, here we go, Becca thought and gulped.

"I didn't need to keep it a secret. After all, what do I have to hide with this beautiful little dame here? I was simply attempting to keep her anonymity, at her own request. She doesn't enjoy the spotlight quite like yours truly here does." Pax chuckled again.

More rambling and another round of questions came, for which Pax's manager, Kenny, stepped in.

Pax was finally able to pull her with him to a limo then, shoving her in.

"Fucking hell," he grumbled and planted his face in his hands. "They're vultures."

His reaction matched her own. "Do you think it worked?"

"I certainly hope so. I don't know what to do otherwise."

They sat quietly and watched as the throng moved outside along with Kenny, who opened the door and slid in in a flash. "Fuck, dude."

"Did it work?"

"I'm not certain. We'll see the headlines soon enough though. You've spent quite enough money on this little venture of yours." Kenny's brown eyes burned back at Pax's, making Rebecca uncomfortable.

"My money is *my* business," Pax grumbled, annoyed, before asking, "What did you say?"

"I said the 'happy couple' would be spending time together at 'their' home."

"You *what?*" Pax retorted loudly.

"Pax, how can you convince them you're *together*—and soon to be wed—if you aren't even living together?"

"Wait. Pax, I can't—"

Pax held a hand up at Rebecca, stilling her words. "Now, just a second, Ken. Why would you say something like that?"

"Because I'm trying to salvage the damage you've done here." Ken's brows shot to his high forehead. "If you have a better idea on how to handle this, tell me."

Pax huffed and looked over to Rebecca, who pulled her lips in.

"It's just temporary, right?" Ken suggested. "I'll go grab a bag of Rebecca's things, and she can stay with you for a few days at least. Be seen coming to your house, be seen out with you. You can't just make an announcement this big, go your separate ways, and expect people to believe you."

He was right. Of course he was.

"Your house is plenty big enough for you to keep your separate spaces if that's what you want."

"I need to go to work, Paxton," Becca interceded.

Paxton nodded to her and took her hand, signaling for the driver to head to the museum.

"Your friends and family need to believe this too, if you're to pull it off. All you need is to have someone get pissed off at you. Then they head to the media and tell them you've both lied to save your asses. Better to just lie to them now and stage a big 'break up' later."

Pax looked to Rebecca for answers. "Your family already knows, but I can tell my people whatever you want me to. I just want you to have your life back, Rebecca. I did this."

Becca shook her head. "No, Pax, *we* did this. You weren't the only one." She took the hand he reached out to her and squeezed it. "Let's be as believable as possible."

"Alright. I'll come pick you up after work, and you'll stay with me for a few days until we can figure out what to do next."

Becca nodded and sat silently, mulling things over as they rode to the Atlanta Museum of Natural History.

When they pulled up, Pax got out and opened her door for her, taking her hand and pulling her in for a kiss. "I'll pick you up at five."

"Thank you," she whispered against his lips. She gave him a smile and kissed him again, savoring it for he tasted so good. She was reeling from his closeness, from his magnitude, from this surreal experience. Despite that the high drama of their situation had been completely chaotic, having this time with him was unlike anything she'd ever known was possible.

He was grinning as he reluctantly let her go, and she moved away, up the steps, and into the museum.

How the hell was she going to break the news to her sister that she was going to go live with Paxton?

"YOU'RE KIDDING, RIGHT?" Quil asked through the phone as Pax moved to the fridge, making sandwiches for lunch. "You're freaking *engaged*? That's loco!"

"Secret's out, bud… Surprise!" Pax tried to sound as genuine as possible. Doing so over the phone was easier than in person though, especially as suspicious as Quillan was.

"I don't believe it! You're a playboy. The last one of us," Trav practically yelled into the phone.

Great, Quil had him on speaker.

"I'm glad to hear it, kid," Linc said, and Pax could see him smiling through the phone.

"Congrats, Pax," Pax heard Brett mumble in the background.

"Talk to your wife, man. Ask if she can let up on my sentencing. Give her some oral or…"

Brett laughed. "She doesn't even want me to look at her right now. I'd be better off giving her a foot rub or a massage."

"Hell, *I'll* give her a foot rub if she'll just end this suspension." Pax sighed, missing his teammates and the game he adored.

"I'll put in a good word for you, bud. We miss you," TJ said.

"I miss you guys, too. I don't like being home. It's weird." And he was getting bored in spite of playing *GTA 5* for hours on end.

"It's only been a few days, you big baby," Quil scoffed.

"Yeah, when you get suspended for simply making out with a hot girl then we can talk, *Hades*."

"Hell, put your feet up and enjoy it," Linc responded back.

"Yeah, yeah, you know I'm itching to sack some QBs. You're the same way."

"Well, when do we get to meet her?" Trav asked.

"You guys wanna come over after practice tonight, and we'll all have dinner together?" Tonight was as good a night as any, after all.

He heard a couple, "Yeahs," an, "I can't tonight," and Quil said, "Sure."

Just then, he heard Madi's voice come on the line, "Pax?"

"Hey, boss," he cooed to the lovely yet commanding Madison McFadden.

"We'll talk tonight."

Great, what the hell did that mean?

REBECCA RODE in silence to Paxton's house, reading his last text.

Pax: I have a surprise for you tonight, if you're up for it that is?

She texted him back with: **Of course.**

She admired the lovely road she was headed down, shaded by trees that hung over her head like a canopy—various shades of reds, oranges and golds as Autumn took the show with its unparalleled beauty. This was her favorite time of year and always had been. Autumns in the south were unpredictable in their temperatures. Sometimes it would be close to seventy degrees on Halloween, so a girl had to have a backup costume or one that was versatile. Not that Becca had worn a costume aside from for work in ages.

Veda, now she was the one who loved Samhain and lived for the fun of it. Speaking of, Veda was pretty pissed at Rebecca and had yet to text her back about staying with Paxton. Well, if a link with an article on serial killers was considered a response.

Now, she smiled as a wrought-iron gate opened, and Pax's house came into view. It was big, beautiful, and looked like something out of a swanky magazine. A marble fountain sat out front of a circular drive and a pink marble front facade greeted her. The structure was of both Greco-Roman and Italian influence, and Becca felt like she'd stepped back out front of her museum and smiled as her door was opened for her.

"Ms. Ryan, welcome. I'm Sonia," the woman dressed in a lovely pale pink dress stated. She was well past middle-age with greying brown hair and no-nonsense brown eyes.

Rebecca moved to take her bag from the driver, but Sonia grabbed it before she could do so.

"Right this way. I'll show you to your room. Mr. Guthrie is expecting you."

Fancy, Becca thought, but truly savored feeling like she'd stepped back in time for a moment upon entering the massive foyer. She looked around in awe at the luxury before her. Shimmering crystal sconces, dark marble floors, high ceilings. The staircase looked as if it'd been hand-carved, the décor was minimal but tasteful, the walls painted a lovely taupe that went with any color one cared to accent with.

Sonia moved up the stairs, and Becca followed, glancing down into a massive room that must've been the living room—or great room, as it was probably accurately referred to. A garden courtyard lay beyond the wall of windows and a set of French doors leading out to it. She yearned to go out and explore; she loved gardens because they made the perfect reading nooks.

Sonia showed her into a guest room that was larger than the apartment she, her mother, and sister shared, and Becca stifled a grunt of surprise as it simply kept going.

"Here's the sitting area and bathroom, although I'm sure you won't be in here much." Sonia winked. "Mr. Guthrie wanted you to feel comfortable, though. He says you're Catholic and old-school."

Old school! Right. Leave it to Paxton to even have his housekeeper believing that they were actually engaged.

"Uh, yes," Rebecca responded in kind. "A girl must stick to her moral code, after all."

"Good way to keep a man in check before the wedding." Sonia cocked a brow. "Perhaps I should've been that way with my own, then I might have been able to keep him in the marriage bed."

Becca's brows rose and she tucked her arms into her chest, unsure how to respond to that.

"Well, I'll let Mr. Guthrie know you're here and give you some time to freshen up. Dinner's served at 6 sharp."

Wow, she even made dinner too? Holy crap! Becca felt like she'd gone to stay at the Biltmore estate.

"Thank you," she replied.

"Of course, dear. And if you need anything, please do ask."

Becca took a deep breath in as she looked around her suite. Now she knew how Cinderella felt stepping into the palace for the first time. She took in the room, its size and grandeur. The crown molding, light fixtures, big, mahogany canopy bed and matching dresser, the gargantuan bathroom with a claw-footed tub, stone shower, and vanity with a built-in settee. She'd died and gone to Heaven. Even the jacks was luxurious.

She began to unpack her belongings, feeling strange as she did so, hanging her dresses up and putting her toiletries away. After that, she combed her hair and touched her makeup up, feeling nervous about seeing Paxton again.

The sounds of gun-fire from a television set rang in her ears as she stepped from her room into the long, open hallway. It drew her to a large media room east of her own with the dark wooden doors opened. She could hear Pax's voice.

"Are you kidding me? Dude, go around me and get that asshole."

Becca heard more swearing and a yell. "Dammit, Maverick, *not* cool."

When she peered in, she saw him sitting in a big beanbag chair, clad in a muscle tank and shorts, leaning forward. He had a headset over his unruly blond locks and a controller in his hands. His head fell only to come up a second later; when he looked up and saw her, he froze.

Uh oh! What if he yelled at her for invading his private space. She took an instinctive step back.

"Becca!" His face lifted into a gorgeous smile. "Hey." He pulled the headset off and threw the controller into the seat before stepping forward to greet her. "How was the rest of your day?"

He stopped just inches from her, and her heart hammered at his closeness.

"Uh, it was... I'm sorry, I didn't mean to invade your space." She motioned to his "man cave." Compared to the rest of the house, this room didn't fit. The walls were covered with a space-themed wallpaper; adorned with posters of various characters, movies, and video games. The furniture didn't match. A black leather couch sat on one wall, adjacent to a huge TV within an entertainment system that could've housed the largest TV set a person could buy. There were knick-knacks, trophies, and old pictures in it. It was the only room that seemed to bear his personality. Becca assumed the rest of the house had been decorated by a designer.

"No worries, m'lady. 'Poseidon's cove' always has room for hot chicks in it." He winked and moved to take her hand. "I had Sonia give you the most comfortable room. I hope it works."

Works? Ha! "Yes, it's perfect. Thank you. You have a lovely home, Paxton."

"Thanks, let me show you around up here."

And he did, taking her in a giant circle. For the next ten minutes, he weaved her in and out of another three guest rooms, three more luxurious bathrooms, a tranquil meditation room, the open-decked veranda, and his messy master suite before they came back to the landing of the staircase.

"I hope you're hungry. Sonia has been cooking all day."

"Oh, I don't mind cooking if she ever wants a break." Becca actually enjoyed cooking.

Pax crinkled his nose. "After a long day at work? Nah, I can't have you do that. I was gonna take you out, but I figured we could hang out here tonight. Maybe take a dip in the hot tub later, if you want?" His grin was hopeful and Becca felt her stomach drop.

"Oh, I don't have… I didn't bring a bathing suit." Just the thought of Paxton seeing her half-naked in a bathing suit made her want to run and hide.

"No worries. I have an endless supply in the pool house, tags still on and everything."

Great! *Now, I have no choice but to acquiesce.*

"You hungry?"

I was but not so much anymore.

"I believe Sonia makes the best veal chops around. Not that *I'd* know," Pax added with a laugh, shrugging. "I'm having ratatouille."

Veal! When was the last time she had that? She couldn't even remember.

"Wow! That sounds great."

Rebecca's belly grumbled in hunger as Pax took her hand and led her down the staircase.

She stopped dead in her tracks when the doorbell rang.

"Oh, I forgot to tell you… I invited my friends to dinner, too."

Friends? *Oh lord.* She'd been nervous enough having it be just the two of them, now she had to plaster on a fake smile and pretend this was just another normal night, despite that this was her first time in his house. As she looked around, she realized she didn't even know where the first-floor bathroom was…or the kitchen. Oh God, *I'll never pull this off!*

"Hey," Pax pulled her into him, mere inches from his frame and cupped her face with the hand he didn't have against her back. "Just be yourself, okay? They're gonna love you." He leaned in and kissed her cheek, hovering there as Becca heard the door open and voices echo in the foyer.

"Well, well, don't let us keep you from greeting the future Mrs. Guthrie," a smooth male voice called out as Pax and Becca continued down the stairs and approached their guests.

Rebecca looked up to see Travis "Ares" Redmond in the flesh, and gaped openly at him.

"Damn Pax, she's hotter than you said, man." He came forward then and gave her a wink as he playfully punched at Pax's shoulder. "I'm Ares, nice to meet ya, queen of the sea."

"Oh, stop it, you stubborn mule. Use your real name. She knows you're *Ares*." A pretty redhead rolled her eyes and gave Becca a bright smile, shoving at the broad running back beside her. "Don't pay any mind to this cocky jerk. I'm Skyla."

Rebecca took the hand offered her and smiled back. "Rebecca. Good to meet you, ADA Larson."

"Ha! A cultured woman. I'm impressed, Pax." She winked at Becca then lifted her chin at Paxton. Rebecca stifled a laugh.

"Now, honey, give the youngster here a break. He's smarter than he looks," Travis retorted.

Pax looked put out and shook his head at Travis. "Go have a drink and stuff it before I tackle you just to get the energy out of my system."

"Save it, groom. Your blushing bride here will want all that energy, I'm sure." Travis smirked and walked away, allowing the next in line.

"Quillan Layton."

"Rebecca Ryan." The "blushing bride" blushed even brighter at the dark-headed stud before her. He could've been a model he was so handsome. All these men were...sheesh. Talk about Gods of the Gridiron indeed.

"Glad someone could settle this wild child down."

"Hey..." Pax frowned. "Don't go there."

"Some of us are more subtle is all I'm saying." Quil grinned. "Introverts know how it's done—si, Becca?"

She gulped at her name on his perfect lips. Damn, maybe she'd chosen the wrong god.

"You've left her speechless, it would seem." Pax grumbled. "Her and every *other* woman around."

Quil patted Paxton's shoulder, then walked off laughing. Becca bowed her head, feeling bad although she wasn't certain why—this was all fake, anyway.

"Pax," came a calm female voice that was laced with both kindness and authority.

"Madi, you look lovely tonight."

"Flattery doesn't become you." She arched a brow at Pax and smiled at Becca. "Rebecca, it's good to see you again."

"You too, Mrs. McFadden. I should congratulate you on your recent nuptials." *And to the gorgeous stud you married.* Brett—aka Zeus—McFadden was tall, broad, and perfectly titled to be the leader of the Gladiators. He had a powerful presence about him that dared one to challenge him, for if they did, they would incur his wrath— well, from the look of him, anyway.

"Thank you." Madison smiled up at her husband, her blue-green eyes softening. He gave her a crooked smile back and extended his hand to Becca.

"Ms. Ryan, it's a pleasure. Brett McFadden."

"It's an honor to meet you. I'm a big fan…of the whole team."

"Of course you are," Madi smarted and immediately Becca's mood deflated.

Brett cut his eyes at his wife in disapproval, but Madi wasn't looking at him, her eyes were trained on Paxton. "Mad—"

"I know what you're doing and I understand, but don't think for one second that this makes it all ok, because it doesn't. Got me? You're still suspended until Friday, and I'll decide whether you play next Thursday night or not."

"Madi?" Pax whined.

"Paxton, we'll talk later. I'm actually hungry for a change, so let me enjoy a meal, please?" She huffed off into the living room, leaving Pax to glance dejectedly at Brett.

"I'm workin' on her. Give me time. She's pregnant; her emotions are all over the place." Brett shrugged and gave Pax a reassuring pat on the shoulder.

When Brett was out of earshot, Becca turned to Paxton, who continued to frown.

"I'm sorry," she whispered.

"It's not your fault." He attempted to smile but it didn't make his eyes.

"She hates me."

"She doesn't. She doesn't trust you…well, me really. Don't worry. She'll get to know you and love you, I promise."

Becca wasn't so sure about that. Madi McFadden didn't appear to want to get to know her. She was an outsider, and by the look of things, Madi didn't approve of this situation.

Pax gave her a reassuring smile and kissed her cheek. "Let's go have a good time, to hell with all their opinions."

Becca tried to settle her raging insecurity as Paxton led her into the lion's den.

She was a mortal woman walking among legendary gods… She was all too aware that history had never favored that interchange.

CHAPTER SEVEN

"I don't *trust* her."

"Why?" Pax grated.

Pax, Madi, and Brett stood in his office in the front of the house while Quil, Travis, Skyla, and Becca were out back in the courtyard having after-dinner drinks.

"Because. She's got her eyes on becoming curator of that museum, and she'll get there by any means necessary…even if that means blackmailing you."

"You don't even know her," Pax defended.

"And neither do *you!*" Madi growled, Hera taking charge. "I had Sloane McBride do a background check on her."

"Why?"

"Because I need to know who she is and what's at stake here. Her father up and left all three of them with nothing. They're dirt poor, in major debt due to her mother's cancer treatments, and her sister is a cheerleader for *our* team. A fact of which I'm certain she failed to mention."

"What? Really?"

"Dammit, Paxton, this is what I'm talking about! You don't even know the woman you're 'engaged' to. This is all a huge mistake on your part. You reacted impulsively, and now the whole damn team is gonna suffer for it!" Madi audibly growled and threw her arms out in frustration.

"Madi, sit down," Brett demanded, taking hold of his wife's shoulder. "And *calm* down."

Madison reluctantly did as she'd been told, taking the leather chair across from Pax's desk. She took in a deep breath, looking from Brett back to Pax.

"Now, Rebecca seems like a fine young woman of high standards, not a gold digger. I'm sure we can figure something out," Brett offered.

"Not with the damn mess he's made out of all this!" She huffed back, cutting her eyes at Pax.

"Mess? Madi, she's my—" Pax interjected.

"Oh, bullshit. Don't feed me that. We all know this is a farce if I've ever seen one. That girl doesn't know you from Adam! It's obvious!"

Damn, was it really?

"Pax, you should have thought this through a little better." Madi shook her head at him again.

"Ok, my love, but he didn't. Now the public believes that he and Rebecca are engaged so he's gonna have to play it out."

"And just how *long* do you intend to do that, by the way?" Madi's angry eyes hit Pax's, and he literally gulped. He didn't have a clue.

"I-I dunno. I mean, I was—"

"At least until this season is finished. February at the *earliest!*" Madi interceded.

"Madi, I can't—"

"You can and you *will*! The last thing we need is anymore tragedies on this team. I didn't pull the best team together this year to have it thrown away on a whim. So, you'll do whatever it takes to make that girl look like you are the happiest couple next to frickin' Romeo and Juliet or you're getting cut."

"What!"

"I didn't stutter," Madi snarled. Pax had never seen her so angry and didn't understand it to save his life.

All he'd done was make out with a girl on a Ferris wheel, but the way Madi was shooting daggers at him right now would led one to believe he'd raped her in a church or something just as vile. He'd really gone and pissed her off...apparently.

"Sunflower," Brett murmured cautiously, squatting down to rub her thighs. "Let's not be hasty and say—"

"I mean it, Guthrie." Madi pointed up to Paxton then. "The only thing I'd better hear from the media about you and Rebecca is about how excited she is for her wedding with you and nothing more. Try me if you don't think I'm dead serious."

With that, Madi shoved Brett aside and walked out of Paxton's office, slamming the door in her wake.

"What the fuck is stuck up her ass?" Pax muttered and frowned at his QB.

Brett sat and pulled a deep breath in. "She just learned last week that her dad plans to retire after we win the Super Bowl."

"Jesus, Brett, we don't even know if we're *going* to the Super Bowl yet. It's still too early—"

"Oh, I know. But he's convinced and so is she. No pressure or anything." Brett laughed without humor. "Trust me, I'm just as perplexed about it as you are. When Jerry was talking about it last weekend, I wanted to puke. Nothing means more to me than my team and our success, but this pressure might just blow my head clean off." He laughed again, and Pax felt bad for his QB.

"I'm sorry, man. Trouble in paradise?"

"No, not at all. I mean, Madi and I are very happy together. Never been happier, in fact. Things have been more amazing with her than I ever thought possible. But with Hunter not even gone a year yet, and now her dad leaving the organization, I think Madi's just scared is all. She's reacting the only way she knows how to."

"Hera *is* protective of her family," Pax reasoned.

"Exactly, so please don't misinterpret her words. She loves you.

She's just out of sorts. This pregnancy hasn't helped things, despite how excited we are… I'm looking forward to the second trimester, that's all I'll say." He grinned, and Pax returned it.

"Maybe she does need some of what I said earlier." Pax elbowed Brett as he stood, in an attempt to lighten the mood.

Brett grinned. "Maybe so. I'll let you know how it goes."

They shot the shit for a little while longer, the tension easing some, then he and Brett moved out to the courtyard to join everyone else.

Madi was laughing with Skyla; It seemed like the whole talk had never happened, but the sting of her words cut Paxton to the core. How could she not see that everything following Friday night's fiasco had been done to protect the team's reputation, not his own? He'd make her understand; he had to. Nothing meant more to him than his career, football, the Gladiators, his brothers—Zeus, Ares, Hades and the rest.

When they all began to leave some time later, Pax hugged Madi to him, willing her to understand. "Hera, don't give up on me," he whispered.

"Don't disappoint me, and I'll have no reason to." She winked and kissed his cheek, all forgotten for the time being.

But Pax had a nagging feeling this wouldn't be the last he'd hear from Madi on this uncomfortable matter. He was left with more doubt than when he'd seen the first headline.

I'm damned if I do, damned if I don't. This was a hopeless situation.

REBECCA ATTEMPTED to smile over at Paxton as she slid uncomfortably into the hot tub later that night. She was clad in a not-so-conservative two-piece tankini—more form-fitted than was comfortable.

Dinner had been lovely and delicious, and the conversation had been fun and light… except that Madison McFadden seemed to eye her like a hawk and have it out for Paxton. Becca had never imagined she'd make an enemy out of the stunning, blonde CEO, but here they were.

"You're even more beautiful free of all your clothing," Pax said over to her, resting his arms on either side of the rocks that lined the lip of the hot tub.

"That's kind of you to say." She pulled her lips in, self-conscious.

"Male opinion, I guess. Typical, right? Sorry," he attempted a recovery. "I mean, you look lovely, Rebecca."

She gave him a little giggle. "I sure could say the same about you." She couldn't help but eye the definition of his neck, deltoids, biceps, and pecs that greeted her from above the steaming, bubbling blue water.

Pax gave her a grin.

She looked down, unsure what to say. This whole hot tub experience was awkward already, to say the least, and she wasn't sure why she'd agreed to do this.

Pax broke the silence quickly enough. "I'm glad you got to meet some of my teammates tonight."

"Me too. They're great, by the way."

"I know we badger each other. It's all in fun, though."

Madi hadn't been badgering him out of fun, it would seem.

As if reading her thoughts, he said, "Look, don't worry about Madi. She'll come around." Although, Becca wasn't sure if he were trying to convince himself or her.

She gave him a weak smile in return and fiddled with her hands in the water. She still hadn't heard from her sister but had spoken with her mother, who was doing "just fine without her." She knew she was worrying for no reason; it was just a couple nights then she could sneak back, but Becca still felt on edge leaving her mam alone.

"You ok?" Pax asked.

"Yeah, just thinking about Mam."

"Is she alright?" His brows furrowed as he asked.

"Yeah, she's—she's fine. I just worry about her. I tend to her at night while Veda works, remember?"

"I thought she was a cheerleader, which I didn't know by the way."

"Oh, yeah, she has several jobs." She wouldn't elaborate about what they all were; Veda's various jobs weren't exactly something Becca was proud of—nor wanted to admit aloud to Paxton Guthrie of all people.

"You make it sound like they aren't permanent."

"No, they aren't." She'd leave it at that. He could draw whatever conclusions he wanted to.

"And you just have the one sibling, right?"

"Yes. I was tasked with caring for Mam at night while Veda worked and vice versa. That was until she got the cheerleading job. It kinda fell into her lap. Her goal is to actually be a model."

Pax's brows went up in surprise. "She should talk to Brooke about that."

"Brooke?"

"Yeah, Madi's sister. She's a model."

Becca couldn't fathom Madi ever wanting to share her sister's number or personal information, let alone a reference. Madi hated her.

"Hey," Pax murmured and came forward, his big frame stopping within inches of hers, making her already frazzled nerves fray on their ends. She gulped. "She'll come around. And if it's any consolation, I'll introduce you to Brooke and we'll bypass the middleman, huh? She's as different from Madison as Veda is to you."

Becca didn't know if that was a compliment or not, but when his hand came up and he fingered a lose strand of her hair that had fallen from the bun on her head, she knew it was a compliment.

Poseidon's eyes sparkled from the glow of the twinkle lights hanging over their heads. His body was too close, too tempting, his lips too kissable, his masculine allure too enticing.

"Let's take this down." He didn't give her time to respond before he came up and pulled her hair from the clasp that held it up. Her curly locks spilled down her shoulders, the ends dipping into the water before she even realized what had happened. "That's better."

"You—you don't like my hair up?"

"Oh, I do. It showcases your gorgeous neck but down… you look so naughty with it down."

Naughty? She didn't have a naughty bone in her body—even if, in this moment, she wished she did. Pax's hand moved to cup her cheek and he came ever closer. Becca's heart pounded hard in her chest. She didn't know whether to go with it or protest, but she tried to relax. If they were to pull this whole engagement off, she couldn't be so quick to weasel away from his touch and balk at his advances.

"I've been wanting to kiss you all night, you know?"

"Well," she gave a huff that was meant to sound more like a giggle but didn't. "Here I am."

"Yes, here you are. Now what ever shall I do with you, my little *naia*."

"*Naia?*" Becca frowned.

"It's Hawaiian for dolphin."

"And Latin for nymph."

He smiled, pleased that she knew that, although she only did because a friend of hers was going to name their daughter that. "Nymph*o* is more like it."

Becca gaped. "I am not a nympho."

"Oh, I bet you're a total closet nympho. Aren't you, Becca?" His smirk was playful and called to some wilder part of her.

"How dare you!"

He laughed again, baiting her, even as he separated the distance between them. He pulled her into his broad, barrel chest, his over-sized muscular arms wrapping around her tightly.

Her breath stilled, and the water seemed to get even hotter. Becca thought she might faint if he kissed her, but he was leaning in. He was going to. He just said he'd been wanting to all night. Now nothing was stopping him from doing so.

"Pax—" she protested, feeling her sex begin to hum even as his lips hovered just centimeters from her own.

"Mmm, I never liked the sound of my name...until I heard you say it, sweetness."

His lips pulled at her own as he softly brushed them over hers—soft as satin and light as a feather. A deep moan answered him and he chuckled before deepening the kiss. Her mouth opened to him, relinquishing control as she let his tongue invade and conquer. His thumb brushed her cheekbone as he angled her head then lifted her. Her legs began to wrap around his waist of their own accord, and she reveled in the feel of his hard-muscled torso touching her half-naked flesh. The wave of turbulence that spiked through her shook her to the core as she moved her arms around his neck, settling herself against him while he pressed her into the wall of the hot tub.

His manly moan made her womanhood ache with a longing she'd never felt before, and she couldn't resist the urge to rub her sex against his tenting crotch. This was better than any fantasy she'd ever had of Pax before—having him here, real and tangible.

"Oh, baby," he groaned as he pulled back to feast on her neck and when he did, he began to unleash something feral inside her. The lapping of his tongue on her flesh had her whimpering like a needy baby for milk. She arched her breasts against his chest and felt a sharp pressure dig into her thigh.

Suddenly, she realized what it was and gasped. She looked into his eyes and the stormy sea she saw there frightened her. He was Poseidon; he had a fury unlike the other gods, a fury for her, and he meant to have her. She gaped, unsure whether to tell him. No one knew! Well, maybe her mom and Veda did, but it was shameful—especially for a woman of her age...

"Oh God, Pax," she cried even as his mouth returned to her throat, sucking, kissing and licking until she was begging with her body for release, rocking her hips against his, as tempestuous as the raging sea she'd seen in his blue eyes.

"Mmm, yeah, baby. You like that?" he asked as he thrust back against her. "Does that feel good?"

She moaned in answer, her hands moving over his bare back and gripping. More, she wanted more. It felt so incredibly good, but she wanted so much more. His mouth moved to her collarbone as if reading her thoughts, his tongue licking the top of her breastbone and lower.

She began to gasp and pant, the noises unfamiliar to her. She felt a pulling of her bathing suit and began to protest only to cradle Pax's head as his mouth fell to the mound of her half-exposed breast.

"Oh, God."

"Name's Poseidon, sweetness," he chuckled as his fingers moved to her upper thigh.

She was a quivering mess now, unfamiliar with the wanton female begging as Paxton's fingertips tickled her groin. Every decent part of her wanted to stop this, but that naughty little nymph he'd awoken wanted to let him go further.

She gasped as he moved the bottoms aside and she felt his fingers touch her where she ached the most. His lips took hers as he thrust a thick finger inside her and she grunted, feeling her body resist slightly at the unfamiliar intrusion.

"Mmm, Becca, you're so tight," he muttered against her lips as she moaned deep and long, loving the feel of him filling a part of her no one ever had. He pulled his finger back and thrust in again, and she squeezed her inner walls around him, getting a groan from him. "Shit, baby."

She wasn't sure if he was protesting or encouraging her, but his finger began to pump into her as his mouth returned to her breast. She arched her hips against him, taking all the pleasure he was giving and absorbing it as his lips moved to her exposed nipple.

She cried out as he pulled it into his mouth and sucked hard, flicking his tongue back and forth over the pebbled bud as his finger continued to torture her. A fluttering began in her lower belly as her body was ravaged by Paxton's loving. Never had she felt such yearning and passion. She couldn't stop herself from relishing each caress as his mouth returned to hers. She felt her soul leave the earth and screamed into his mouth, her body spasming and quaking around his finger.

"Oh, oh, Pax," she whimpered as her hands gripped his broad shoulders, and he kissed her cheek, chuckling.

"Damn, that was hot as fuck, baby," he said, pulling back as he looked down at her bared breast, thanks to his voracious hands. "Look how hard you got me."

He pulled her hand to his crotch, and she gasped in surprise at the swollen member suddenly in her bare hand; somehow her hand had gotten into his trunks and now, his hard sex was in her palm. Damn, it was fascinating. The length and thickness of it as she stroked him in her fist. Oh, the sounds he made as she did so; she was aroused all over again.

OMG, I'm touching his penis. Holy shit!

"Mmm, Becca," he grated through his teeth, looking back into her eyes with such want that her heart threatened to beat out of her chest.

"Pax," his name was a whisper on her lips as she leaned back in for another kiss.

He kissed her back, his tongue raiding and pillaging every square inch of her mouth as she fought to contain the emotions erupting within her.

Suddenly, he was turning her and pulling at the bottoms barely hanging around her thighs, moving toward a jet.

"Pax?" she asked confused even as he pressed her aching sex into a pulsing jet of water. Her gasp was sharp with equal parts objection and desire as he hovered her over the blast of water, his finger moving back inside her from behind. "Oh my God," she whimpered as his lips returned to her neck, his hand to her breast, squeezing as if he owned it.

"Yeah? I'm gonna make you come again, my little *naia*. Come, then it's my turn to come."

He pulled her hand back to his erection and she gripped it possessively. A surge of pleasure rose between her legs and spread deep in the hollow of her belly.

"Paxton."

"Oh yeah. Say my name, sexy lady. Give me your moans. I want them all." He beckoned as he began to bounce her up and down over the jet that shot into her most secret spot. He began to thrust against her gripping hand, moving his pelvis into her bottom while he tormented her with the jet of water and his finger thrust into her.

"Oooh," she cried as another orgasm assaulted her, making her succumb to both the water and her captor, Poseidon, the god of the seas.

Paxton was quick to follow. He roared into her neck as he latched on, biting into her shoulder and pulling her into him, groaning his release as he arched up into her fist over and over again. His moans and grunts subsided slowly as they both came back down to earth, their heart rates and breathing returning as he continued to stroke her breast and swollen bud.

"Oh shit, Rebecca. That was amazing, my sweet." He kissed her shoulder before turning her abruptly around. "Mmm, now I wanna bury my cock inside that tight little pussy."

He began to jerk his trunks down and pulled her legs back around him. That's when Becca started to panic. His hands roved her body, and he took her lips again.

She grunted and pushed against him. "Wait!"

Paxton's deep blue eyes stared deep into hers. "What's wrong?" he asked, and Becca's cheeks flamed red in shame.

She felt more exposed at that instant than she ever had in her entire life, their naked sexes mere inches from one another, his hungry lips and body ready to devour her whole.

He stroked her hair, and Rebecca looked away, humiliated by the tears gathering at her eyelids.

Her lips began to quiver even as Pax cooed, "Becca, baby, talk to me."

"I'm sorry, Paxton. I—I can't…"

"Ok, that's ok. We don't have to," he reassured her. "I didn't mean to be pushy. I just— You're just so damn irresistible, sweetness." His crooked grin stilled her.

She gulped and willed her backbone to straighten. "It's not that I don't want to, I-I—"

Oh God, just say the words, you damn coward!

"Pax, I'm a virgin."

CHAPTER EIGHT

H ad he heard her right? Had she said...?
   "I'm a virgin," she repeated, her face tightening as she lifted her chin.

Holy shit balls! He'd not been expecting that. Not in a million damn years. Sure, she was quiet and introverted, but she was hot as hell. How on earth had she come this far in life and not gone all the way with anyone? She wasn't new to being touched or orgasms...was she?

"Becca, I'm sorry."

"Why? I'm not," she retorted.

"Well, I mean, if I'd have known I would've—"

"What? Not done what we just did?"

Hell no! He would have done that either way. He probably just wouldn't have been as...well, as forceful. God knows, he hadn't wanted to scare the poor thing. She didn't look scared though.

"I just wish I would've known... so I didn't hurt you."

"I think you saw that you didn't hurt me, *a rúnsearc.*"

Pax laughed. "Did you just call me a ruined *shark*?"

"*A rúnsearc.* It's Celtic for..." She blushed. "Never mind."

Whatever it was, it sounded sexy on her lips, and he grinned only to frown. "Sweetness," he touched her cheek again, "why didn't you tell me?"

"And when was I supposed to do that? As I was having my first orgasm that didn't come from my own hand?" Her voice was raised and his brows followed.

"Becca, you...?"

"Wow, that sounded even worse out in the open." She began to pull away from him. "I...I think it's time I retired for the evening."

"Becca, come on. Please?"

"No, I-I should go. Thank you for..."

She didn't finish as she extricated herself from him and moved to the steps.

What could he say? There was nothing *to* say.

He watched her walk away, her tight little rear-end in the bikini bottoms, her dark hair so long it almost touched that plump ass of hers.

A virgin? Holy shit! He'd never been with a virgin. Never dreamed he would ever be in the throes of passion with one, and it turned him on like never before. Before, it would have just been like any other time. But now, it was gonna be so much more. He would be the first to claim her. The first man to be inside her. The first man to possess her body. Being the first man to love a woman as sweet and soft and stunning as Rebecca Ryan made Paxton ravenous. He'd given her the first orgasm she'd ever had that wasn't self-inflicted. And he felt like fucking Superman. He was suddenly completely fascinated with ruining her.

"I'm a sick man."

But he knew deep down it wasn't because he was sick or mental or insane. He was simply digging this chick. For the first time in a long time, he felt something again. And it was desire—sharp and poignant. But it was also something else, something deeper, something he'd not wanted since he was much younger. A relationship. A real relationship with a woman who would mean more to him than just a simple fuck.

His father, Glenn Guthrie, had left when he was just a child—at the ripe age of eleven. He and Pax's mom, Tara, had fought for years. Prior to finding out he was adopted, Paxton had always assumed it to be because his father wondered about Paxton's legitimacy. Glenn and Tara had adopted him when he was a baby, but he'd not known it until Glenn was out of their lives.

Pax had never looked anything like his adoptive father—what with his bright blond hair and sky-blue eyes. He had deeply tanned skin, while his father was fair, freckled, and red-headed. Even as a child, Paxton had noticed the many differences in them and questioned it. His mother, Hawaiian by birth, had never confirmed nor denied exactly why Glenn left when Pax had asked her, but it had destroyed them both when he filed for divorce and walked out of their lives. It was a raw wound in Paxton's open heart.

His mother had come clean by the time Pax was fifteen about his adoption, but it hadn't mattered. In his eyes, he was an unwanted child, abandoned by both his biological parents and the man who'd raised him until he was eleven—whether he was genetically his or not, it had cut Paxton to the core.

Since then, he'd not had a steady relationship—nor *any* relationship, really—save for with his mom and uncle Kawai, his mother's brother.

It had been awkward at first. Pax had so much anger after his father left him that anyone in the way took the brunt of it. But Uncle Kawai was tough, took no shit from him, and pushed him into football to get his focus on something physical and out of the trouble he knew Pax would've gotten into had he not had an outlet to focus his anger. At the time, Pax threw the love he tried to show him back in Kawai's face at every turn. Now he was one of his best friends. Kawai was the reason Paxton Guthrie had become a legend, a god of the gridiron, all because he hadn't given up on the violent, broken little boy—the one whose father would never love him.

Now, he pulled himself from the jacuzzi and cut the jets off, feeling like the biggest son of a bitch in the world.

BY THE NEXT MORNING, Pax had had time to figure out what he might say to Rebecca.

He showered early and came downstairs for breakfast, hoping to see her and apologize for his brutish behavior the night prior.

She looked as beautiful as always, hair up in a ponytail, glasses on, reading a book the size of Texas as she dined on fruit, eggs, and a croissant that took up half the plate. Her porcelain skin was slightly exposed, her cream tank top highlighting the subtleties between the two colors beneath a rust-colored cardigan. Did the woman own anything that wasn't a sweater?

"Morning," he said as he took the seat next to her. Sonia met him with a steaming mug of coffee and a plate. "Thanks, Sonia."

"Of course, Mr. Guthrie."

He smiled over at Becca, who wasn't looking at him. She appeared entranced in the novel. He tried again. "Did you sleep well?"

Finally, searing emerald eyes met his over the top of her book. "Don't you know that when a book is open, your mouth is to be closed?"

"Ouch," he leered. *I guess I deserve that after the mind-blowing orgasms in the hot tub, huh?*

"I apologize." She puckered her lips and closed the book, dramatically—*in his opinion*—laying it down on the table. "I should've waited, but it was getting exciting as—" She looked off, bashfully, and he couldn't help but smile at her.

It was good to see her so passionate, regarding anything, but a book in particular.

"What's it about?"

"Oh, it's the fifth book in the Outlander series—*The Fiery Cross*."

"There are books, *too*?" he asked in surprise.

She frowned at him as if he'd been hiding under a rock, he blushed. "Don't tell me. I'm only on Season 2. They're in France."

"Oh, you have a-ways to go then."

He smiled as he took a bite of his croissant. When he swallowed, he said, "So, I've been thinking... What if we host a party?"

"A party?"

"Yeah, a way to introduce one another. To more than just my close friends. To the whole team and *your* friends, too. Halloween is Saturday, and we have a Thursday game next week, so that will be our off day."

"You want to have a big party in seven days?"

"Why not? It'll be fun. We can dress up!"

"I dunno, Pax. I—"

"You're an introvert, I get it. But it will be fun, I promise. We can be Claire and Jamie. I'll get a kilt and a wig and..."

Becca was laughing hysterically. "Oh my goodness. You'd wear a kilt?"

"Sure. It's Halloween. I'll even go without my skivvies, just so it can be true about what they wear beneath them." He winked and her eyes changed for a moment before she looked down, her cheeks as red as the strawberry jam on his pastry. "Speaking of. I'm sorry about last night...well, embarrassing you, anyway. I didn't mean to."

She finally looked up and smiled. "It's alright."

"I don't regret any of it, I want you to know that. I just— Well, I wish I would have been more prepared."

"No way to prepare for a twenty-four-year-old virgin," she smarted.

"You make it sound like you're forty. There's nothing wrong with being a virgin at twenty-four, nothing to be ashamed of."

"I'm not ashamed, just..." She looked away again. "I'm proud of being a virgin."

"Well, good. As you should be," he replied and took her hand. "Becca, millions of people regret their first time, myself included. I did it because all my friends were and I didn't want to be 'uncool.' You have something that few of us ever get; the power to really choose for yourself who you give yourself to the first time."

"I wanted it to be special. Call me a dreamer, naïve, whatever. I wanted to give my virginity to someone who deserves it, not just get rid of it at the first opportunity."

"That wouldn't be me then." Pax frowned, knowing he wouldn't have deserved a gift so valuable. Though he hadn't taken her virginity—well, not yet anyway—he'd taken something just as precious.

"And how do you know I've not been saving myself for *you* and you alone, Paxton Guthrie?" His brows went up in answer, surprised by the boldness of her statement. "Do you know how many posters I have of you on my walls?"

Was she being serious? He couldn't tell. Her intelligence far exceeded his own. He smiled though when her dark brow rose. "I'm gonna guess at least ten," he answered.

Becca didn't reply, but her porcelain cheeks turned red as her eyes lowered.

"A twenty-four-year-old virgin, eh?" He winked. "Do you have one of those special candles we get to light on Halloween night?"

She laughed out loud. "This isn't Salem, but I'm sure I could find one… if that will bring you to my bed."

Mmm, he wanted to be in her bed, even if he *didn't* deserve it. "It wouldn't take *much* to bring me to your bed, *Sassenach*."

"Oh *God*, please don't say that word like that." She moaned. "Holy mother—" She fidgeted in her seat and pulled her lips in—and he was growing an instant erection at her reaction.

"Damn, sweetness. I didn't realize I'd get *that* kinda response out of you. Now, I'm going online right this minute and ordering a kilt." He pulled his phone from his pocket to do just that, but Becca grabbed at his hand.

"I think you should be Poseidon for Samhain, not Jamie."

"I don't think so... Poseidon won't score me the points that a kilt and highlander gear will. Not after you practically *came* at the word—"

"*Don't* say it again."

He smirked and looked her over, wanting to feast on her even more than the food that was in front of him. "Rebecca Ryan, you're just full of surprises, aren't you, *naia?*

"You have no idea."

"Mmm," he hummed, his eyes raked her over. "I can't wait to find out."

"I'll just bet you would. Play your cards right and you *will*. Now, order a costume for Poseidon. I have my own surprise in store if it's a Halloween costume party you want."

With that, she winked, stood, grabbed her book, and walked off, leaving him to gape at the tight little mini skirt she wore. It was red plaid and made her look like a delectable little schoolgirl.

Fuck! She was so damn hot, and he fantasized about what lay beneath that pleated skirt.

That thought would drive him nuts all day.

ON SUNDAY, they watched the game together. Pax felt resentful and annoyed that he wasn't there with his team. But Becca was on the couch with him, cheering and rooting them on alongside him, which made the ache a little easier to bear.

The Gladiators won against Houston, but only by a field goal. The game was a teeth-clencher the whole time, and he and Becca realized how long they'd been holding their breaths when it was over because they both collapsed in relief.

They'd spent the remainder of the day planning out their party for Saturday and figuring out their guest list. It was gonna be fun, and Pax was looking forward to it. They worked out around three

PM. Later that night, they watched the Packers vs. Bears game. He got a treat he wasn't used to eating during football season—blackened Mahi-Mahi tacos and fries—courtesy of Hooters off GrubHub.

On Monday, Becca went back to work. Pax got an early call telling him that his suspension was over and that he could come back to the complex at eleven for their team meeting. Wednesday would be a half practice, since their game was on Thursday. Pax was pumped that he was back at it, ready to prove himself.

He strolled through the halls like a bird uncaged, his mood lighter than it had been since his fall from grace. He was brought up to speed on the plan for Thursday's game during the meeting. Following a vigorous workout, Pax changed and was heading out to the field to practice with the defense when he noticed a newly-hung sign above the tunnel.

"An invincible determination can accomplish almost anything and in this lies the great distinction between great men and little men. —Thomas Fuller," it read.

"That's a cool message," he stated, thinking aloud.

"Yeah, Quil found it. He said it fit our theme this year." Brett shrugged with a grin.

Pax nodded to his QB and his chin rose as he patted the sign and strolled out to crush his routes.

After practice, he showered and told the guys his plans for a Halloween party.

"A Halloween party?" Trav replied eagerly. "Sounds like a blast. Let's do it!" He gave Pax a high five.

TJ was on board too, and they encouraged Brett, who was unsure due to his wife's recent grumpiness.

"Oh, c'mon. It'll be fun," Linc insisted.

Quil looked like he might barf, and Pax patted him on the back. "Now, Hades, don't look so grim."

That got a laugh out of all of them, and Trav put his finger up as if to say, "Eureka."

"Hey, that's what we should do. Dress up like our god names." He rubbed his bearded chin in thought. "My future wife is gonna make one fine Aphrodite."

"What the heck does Lazarus even dress like? I'm gonna look like an idiot," Linc grumbled.

"Nah, you'll figure something out. Be creative. I can't wait for you guys to see my Poseidon costume," Pax replied, happily.

"Do I *have* to dress up?" Quil's scowl deepened.

"Oh, c'mon, chicken shit. If I have to wear this stupid wig with lightning bolts," Brett retorted and pointed to the Zeus costume he'd found online on his phone, "then yes, you have to dress up, too. Hell, you're Hades, wear a damn black cloak and bring a scythe."

"No, it has to be legit. No cheatin'," Trav scolded.

"Fine," Quil whined. "Is this kid friendly? You know my *hija* will want to trick-or-treat first."

"Yeah, the twins too. It's their first Halloween where they're old enough to know what's going on," Linc agreed.

"Sure, bring 'em. I'll have a room set up for the kids to play and hire some good baby-sitters. This way the adults can play," Pax recommended.

"And play we shall." TJ's brows bobbed and he nodded.

Once Pax left the complex around three, he headed to Rebecca's museum. He wanted to see his girl, so he parked and walked up to the old brick structure off the main road. He'd just headed inside when he saw her talking to a large group; she was about to lead a tour, so he quickly paid for a ticket and joined them, pulling his ball cap down tighter on his head to be as inconspicuous as possible.

She gave him a wink, noticing him right away, and beckoned everyone forward, stopping to discuss the remnants of Civil War memorabilia in the first room.

"As you know, the Civil War was one of the bloodiest stains in America's history and some of it was actually fought in our backyard."

She spoke of the Battle at Chickamauga, the first major battle on Georgia soil with the second highest casualties following Gettysburg. Then about the Battle of Kennesaw Mountain and how strenuous the trek up the mountain was while hauling both horses and heavy cannons atop wagons. Pax looked around at all the uniforms, both Confederate and Union, the leftover tins, bullets, and muskets displayed in cases with backdrops of maps. It stilled him to think about brother fighting brother. He thought perhaps he and Becca should take a hike up the mountain next weekday; he'd never been.

They next moved into a room where arrowheads, tomahawks and headdresses, and the wardrobe of a Cherokee warrior were displayed on a wax mannequin. Becca gave them a rundown of the Georgia Indian War of 1782, then they moved on into a separate room where a primitive human was displayed along with cave drawings. A giant sea creature greeted guests on one wall of the next room, a sasquatch on another. The next rooms housed Egyptian hieroglyphs and Roman Empire memorabilia. All the while, Rebecca wove a fascinating tale about the ancient contents behind the glass. She was an enthralling storyteller, dropping and raising her voice as if acting out a clandestine play. She was animated and answered each question brought to her. Pax had never felt more captivated in all his life. She knew her craft and knew it well. When she let the patrons explore an opening room displaying everything from planets to insects, he moved forward to speak to her.

"Well, well, Ms. Ryan, history has never been hotter, I don't think."

"I hope I wasn't too boring." She blushed and looked down at the heeled-toe she jutted out.

"*Boring*? On the contrary, m'lady. If I'd had a history teacher as sexy and mesmerizing as you are, then I definitely would've paid more attention in class."

"Did you learn anything aside from my bra size, Mr. Guthrie?" she scolded.

He leaned in and whispered, "I've had your plump breasts in my hands, sweetness. I don't need your bra size."

She gaped as he pulled back and winked.

"Besides, I was actually paying attention to the stories, believe it or not…while *also* admiring your ass in this pencil skirt."

"Pax," she scolded and swatted his hand away.

"Seriously, this is great." He gestured as he looked around. "I can tell you're passionate about your work. You're a wonderful storyteller."

"Thanks, but you're probably just biased."

"Maybe so, but still. If I wasn't into history before, I am now for sure." He gave her a knowing smile, and her porcelain cheeks reddened further.

Just then, a strange-looking man in a hooded sweater came up and cleared his throat. "Rebecca, you were wonderful as always."

"Oh, why thank you, Jeremiah."

The man Becca referred to as Jeremiah eyed Pax with suspicious, angry brown eyes that he narrowed. He gave Pax the once-over as he said, "You must be the fiancé."

"I am. Indeed. Tagging along to see my beauty in all her glory."

"Never seen you in here before." The answer was leading, but Pax didn't take the bait.

"Paxton Guthrie. It's good to meet you, Mr.…?" Pax extended his hand to introduce himself.

The stranger didn't take it, looking as if Pax had presented him with a handful of shit. Pax pulled his hand back, grateful the weirdo hadn't shaken it.

"Rebecca, you look lovely as always. I'll see you later."

With that, Jeremiah walked off, leaving Pax with a knot in his gut; the guy was a total freak.

"I don't like him," Pax grumbled as he took Becca's hand in his.

"Yeah, me either, but not much I can do about it."

"Does he come here often?"

"At least once a week," she confessed.

"Just don't ever let yourself be alone with that weirdo." Pax looked over to see that Jeremiah had stopped at the wooly mammoth display and was glancing back at them with a nasty scowl on his face.

"Becoming the protective bridegroom, are ye?"

"Hell yeah, I am. I don't like the way he looks at you."

"Jealous much?" Becca giggled, and he stroked her palm.

"Very. You're mine, little *naia*. Poseidon doesn't share."

Rebecca giggled again. "Well, *Poseidon*, you should put your trident away. My boss might not like your closeness during the public tour."

"Mmm, do I get a private one later, then?"

"Do you want one?" The green eyes that scorched his made him hot all over.

"Don't tease, Amphitrite. Poseidon is a furious god, after all."

Rebecca all out laughed then, the sound echoing through the halls, making her blush red once more. She pulled her lips in and looked down before finally saying, "So, you did some research did you, sea god?"

"I did. She's Poseidon's queen."

Becca's face grew serious and she cleared her throat, pulling her hand from his. "Well, I should mingle for a moment, see if anyone has any questions. I'm off in a half hour. Wanna meet me out front then?" She was dismissing him.

What had he said? He didn't sulk, for Pax wasn't one for sulking. He nodded. "Sure."

"Keep looking around. You might find some other areas of interest." She winked and turned to walk into the crowd of people.

Pax watched her. So professional. So classic. So beautiful. So perfect. How was this woman still single? It blew his mind even as he rounded the bones of a brontosaurus that took up the expanse of the room so he could still follow her with his eyes. He was still leery of the psycho man who also continued to watch her with growing interest, making Poseidon's fury rage within.

When Rebecca excused herself from the six people who'd gathered around her to assumedly ask questions or speak on history, the man accosted her.

Pax couldn't hear what the asshole was saying, but when he grabbed for her wrist, Pax stepped forward, only to be blocked by a little boy who beamed up at him.

Uh oh, he'd been recognized.

"Hey, buddy," Pax began, looking from Rebecca to the boy in front of him.

"I know who you are."

"Well, let's not advertise it, ok?" Pax winked then looked apprehensively back up to see Becca and the man arguing. He had to get rid of this kid. "Want an autograph?"

The boy, clad in a crimson Gladiators hoodie, nodded vigorously.

"Alright, I tell you what. Go grab a pen for me at the front and don't say anything, and I'll sign whatever you want. Deal?"

"Deal." He jumped for joy before turning to do as Pax asked.

Pax didn't fail to notice that Becca was rubbing her wrist where the prick had grabbed her. Where had that SOB run off to?

They would be discussing that very shortly as Pax pulled every bit of willpower he possessed, attempting to contain Poseidon's wrath as the boy came running back to him.

"So, are we gonna talk about what Jeremiah did?" Pax finally asked at dinner when they were halfway through.

The tight lips and narrowed brows immediately alerted Rebecca not to divulge too much.

They were seated in the back of a small and quaint little French bistro downtown. It had always looked inviting, and Becca had suggested it after Pax asked her where she wanted to dine. They'd walked in and had been immediately sat. Becca'd then witnessed the perks of fame, as well as the downside, as people had gasped and pointed when they'd walked by. Pax had nodded, giving them his beautiful smile as his palm settled on her lower back.

He was so devilishly handsome, no one could deny that fact. Handsome. Beautiful. And built like a tank. And she wanted him with a passion that blinded her to anything else. Here she was so close to giving her virginity away before marriage, but to a man she'd secretly worshipped unbeknownst to him for a long time now. The other night in the jacuzzi had been so passionate, so raw, and she'd been so close to having him inside her. It was all she'd thought about for the last two days.

But they hadn't been intimate again, and she wasn't sure if it was because he didn't want to or if he was thrown off by the fact that she was a virgin.

"Rebecca?"

She looked up into those stormy blue eyes of his—stormy with a rage she'd only seen on the gridiron—and she gulped. Pax was usually always smiling, but she was seeing another side of him right now; it began to frighten her.

"You want to tell me why that bastard grabbed your arm?"

She looked down, shame seizing her.

"You made him seem like some distant admirer, but that wasn't how it looked when he *assaulted* you."

She looked back up then down again, not sure what to say on the matter.

Paxton huffed out and took her chin in his massive palm. "Tell me. Why did he think it was okay to touch you?"

"He's, well, he's sorta my ex-boyfriend," she muttered under her breath.

"What?" his sharp tone echoed loudly off the cavern-like ceiling of subway tiles surrounding them. She'd never seen him so riled up, the sweet gentle giant now a raging Hulk.

Rebecca gulped as fear seized every cell of her body; she was unable to move, unable to speak.

"You're *fucking* joking, right?" Pax's voice wasn't as loud as before but was equally as belligerent, and Becca looked around for a quick escape. "Wait." Dark eyes held hers as his hand turned her face back to his. "He's done that before, hasn't he?"

She didn't want to talk about it. It was the past and things were fine now and...

"Becca, talk to me. Right the hell now." His commanding tone had the intended effect, and Becca couldn't hold in her tears—the fear, the regret.

She felt Pax's arm move around her shoulder in the booth they sat in, and he pulled her into his chest, cradling her head as he let her compose herself. She did so quickly, all too aware of the eyes on them.

"I'm sorry, sweetness. I just— I don't handle men abusing women well, as you can see. I didn't mean to frighten you. Hulk smash comes to mind, is all."

She couldn't help but snicker as she looked up into his sincere eyes. She took her finger and traced the lines of his face, smoothing his frown, and running her fingertip along his square jaw—so handsome, so sexy. "I understand. Veda would kill him if she knew he was still coming around the museum."

"Not if I get to him first," Pax added with all seriousness.

"It wasn't..." she trailed off, unsure how to start. "He was a regular 'fan' of my tours and one day asked me out for coffee. He seemed genuine enough and was always dressed in suits when he came in. We went out for coffee and things went well, so I agreed to have dinner with him. Again, he seemed kind and charming so we started dating. A month or so went by and he got confrontational with one of my patrons during a tour one afternoon and was kicked out of the museum. His whole demeanor had changed; he'd gone from benevolent to possessive almost overnight and demanded I quit working there. I refused and broke things off with him. He harassed me for a while. I had to change my phone number, and we even added more locks to the apartment. I assume Veda must have threatened him or something because months went by without a word. Then one day he showed up out of the blue and apologized, but things have been quiet..."

"Until today," Pax finished, and Becca nodded. "Look, I don't get a good feeling from this guy. I mean it when I say not to be alone with him. He's threatened by me and for damn good reason."

"Ok, *Poseidon*," Becca smarted.

"Poseidon nothing! I'll shove my fist down his throat if he *ever* touches you again."

"You sound a little possessive, Hulk." She tapped his nose with her finger.

"I don't share what's mine, I already told you that."

Becca practically swooned; it was the second time he'd said she was "his." That fact thrilled her and made a shiver run down her spine. How delicious it would be to let him officially make her *his*. "Down boy."

He gave her a crooked grin and leaned in, his face inches from hers. "This *boy* doesn't want to get down. Well, actually he does; down and dirty with his sexy little virgin."

"You're too much, Pax. Pervert," she baited.

"Right? Ever since you told me, it's all I've thought about. *Deflowering* you. Exploring every inch of you, making you beg for me to shove my—"

"How was everything this evening, Mr. Guthrie?"

They both jerked apart with a start. Pax cleared his throat, answering the server with, "Delicious," as his eyes roved back over Becca. "We'll take the check, please?"

"Madam, were the haricot vert cooked to your specifications?" the waiter asked, oblivious to the sexual waves rocking between Becca and Paxton.

"They were perfectly al' dente, Dante. Thank you so much," Rebecca cooed.

The server nodded and took their plates away, and Rebecca exhaled sharply.

"Fancy, Ryan. You're a woman of class, you know? A rare emerald in a sea of pearls."

"Emerald, huh?"

"Like the color of your eyes... stunning."

His nose against her jawline sent yet another shiver down her spine, and she couldn't wait to have his lips on hers once again.

When they got back to the limo, he was pulling her across his lap, the hard ridge of his cock digging into her pubic bone through her skirt.

"Mmm, Pax," she whimpered as his mouth fell to her collarbone.

"I'm gonna make you come again for me, my sexy little virgin bride."

She gasped as his hands moved into her cardigan and his mouth took hers. She thrust her tongue in, gripping his shoulders as she unleashed her passions upon him.

When Paxton pulled her tank top up to expose her lacy black bra, he was the one moaning.

"Damn, I thought virgins weren't supposed to wear naughty lingerie like this."

She giggled as he kissed the round mounds with calculated precision, his tongue darting out to tease. "Stereotyping is rude, Poseidon."

Rebecca ground their hips together as he continued to torment her flesh. She sucked in a gulp of air when he unclasped the front clasp of her bra and held her breath as his eyes took in her nakedness.

"Baby, you're so beautiful." His voice was reverent as he cupped her breasts in his massive hands, testing them and running his fingertips over her rigid nipples.

"Oh Pax," she cried as his head fell and his lips enveloped a nipple, taking half her breast into his mouth. His hands fell to her hips and rocked her against his steely erection.

"Fuck, baby, you feel so damn good."

She'd have to agree as her hands moved to unbutton his shirt, and he gripped her bottom, thrusting himself into her. She could feel the head of him slide through her covered folds and moaned loudly as her hands sought his naked chest.

His muscles were so smooth, so cut, so manly, and she felt her orgasm building as his hungry mouth moved to the other nipple, tormenting her with an eager tongue.

"Mmm, Pax, yes, oh baby."

"Come for me, sweet girl."

And as his teeth nipped at her flushed skin, she did, gasping and crying and dry-humping her fake fiancé's crotch like he was the answer to all her prayers—for he was, in all his glorious sexual allure. His half-cloaked chest rippled as he arched against her, his brows furrowed, his mouth opened as he groaned out and found his own release. His eyelids fluttered and his hand sought her breast, squeezing as he gasped her name. She could feel the wetness pool between her legs and attempted to catch her breath as she watched him looking her over.

"Damn baby. I can't wait to see what it feels like being inside you. This was one hell of a preview though, I have to say."

She smiled. She tended to agree. Although there was some part of her that was sad to see her virginity go, she was glad she was going to be giving it to him—to Paxton Guthrie, her *a rúnsearc*—her secret love and keeper of her heart.

He cupped her face as he recognized her doubt. "You ok, *naia*?"

She nodded, afraid to speak.

"I'm in no hurry. I want you to know that."

Ah, only because he was so intrigued by the fact that he would soon be sleeping with a virgin—just another tick-mark on his belt, she was sure. For her, it would be the opportunity of a lifetime, but for him, she would just be another woman in the long line of them.

Suddenly, that bothered her. A lot. She gulped.

She would just have to make him wait. So that she made sure she *was* special to him. She wanted him to remember her, miss her, and want her long after this fake engagement was over.

She would do everything in her power to simply drag this out as long as humanly possible.

CHAPTER NINE

"Hi, you must be Becca," said a lovely, tall, slender brunette with blonde highlights. She favored Madi. *She must be her sister.*

"I am. You're Brooke, right?"

"That's me." She gave Becca a crooked grin.

"Pax said you're a model."

"Brooke's many things; model is *one* of them," snorted another stunning blonde with an Australian accent. "I'm Valeria, but you can call me Val. Good to finally meet you." Val stuck her hand out for Becca to shake, and she did, with a smile.

"Linc's wife, right?"

Val nodded. "You've met Linc?"

"Oh, no! Not yet. I—"

"She's a fan of the team," came the cautious voice of Madison McFadden. "Of course she knows the players...and wives."

Becca gulped at the blue-green eyes that held hers. How in Hell was she ever going to prove herself to this woman?

"Hell, can you blame her?" Skyla piped in and grabbed Becca's arm. "Paxton Guthrie. What's not to swoon about 'Thor of the gridiron'?"

Pax really did favor Thor with his long, blond curls covered by the helmet when he played. Of course, it was a sweaty mess before the game was over—and it haphazardly gave something for the opponent to grab onto—but it was his signature feature.

"I was a big fan too, you know?" Sky continued as they took seats overlooking the field.

The luxury box was swankier than Rebecca could've anticipated with comfy leather seats, large TV sets so that one had a view of the game from any place in the room, an antique bar, and a buffet of various foods. The old wooden bar sat in the corner of the box, not obstructing the view, and appeared to house a full stock.

"You were?"

"Oh yes. Travis and I were classmates in high school, and I followed his football career over the years." A blue eye of the gorgeous redhead winked.

Becca hadn't known that. So, she wasn't the only "outlander" then.

"So, the date was all a bunch of BS, huh, Bec?" Brooke asked bluntly.

Rebecca didn't fail to notice Madi had turned to watch her, eyes slanted. Becca gulped.

"Well, uh..."

"Linc said that Pax said—"

"Can it, Aussie Barbie, and let the woman speak." Brooke elbowed Val.

Becca felt the heat in the room rise as all the women—Val, Brooke, Madi and Skyla— turned their attention to her. Oh God, she couldn't lie to them, but she had no choice but to do so. After all, Pax had told her they had to make this seem as legit as possible. They'd even created a story to cover their tracks, and she wore the ring on her finger to help with the validity.

"It was his romantic attempt to propose."

"Where'd y'all meet?" Val asked.

"My museum. He was in a tour group."

"Paxton likes history?" Madi asked and planted her hand on her hips.

"Oh he *loves* history," Becca stated matter-of-factly. They'd discussed it many times before. And she knew which history he loved best. "He's a fan of the ancient civilizations—Egypt, Rome, Greece."

"That's because he loves to play the game *God of War*." Skyla smiled, knowingly. "Yeah, he plays with Travis over the headset sometimes. I'm sure you've heard him yelling at Maverick?"

Becca laughed. "Ah, yes. He does do that."

"How fun! So, you're the curator?"

"I'm one of the historians, but eventually I would love to be a museum curator." Becca smiled back at Val who asked the question.

"History; so much we can learn from it but seldom do," Brooke remarked and threw a glass of amber liquid back. "Want a whiskey, Becca?" she asked as she rose to her feet.

"Umm, yes, please? Jameson."

"Aye, *Irish* whiskey, eh?" Brooke winked. "I thought I detected a hint of an accent."

"Irish, huh?" Skyla smirked. "I got some Scottish in me from my mom's side."

"Brett's Scottish, too. I mean, obviously... McFadden." Madi smiled genuinely for the first time since Becca had met her. "Where in Ireland?"

"Doolin."

"Ah, Hunter and I visited the Cliffs of Moher. It was one of the most beautiful things I've ever seen. We were married in Galway."

"Oh, I didn't know that. We moved here when my sister and I were eight. My Gran and Gramp are still there. Maybe one day I can go back and visit them."

"It's beautiful there. Brett and I are planning to visit Scotland next year. I can't wait."

Becca smiled at her, suddenly getting the feeling that Madi might not be out to get her after all. There was a kind person hidden behind that ironclad mask of hers. Perhaps Madi was just being cautious about Becca and Pax's situation. After all, she was the CEO of the Gladiators, and it was her job to protect her team, like it was her husband's job to lead them.

"One Irish whiskey for the wee lass," Brooke said in her best attempt at an Irish accent as she handed Becca the whiskey glass.

Becca laughed and shook her head. She rose her glass and said, "Slàinte mhaith."

"Slaw-cha what?" Val asked

"Oh snap! She knows Gaelic?" Brooke's brows went up, impressed.

Becca smiled. "It's Irish actually; the Scots speak Gaelic." Becca pronounced the word like "gal-lick," getting a confused look out of all them which made her laugh. "Our languages are totally different despite that they have similar roots."

"Wow, who knew?" Val stated with a giggle.

"Who are you kidding? No one understands your Aussie ass either," Brooke mimicked.

"Oh, bugger off, you bogan," Val smarted back in her best Aussie accent.

They all laughed, even Madison.

"You two, zip it. Here come our men," Skyla looked out the box to see the Gladiators taking the field. Glorious in their crimson, gold, and white jerseys. They were larger than life, figures of true legend —Gods of the Gridiron.

"So, Pax said you live with your mom and sister… Is your father dead?" Brooke questioned, brazenly.

Becca looked over to Madi, those eyes watching her again. Why was she so suspicious?

"Aye, he passed three years ago. A sudden death. Heart attack." Becca failed to add that he'd simply up and left them all one day, when Veda and Becca were just teens. She'd heard about his death from their grandparents back in Ireland. The blow still felt just as sharp; she'd been a Daddy's girl.

"I'm so sorry," Val patted Becca's shoulder.

"Thank you."

"Oh, look at my sexy Ares. He's so handsome," Sky interrupted, seemingly to bring the topic back to something more comfortable.

The camera zoomed onto Travis talking with a sportscaster about the game. His pearly white smile was devilish as he spoke into the mic with an air that rivaled that of his Greek god counterpart.

"Well, Erin, I know I'm ready to get to plowin' that field." He winked into the camera.

"Gah, I can't wait to celebrate the victory with him tonight," she murmured.

"Yuck," Brooke gagged dramatically, shoving Skyla.

"That delicious ram will be plowin' more than *that* field tonight, especially if they win."

"You two are ridiculous," Madi scoffed playfully and sat down beside Skyla.

"What? Like you and Brett are any different, preggers!" Skyla snorted in response. "Don't tell me you don't do that same exact thing with Mr. Dead-serious Zeus?" Sky taunted Madi.

"What Zeus and Hera do in the privacy of their own bedroom is of none of your concern." Madi glanced at her, attempting to stay serious even as her cheeks flamed.

"Bunch of freaks, y'all are! They only think I'm the wild one. It's the quiet ones you gotta watch out for, I always say." Brooke elbowed Becca, who grinned subtly. "What's big ol' Poseidon like in the bedroom?"

"Oh, I—" Becca felt her cheeks flame in response. "Pax is—" But she knew she couldn't lie about this. "Well, he's quite gentle, surprisingly."

"Gentle, but rough when need be, I bet," Val encouraged.

To the contrary, but she couldn't say that because she didn't know for certain. Becca shrugged. "We haven't—"

"You haven't slept with him?" Skyla asked, surprised.

Becca shook her head, fearing she'd destroyed everything all at once.

"Good for you!" Brooke added. "Keep the big lug waiting, serves him right."

"Brooke," Madi warned, tilting her head.

"What? She's his fiancée, she has to know what a man-whore he's been. I'm sure he's told her."

He'd told her nothing of the sort. Although Becca could've already guessed as much and pretty much had. But hearing the words aloud gave the term a whole new meaning.

When Becca dared to look up, they all stilled. She swallowed down her hurt.

"Oh, Bec, I'm sorry. I didn't mean—"

But Rebecca was already standing. "Excuse me, please? I need to uh, freshen up before the game starts."

Becca practically ran to the bathroom just feet away and threw herself at the sink, turning the faucet on and splashing water into her face.

She was surprised when she turned to see Madi propped at the corner, dressed as regal as always in a flattering crimson dress with a small Gladiators logo embroidered above her left breast.

"Why did you agree to pretend to be his fiancée?" she asked.

Becca shrugged. "It seemed like a fool-proof plan at the time."

"Fool-proof, ha!" Madi laughed. "The media is going to dig and find the truth. It's only a matter of time. He can't be placed in the museum until just yesterday, so you're gonna have to come up with a new story."

Becca's jaw dropped.

Before she could speak, Madison continued. "Yes, I'm having you watched. Don't look so surprised. It's nothing personal, Rebecca. I have an asset to protect—my team." Madi huffed, as if this was as uncomfortable for her as it was for Becca, but that couldn't be possible. "How much money do you want?"

"What?" Becca asked incredulously. "Why would I want money?"

"Isn't that why you would agree to this in the first place? Your sister bounces around like a ping-pong ball, your mom is having rounds of chemo to treat cancer for the second time now, and you're not exactly living 'high on the hog' I see."

Becca gulped, so that's why Madi didn't like her; she thought she was out to con Paxton.

"At least if y'all haven't slept together, you can't bribe him with a baby. So, what'll it take to get you out of the picture?"

Becca looked down. The smart girl in her would just take the bribe. She sure as hell could use the money, but she didn't like hand-outs. She'd worked hard to get where she was. Taking money from Madi would make life easier, but at what cost?

"I don't want your money, Madison." Rebecca held her ground. "What happened that night wasn't planned, but our chemistry was undeniable. I wish it wouldn't have happened the way it did, but wishing gets us nowhere. Pax has put a lot at stake to save face for both of us. Now, what kind of person would I be if I just walked away and called him a liar after all he did to help me?"

Madi evaluated her for the longest time. Becca felt like she was being held under a microscope before Madi finally gave her a big smile. "That was the answer I was hoping for. Well, in that case, you'll have to keep the ruse up until after the Super Bowl. Are you willing to do that?"

"I'll do whatever it takes. Paxton has done so much for me. I owe him that much."

"Well, then we have to change your story. You're the friend of a friend of mine, and you and Pax were introduced at a party we threw back in July. You've been talking since then."

"July? That's only—"

"Three months. But as you said, your attraction was undeniable and you plan a long engagement." Madi winked.

"Ok, that's more believable." Becca agreed.

"More believable than Paxton Guthrie going of his own volition to a museum," Madi stated sarcastically, getting a laugh from Becca.

"I guess it sounds more believable *now* than before he met me, huh?"

"Very much so. And don't listen to those girls." Madi waved her hand dramatically. "Pax is a big flirt, not unlike Travis, but he's no worse than any of the rest of them, if you understand my meaning."

Becca couldn't hide her blush, nor the jealousy that tore at her heart thinking once more of the hordes of women Pax had probably taken to bed over the years.

"So, I hear Pax is throwing a Halloween party on Saturday?" Brooke asked, turning to watch Becca and Madi coming out of the bathroom, arm in arm.

"You *are* coming, right?" Becca asked Madi, who stopped at her question.

"Sure you want me to after how rude I've been to you?"

"Of course. Pax adores you."

Madi gave her a warm smile and patted her arm. "Ha! He's like all the other guys. He's simply tolerating me right now. I'm hoping the second trimester will be easier." She winced.

"Oh, you're pregnant? You're so slim, I didn't even notice." Rebecca's eyes fell down Madi's front.

"Well, Sky and I both are due pretty close to the same time. We're still very early along."

"Well congrats, ladies. That's wonderful news!" Becca said, congratulating them both with smiling eyes.

"And don't worry, I won't tell my husband," Madi whispered and winked at Becca, pulling her back to the seats with the amazing view of the field.

"Tell him what?" Becca wondered aloud.

"That Pax adores me." Amusement danced in Madison's eyes. Before Becca could reply she said, "Although he sure has a hard time keeping his eyes off *you*."

Becca blushed again. She resented even adding blush to her

cheeks anymore, since her color was perpetually pink anyway, it seemed.

"And yes, I'll be there. I'm looking forward to dressing up as the queen of the gods." Madi gave Becca a smirk.

"See! Told y'all," Brooke smarted. "The quiet ones. It's always the quiet ones."

PAX WATCHED with bated breath as the QB's eyes caught his through his helmet. The man's feet shuffled and he gulped. He looked left, he looked right. But it didn't matter, because the fury of Poseidon was about to rain down on his parade and crush his dream of a Hail Mary. It was fourth and long in the fourth quarter at the two-minute warning. The Gladiators were up by two TDs, and by the QB's piss-poor give away reaction, Pax knew exactly what he planned to do.

When the QB called for the snap and stepped back into a shotgun formation, his receivers running to take the field, Pax didn't chase after them. Instead, he ran through the huge hole the line had made and rushed the QB, who gripped the ball like it was his lifeline.

Too late, buddy, Pax thought as he launched at him, tackling him to the ground for a sack. He rose in triumph over the sprawled QB, smirking as he looked up at the roaring fans in the stands. He took his stance, feet together, slamming his right arm down like he had a trident there and crossed his arms over his chest.

The crowd ate it up, chanting, "Po-sei-don, Po-sei-don." Pax made sure to flex his biceps as he roared with all the fury of the mighty Poseidon, then clapped Linc's back as he grabbed him up for a victory embrace.

They were gonna win. Pax had stopped the opposing team's forward progress with one damn good sack; his second of the game. When he got back to the sidelines, Brett gave him a crooked grin and patted his helmet.

"My king," Pax murmured obediently, getting a laugh out of Zeus.

"Well done, Poseidon. I knew you'd be releasing that Kraken today."

"Only on your command, brother," Pax joshed as Brett shook his head in amusement.

Seven games, seven victories, now to just keep doing what they were doing… the Super Bowl might not be too far off.

Pax was distracted by a dark head of hair running towards him as he moved to the fifty-yard line for a better view; she looked so much like Becca that his heart hammered for a moment. However, he was confronted by the angry eyes of her twin sister, Veda, whose face was heavily made-up.

"Where's Bec?"

"She's fine. She's up in the box." Pax pointed to the luxury box tucked high in the stands.

Veda's scowl deepened, and she looked him over with growing contempt. "If you so much as think about touching her, I'll fucking leave you with a pitiful flap of skin not even remotely resembling a dick. You'll be having to piss through a thin plastic tube by the time I'm done with you; you'll be totally banjaxed. Got me?" she growled, looking fairly intimidating in her crimson, white, and gold cheerleading uniform which hid most her chest and the upper portion of her thighs. Her tattoos were covered by heavy makeup and her nose ring had a clear piercing that he couldn't see; he only knew it was there because he'd noticed the little diamond in her nose when they'd first met.

Pax put his hands up in surrender. "Yes, ma'am," he smarted.

"I'm not fuckin' kidding, you gobshite."

She huffed off as quickly as she'd come, but no one really seemed to notice as Pax's team was taking the field, celebrating their victory.

Pax looked up at the box, unable to see Rebecca, but was eager to celebrate with everyone later. They'd worked hard for this win, and Pax was so grateful to have everything back to normal.

He ran onto the field to congratulate his QB on yet another victory.

"H," Becca said to her sister as she came into the apartment with a bag of groceries.

Veda didn't even budge from her perch in the chair, her green eyes glued to the screen of her laptop. It looked to be *The Witcher* she was watching, if Henry Cavill in a hot tub half-naked was any indication.

"That's a good one." Becca pointed to the screen, setting the bag down on the Formica kitchen counter. She unloaded the groceries she'd gotten for dinner tonight. She was making colcannon, lamb shanks, and roasted carrots along with the second loaf of brack for dessert that she'd made at Paxton's that morning.

"Mmm, it smells delicious in here," Pax had said, coming into the kitchen after his workout earlier. "You making a cake?"

"Yes, barmbrack. It's a fruitcake."

Pax had wrinkled his nose. "Isn't fruitcake a Christmas thing?" he asked and sat at the island opposite her.

"Well, in Ireland, Mam would make them before Samhain and throw little trinkets into the batter." Pax's brows rose, and Becca laughed. "It's similar to what they do in New Orleans, with the king cakes. If you find a coin, it means you'll be wealthy and a ring means ye'll be married within the year."

"Well, that's fitting." He'd winked. "Teasing our unsuspecting guests, I see."

"Oh, Samhain is a *big* celebration in my family. We have all kinds of traditions."

"I'll bet." His grin had widened into a smile. "You're a Celtic druid, aren't you? Gonna go out and dance naked while the moon is full around a bonfire? I'm down." His eyes moved over her apron clad body with growing interest. "So long as I don't have to be sacrificed."

Rebecca had laughed. "Oh, not the lord of the manor, of course."

Pax had hired a decorating company. They were there now, while she was gone, to turn the entire bottom floor of his house into a magic wonderland. Becca decided to come see her family tonight and make them dinner so she wouldn't be in the way. She wasn't exactly sure what Pax had them doing but was eager to see when she got back later that night.

He had a catering company coming to prepare and serve the feast tomorrow, of which she was grateful for. Cooking for that many people was never an easy task.

With the food now laid out for her to begin prepping, Becca looked over to Veda who, again, ignored her presence.

"Don't you have a party to plan?" Veda grumbled with clear disdain.

"The decorator is there now with Pax."

"Oh, of course he hired people!" Veda rolled her eyes, drawing her bare legs beneath a floral blanket.

"Where's Mam?"

"Napping."

"Vey."

"Shh," she shushed her sister as she turned the volume up on the laptop so she could hear the dialogue coming through the small speakers.

"Dammit, Veda. I know you're mad at me but—"

"Mad? I'm not mad, sister. It's you who's *mad*!"

Here we go, she thought.

"Did it ever occur to you to think about someone other than yerself?" Uh oh, she must be fairly angry; her Irish got more pronounced when she was.

"What? How could you—?"

"Mam and I have been harassed by the media ever since—"

"Don't you dare! You're the one who put me up to this cac in the first place, so you don't get to blame me now that I've tried to do what's best for *all* of us. It will die down…eventually."

"No, it won't! Your brush with fame has put us all in the limelight, even if we didn't wanna be."

"Now just stall the ball! You want the limelight more than anyone I know."

"Aye, I did. Until I got it," she grumbled and pushed the laptop away. "Now you're jeopardizing your good name by living with him like some common harlot."

"Oh, tarbh. I'm not. I'm sleeping in my own room. And what do *you* mind, anyway? You certainly don't bother to act less than a slag yerself!"

"This has gone arseways, Bec. I say you get out while the getting is good. Your craic is over."

Becca just shook her head in response.

"Oh, don't be a mog. He's gonna break your heart. I can see it in his face; he's a chancer if ever I saw one."

"I can't just call the whole thing off now, Veda. I have to wait."

"Why?"

"Because. He doesn't need the ill repute either. He's a good man, even if he's a player. He helped get me my job back and cleared my name too."

"For his own cause."

"No, sister. For me."

"Ach, keep tellin' yerself that." Veda crossed her arms over her chest. "And then you go and blow me and Mam off, of all the days but Samhain."

"You're invited. The two of you."

Veda rolled her eyes.

"I came to invite you." Becca softened her tone and moved toward her twin.

"I saw you made brack." Veda lifted her chin over at the lovely loaf perfectly sealed in plastic wrap sitting on the countertop.

"I did. Try it. It's as good as mam's any day."

"I heard that." Her mother stepped out into the hallway. "Well, let's have a taste then, eh?" She winked as she took a seat in the armchair across from where Veda sat, and Becca hurriedly retrieved a slice of the cake.

"Mmm," her mother said as she bit into it. "Added in a splash of fresh whiskey, did ye?"

Becca smiled. "Just like you taught us."

"It's fine, lass. Fine barmbrack indeed, my girl." Her mom leaned in and kissed her cheek. "Now, why were the two of ye eatin' the head off the other?"

"Veda's mad at me."

"Am not!"

"Oh, stop it, you two. Don't make a holy show out of everything. You're sisters, twins at that. Try and be nice to one another. Becca, what're ye making us for dinner?"

"Our classics, Mam. Then the brack for afters with Irish coffee, of course."

"Little whiskey for me."

"Eh, she's likely to get buckled if you don't," Veda laughed. "She can't handle her liquor like she used to." Veda winked.

"Lord knows I could still drink you both under the table if I wasn't on all these meds."

They all laughed at that, and Becca popped up to get their dinner started. She'd gotten the potatoes to boiling and the lamb and carrots into the oven when Veda finally came in to help her chop the kale—assumedly her anger cooled for the time being.

"I'm sorry, I've been on the outs with you gone."

"I know. I'm trying though, Veda. I have to make it look real. If Pax and I aren't together, people won't believe we're engaged."

"Sure look it. Who's all coming to your party?"

"Well, most the players, I reckon...and I had hoped you and Mam, too."

"Will Quillan Layton be there?"

"Aye." Becca smirked, getting a smile out of Veda. "You fancy him, don't ya?"

"What's *not* to fancy? He's gorgeous."

Becca giggled. "Yes, he is that indeed."

"Well, in that case, I need to make an appearance for sure." Veda's smirk turned sinister.

"Oh, well. I'm glad to hear it. Whatever will you wear, sister?"

Veda's laugh was maniacal. "I got a few costumes up my sleeve."

CHAPTER TEN

"Holy mother of Zeus!" Pax gaped openly at his gorgeous fake fiancée as she met him at the top of the stairs. She wore a figure-flattering white ombre V-neck dress outlined with gold braided cloth. Golden ropes cinched the fabric at the collarbone; the sleeves opened from the forearm, flowing outward and leaving her upper arms exposed. Her cleavage was ample and her shoulders were half-bare; Paxton's desire was full throttle. His eyes moved down over her. A gold belt below her breasts created an empire waistline and the bottoms of the sleeves and dress were teal as if dipped into an aqua ocean of dye. Her dark hair was braided and pinned back with a starfish; a gold tiara topped it. Her eye makeup was thick, accenting those piercing green eyes of hers, and her lips were coral.

"Who the hell are you supposed to be?" he asked, breathlessly.

"I'm Amphitrite, Queen of the Sea," she answered, separating the distance between them. "I'm Poseidon's bride *of course*."

"Of course you are. And a stunning bride you are, Becca." Too bad he hadn't invited a priest, he would've made it official right then and there.

Becca giggled, pleased with his assessment. "Pax, you look mighty handsome, I must say. I love this." She stroked his thick five o'clock shadow, the one he'd let grow and trimmed close since no-shave-November started tomorrow.

She looked him over. He knew he looked ridiculous. His bare arms and upper torso clad in the toga-like garment that was as thin as underwear, head adorned in a gold crown that appeared to be fashioned of coral reef and seashells, holding his golden three-pronged trident he'd ordered online; the damn thing was heavier than he'd thought it would be. The gold sandals that laced up his feet and shins were probably his least favorite part of the outfit; he felt like a complete fool.

Becca stroked his beard, and he could've moaned aloud; it felt good to have her soft hands on him. He smiled big.

"Too bad we have a party to attend, my sexy goddess. Otherwise, I'd pick you up, run into my room right now, and take a swim in your irresistible sea."

Becca's mouth opened slightly, taken aback by his blunt words.

"Jeez, I'm sorry Bec. I didn't mean to sound so crass. It's just… well, you look amazing."

Becca shook her head and looked down, pink tinting her high cheekbones. "No, it, it, uh… it had the intended outcome."

Pax's brows shot up just as the doorbell rang, and he took in a deep breath.

"Well, shall we, my fiancée?"

She nodded and took his extended arm as they moved down the stairs.

Paxton laughed as Brett and Madi entered. Brett looked even more ridiculous than he did, with a long, curly white wig and a matching beard. His garment was even more thread-bare than Paxton's, revealing his broad chest, torso, and biceps. He also wore golden sandals, so Pax didn't feel so alone in his plight. Brett's brows drew as he held up a big, shiny thunderbolt.

"I smite thee, mighty Poseidon… for making me wear this silly shit!"

Madi laughed loudly, looking lovely in her own white and gold costume, showcasing her tall, curvy figure. "We're the first ones here, huh?"

"You guys look great," Becca said and pulled Madi in for a hug.

"The internet. Thank goodness for it, otherwise we'd be in regular clothes. Dressing this one up was no small task, I assure you."

"Oh, I bet," Pax joked with Brett and shoved at him. "But if anyone can pull off Zeus, it's you, brother."

"It's a good thing it's not cold out." Brett grumbled and crossed his arms over his chest.

"Patience, my love," Madi cooed. "The night is still young. You'll be rewarded for your sacrifices later, I promise." She winked at Pax and Becca, getting laughs out of them.

"I better, Sunflower, I damn well *better*," Brett glowered over at her.

Madi giggled and grabbed Becca, pulling her through the beautifully-decorated foyer.

The designers had made it look like Hogwarts, with "floating candles" hanging from the ceiling below a twinkling starry nightscape. The resulting decor had a magical effect.

Next in was Quillan wearing baggy, black linen slacks, an open black leather vest, a black and crimson cloak, and crimson red accessories. He had a "broken" golden crown on his head and a smirk on his face.

"Quil, you look awesome as Hades, man. Didn't expect you to actually dress up!" *Or not wear a shirt*, Paxton thought. Quil was the most modest of them…usually.

Quil laughed, "This was fun. I have to admit."

"Where's Quinn?" he asked.

"Oh, her nanny volunteered to stay after I took her trick-or-treating. She was exhausted after her sugar rush finally ran its course. Remind me again why parents are such gluttons for punishment on holidays?"

Pax laughed. He wasn't a parent yet but understood what Quil meant.

"Besides," Quil continued. "I'm getting my drink on tonight." Quil's brow arched and Pax laughed again.

"My man, come on in. Make yourself at home."

Pax greeted Trav and Sky next, both impeccably dressed—in similar Greek-style fashion as Paxton was—as Ares and Aphrodite. Linc and Val were the last to show up, followed by TJ; all dressed in comparable attire, TJ fronting as Hephaestus, the nickname Linc had recently coined him.

Everyone piled into the kitchen as drinks flowed and servers came around with trays of food; petite fours, hors d'oeuvres, crudités, and mini versions of classic favorites.

"Quil," Becca cooed sassily, "did you come out tonight trying to get a wife?"

Quil smiled as Becca's finger pointed down his torso, making Pax heatedly jealous, but brushed off the comment. "No, *amiga*, just having some fun."

Madi smirked, and Travis punched at Quil, calling him a show-off.

Paxton had wondered when Quillan was gonna lighten up a little. He'd not shown interest in dating or women, save for going to the occasional strip club, since his wife had died over a year ago. If he had a side piece, he wasn't telling. But Pax was sure he was simply staying single to focus on his daughter. As much as Pax commended him for that, he still wished Quil could find someone. He seemed so lonely sometimes.

Hell, who was Paxton Guthrie kidding? He was one to be talking. But he still had some years to go. At only twenty-five years old, he wasn't in any hurry. But he wasn't gonna kid himself, having Rebecca Ryan around was starting to become greatly enjoyable. She was fun, smart, kind, and giving. And he loved spending time with her… and looking at her gorgeous figure.

Tonight was the barest he'd ever seen her chest and arms—in clothes anyway—and he was liking what he saw. She kept eyeing him, and it made him feel good—and aroused, at the sparkle in her eyes. He was eager for what would happen tonight when everyone left, for she seemed to have a boldness about her in costume that she didn't in real life as she twirled and showcased her outfit to the girls.

She and Madi seemed to be over the tension that had once been between them, and although Pax wondered what had changed, he was ever grateful that they were getting along now. All the girls seemed to like Rebecca, and as he saw Brooke walk by and hug her, his heart soared. Becca gave her a big smile and complemented her costume. She was clad in a well-accomplished She-Ra costume. It was fitting for her and the Greek god theme they'd apparently imposed on everyone.

"Damn, she's smokin' hot," TJ growled next to him.

Pax warned, "You'd better be talking about Brooke and not my fiancée, you asshole."

TJ laughed. "Don't get me wrong. Becca's beautiful, but I'd love to tear that big ass of Brooke Taylor's *up*."

Pax snorted with a laugh, almost spitting his rum and coke out. "Damn, dude, ease up on the Crown." Pax motioned to his drink.

"I know. Fuck, I'm sorry, but she's fine as fuck."

"I didn't know she was your thing."

"I'd like to ruin her with my *thang*. Think she could handle ten inches?"

Pax sincerely doubted TJ had ten inches, but the look on his round face gave nothing away. TJ wasn't unattractive—well by women's standards anyway, Pax guessed. He was tall, big, and stocky but not fat. His chest and biceps were bigger than Pax's were and he was a couple inches taller. He was probably of German descent if Pax had to guess with his dark brown hair, tan skin, and dark eyes, but wasn't sure. TJ had big lips, a long nose, and high cheekbones with a round face and square jaw. Pax had seen women throw themselves at the man, so there must be something fairly alluring about him. But Brooke had never seemed to see TJ as anything more than a friend.

"I dunno, TJ, bud. She doesn't really mess around with football players. Seems like her unspoken rule." Pax shrugged. Besides, there were rumors she preferred the company of women to men anyway.

"Rules were made to be broken."

Pax rolled his eyes and patted his teammate's big back. "Well, good luck with that, my friend. I think you'll need it."

TJ grinned presumptuously and walked over to the girls, turning his flirt on and getting them to laughing.

Paxton headed back to the bar for another round, then he stopped in his tracks. A lovely, fair-skin brunette he recognized was standing in the doorway, clad as Medusa in a dark dress with gold embellishments, a black masquerade-type mask, and a crown of fake snakes, arms crossed beneath her breasts. The only reason he knew who she was since the mask covered a decent portion of her face was the familiar tightness of her lips, ever present when he was around, and the fact that she was the spitting image of his fake fiancée—tattoos and piercings aside.

"Veda! Glad you could join us," he stated as he came to a stop in front of her.

"Thanks for the invite... *god* of the sea," she smirked, and Pax frowned. Would this woman ever stop hating him long enough for him to try and befriend her? "Nice pad you got here!" She looked around, admiring the luxurious and open concept home of Paxton's.

"Thank you and welcome. Enjoy yourself."

"Right," she smirked again and uncrossed her arms, taking a glass of champagne that one of the waiters brought over. "Happy Samhain."

"Sow-win?"

"It's Gaelic for Halloween, idiot," she mumbled under her breath.

"I knew that. I just wanted to make sure I was pronouncing it correctly," he smarted back. To be his fake fiancée's twin, she wasn't anything like sweet Rebecca.

"Well, at least you can get *something* correct." Her green eyes lingered on his for the longest time before she walked off, heading toward her sister.

Pax huffed out. Dammit, why did she hate him so much? And how was he ever going to prove himself to her?

It was just gonna take time, he figured.

Time and a hell of a lot of patience on my part.

BECCA LAUGHED as she cut into the barmbrack and handed Quillan a piece.

"Sláinte," she stated as she toasted his drink, slinging her own back and waiting for him to bite into the traditional Irish fruitcake she'd made yesterday for tonight's Halloween celebration.

Quil gave her a crooked grin and took a bite, giving her a nod as he tasted it. "Damn, for a fruitcake this shit is good," he answered after he chewed and swallowed.

"Told ya," she giggled and patted his forearm.

She turned to see her sister dressed as Medusa and laughed, pulling Veda to her for a hug. Veda embraced her back but stood there, looking ill at ease with all the strangers around.

"Ow, dammit," Quil grunted as he pulled the cake from his mouth and fished out something metallic. "What the hell?" he asked as Becca covered her mouth, knowing full well what he'd bitten into.

"How did a *ring* get in there?" Quil asked, holding up the golden jewelry with his thumb and index finger.

"Uh oh!" Pax exclaimed. "You know what *that* means?"

Quil looked to Pax as if he'd lost his ever-loving mind.

"You'll be married within the year," Becca added. "Barmbrack is traditionally a fortune-telling cake, you know?"

"Married! Right? I think not," Quil's brows rose in defiance.

"The brack never lies," Veda added and looked Quil over with growing interest.

Everyone had stilled, as if only noticing Veda—aka Medusa—for the first time, what with all the drinks going around, the darkness of the entire house, and general joviality of the festivities.

"Oh, everyone. This is my twin sister, Veda. Veda meet Quillan Layton." She figured she might as well start with Quil, since their eyes were already zeroed in on one another.

"Call me Quil, *señora*," he replied and extended the hand that he wasn't holding the ring with to Veda. "It's a pleasure."

"The pleasure, Mr. Layton, is *all* mine."

Oh boy, Becca thought and began to pull Veda's shoulders around so that she could meet everyone else. She took her arm and introduced her to them all, finally stopping at Brooke, who looked Veda over as if she were a juicy piece of meat.

"Brooke Taylor," Brooke cooed as she shook Veda's hand.

"You look so familiar," Veda answered. "Aren't you a model?"

"I am. I'm flattered you recognized me."

Oh lord, here we go. Booze and sex; they were such familiar companions. As much as Brooke had proclaimed to be a practical pansexual, Veda wasn't. She fancied men. Brooke had testified last time they were all hanging out together that, "Sex is sex, it doesn't matter who it's with, the end results are always the same—orgasms."

Becca felt that it wasn't like that at all. But, then again, she'd not experienced all that sex had to offer yet, so maybe she wasn't a good judge of the act.

She left the two to talk and walked back over to her god.

"Mmm," Pax said and pulled her into his hard chest to hug her. "Are you having fun, my queen?"

Becca giggled and pulled back to look into his handsome face. "I am, my god of the sea. Are you?"

"Indeed. Although, I have to say, I can't wait to have you all to myself soon."

Soon? The party had just begun and Becca highly doubted he would take her off to one of their rooms for a quick rutting. Even if it sounded enticing, she wouldn't run out on their guests either and gave him a reassuring smile.

"So, what other traditions do you druids have on Samhain?"

Becca's brows went up; he'd pronounced it correctly this time. "I'm impressed."

"I asked your sister if I said it right."

Becca giggled again, the booze was making her all giddy. "Well, we can always dance around the bonfire."

"Naked?" he asked, his brows rising provocatively as his hand settled on her hip.

"Hmm, not tonight, but it will be *almost* as alluring."

"You, my sweetness, are *always* alluring." He leaned in and ran his nose along her jawline, making her shiver and goosebumps run the length of her exposed arms, her nipples hardening into painful peaks.

"Mmm, Pax," she murmured into his ear.

"Fuck, baby, don't say my name like that. You're making me hard," he groaned breathlessly in her ear and kissed her beneath the lobe, getting another shiver from her.

She pulled back to look in his eyes and gulped at the intensity there. Damn, their attraction was unquestionable.

Suddenly, Becca was jarred by a light shove from behind, and Pax frowned over to her right. She looked to see TJ there, grinning from ear to ear.

"Brooke says the Druids danced naked on Halloween night."

Becca gulped; so they'd overheard the conversation it would seem. She looked to Pax with uncertainty then nodded back at TJ.

"Ha," he answered back. "Sounds like a fucking fantasy come to life." He looked back to Brooke, who sassed with a duck face. "Let's see you do it then, fancy pants. All talk and no damn action."

"What do I get in return, big boy?" Brooke's eyes twinkled vindictively.

TJ laughed heartily; it was very clear that he was ossified. "Oh, I'll give you something all right." TJ grabbed a handful of his package, making Becca balk and Pax snort in laughter.

"Jesus, TJ, there are ladies present, you lug," Pax scolded.

Becca giggled then and kissed Pax's cheek.

"If it's smaller than six inches, I don't want the damn thing," Brooke teased.

"Oh, it's a *hell* of a lot bigger than six inches, darlin'. In fact, I don't know if you can handle all of it."

What the hell was happening here?

"So, let me get this straight... I dance naked in front of this entire group around that bonfire out there, and I get your cock in return?" she asked, her chin rising.

"Yes ma'am, all ten long inches of the fucker."

Becca tried to cover her gasp as all eyes stayed riveted on Brooke and TJ's interchange.

Brooke's eyes glazed over with something that looked to be a mix of lust and challenge and she stuck her hand out. "Deal!" She took his hand and pulled big TJ with her out of the kitchen.

"Becca, get your ass out here," Brooke called back. "You're gonna show me how the witches dance so I can get a hefty dose of cock tonight."

Becca looked back at Paxton in shock, her cheeks flaming red.

"You heard her, baby doll. Every girl needs her fix." He winked and patted her bottom softly even as he turned them to follow the crowd which now headed outside toward the raging bonfire that had been set in the firepit.

Holy mother of God! What had she started?

"OK, I don't get it... Was she not just hitting on me earlier?" Veda stated in surprise as a naked Brooke Taylor jumped astraddle of a standing TJ Rawlins. He gripped her ass and pulled her to him, his head falling to hers for a smothering kiss.

Becca shrugged. "Apparently, she prefers the 'mountain that rides' tonight," she offered, likening TJ to a ginormous character from one of her favorite fantasy series.

"What's the matter, Medusa?" Quil teased. "Were you craving pussy tonight, baby doll?"

Becca's eyebrows hit her forehead; she'd never heard Quil so crass. Then again, she'd never seen him three sheets to the wind either.

"Feck off, Hades," Medusa sassed. "For your information, I don't eat pussy. I only swallow cock, thank you very much."

Dear God, one night of drink and merriment apparently led to a bunch of foul-mouthed, randy hooligans who wanted nothing more than to shed their inhibitions and go at it like a bunch of rabbits.

Becca blushed and looked away while trying to extricate herself from the conversation slowly veering off in another direction.

"Medusa was always a good *snake*-handler, I assumed," Quil went on.

Veda snorted. "Assuredly."

"I'm glad to hear it, *dama serpiente*. I was wondering if you might wanna dance with the devil tonight, seeing as you seem unafraid of flames and all."

Damn, what a line! Good for Veda though, she'd been highly interested in Quil. Now it seemed he, too, was interested in her.

Japers! Becca thought as she looked around, seeing TJ shoving Brooke to the side of the house, making out like a bunch of teenagers. Tonight promised sex for many people, it appeared. Maybe tonight was the night for her and Paxton, after all.

Becca found him talking with Brett and Linc and tucked her arm in his as she motioned for him to herd everyone back inside and away from the couple about to fornicate before their very eyes. Brooke was moaning like a banshee as she practically ate TJ's face, his hands roving her bare body.

Pax took the hint and led them all back inside where a speaker was playing music. He pulled Becca into a slow song from *Phantom of the Opera*, and Becca smiled when she saw Quil do the same with her sister. So, that's what he meant by 'dancing with the devil.' Becca laughed under her breath.

"What's so funny?" Pax asked and pulled her closer to him, his hand searing her exposed back in licking flames of desire.

"Oh, nothing." Her eyes sought his baby blues, and he smiled big.

"Having fun?"

"Aye, I am. You?"

"Lots, save worrying about having to shock the pool after TJ and Brooke are done in it." He rolled his eyes dramatically as they looked out the giant window to see the two plunge in, clothes and all. Rebecca laughed.

"To say I'm surprised is kind of an understatement. Although I knew Brooke had a bit of a reputation, seeing it in action is quite something else."

"Yeah..." Pax trailed off, looking away. Whatever he knew or had seen in the past, he wasn't apt to say. It made her admire him all the more. "You looked lovely dancing amid the flames of the bonfire, by the way."

His wide, bright smile made her tummy flutter. God, he was so handsome. Big, tanned, beautiful. Everything she'd ever wanted in a man—well as far as looks went. She was still getting to know him, after all.

She blushed, ashamed that her thoughts hovered on sinful as she thought about what the rest of him looked like. She'd not seen him fully unclothed yet, and the thrill of it held her enchanted. She looked over to Madi and Brett, who'd shed his wig and beard a while ago. He smiled so longing at his wife, placing his palm on her lower belly, that it made Becca's ovaries hurt.

As much as she'd daydreamed about Paxton Guthrie, wanted him —and had for so long now—she wasn't sure he'd ever give her that look. That look that said more than words ever could. He wanted to bed her. He'd said that. But when he'd finally lain with her, would that be it? Would it be over? The thrill spent? She suddenly didn't want to know. She wasn't ready for it to be over. It had only just begun. Perhaps she should hold onto her virginity a little longer. Make him work a little harder to earn it. Wasn't that what smart women did? Waited for men to respect them?

She didn't know much about men. Her father and mother seemed to have a decent relationship. He'd respected her mother... for a time, until the sickness surrounding him was too much to bear and he'd abandoned them. Of course Becca wanted respect and trust in a relationship, too. She wasn't sure why she'd not dated much over the years. Maybe it was due to the ongoing fear of abandonment.

Veda appeared to be oblivious to love, or at least appeared not to want it. Perhaps their fears were fashioned from the fact that they were afraid to lose anymore loved ones, which prevented them from seeking love. After all, things had been touchy with their mother's cancer for years. Well to sick, active to remission. It had been a rollercoaster of emotions and treatments and prognoses over the years.

As if sensing her hesitations, Pax cupped Becca's cheek in his big, calloused palm. "What's the matter, my little *naia*?"

Becca smiled back up at him and shook her head. She didn't want to ruin this perfect moment with him. He was so gentle, his massive body felt so secure pressed to her own, so solid, so unbreakable. His hand lowered to her bottom again and squeezed lightly.

"You look beautiful tonight. A true goddess, Rebecca."

She sighed wearily; the twinkle in his eyes was back. Instead of thrilling her, this time it frightened her a little. She thanked him all the same.

"It's true. I really like this outfit. Maybe you should wear it for the rest of the night." His brow rose and he added, "or perhaps I could tear it off you."

As much as these words had been what she wanted to hear—

especially upon seeing Brooke and TJ together—her fear of going all the way took front and center now. In her dreams, intimacy with Pax had been safe. Now as a potential reality, it made her self-conscious, unsure, and nervous.

"Hey." Pax's finger moved slowly from her cheekbone down to her neck. "It's ok if that's not what you want."

She shook her head. "Paxton, it's not—"

"God, I love how you say my name."

She didn't think she said it any different than anyone else did, but she wouldn't argue.

"I just want you to know that I won't pressure you into something you aren't ready for. I care too much about you for that."

She couldn't help how her heart swelled at his words. Could he really be as sincere as he seemed? She leaned into his chest and tilted her face up to his, anticipating and savoring his plump lips as they brushed hers. He moaned and slanted his mouth, deepening the kiss almost immediately and his big arms coiled around her, holding her tightly as hers wrapped around his neck. His kiss was slow, soft, unhurried. She relished in the feel of it, of him, his lips, his tongue, his hard body pressed tightly to hers, and the brush of his hardening length along her thigh. She was touching the precipice of some great crest, a wave perhaps, unstable and undulating. She feared what would happen when it crested, for waves eventually met the shore with a jarring crash.

She pulled back when an elbow hit hers and yelped, rubbing at it.

"Damn, sorry, Becca," Ares stated apologetically.

"Hey watch out, you clumsy ram," Poseidon sneered. "Touch my goddess again, and I'll have to unleash the Kraken."

Skyla snorted, rolling her eyes as Travis turned from her to face off with Paxton.

"Do I sense a challenge, Poseidon?" He stopped and planted his hands on his hips.

"You dare to challenge me in my own sea, Ares?" Pax smirked, the thrill to spar great within the furious god.

"Oh lord, here we go!" Sky stated with exasperation. "Boys, you can't wrestle in the—"

Her words were cut short as too brawny bodies hit each other with a hard thud and dropped to the floor, making the record on the turntable skip and stop.

"It was an accident, you angry oaf," Trav said as Pax slammed his head to the floor and pulled his arm behind him. He grunted and twisted, breaking the hold and shoving Pax.

"Doesn't matter. You started this shit, Ares," Pax stated. He then groaned as Travis threw all his weight into Pax's hips, flipped him over, straddled him, and put him in a headlock.

"Say uncle and I'll let you go, junior," Trav leered in triumph.

"Fuck you, asshole. Let me go." Pax's face was turning red, and Becca started to panic, only to breathe in relief as Pax's fist hit the rock-solid, tree-trunk-like thigh of Trav's.

"Ow, do it again and see what you get," Travis grated as he took Poseidon's crown off and threw it aside, only to rub his clenched knuckles into Paxton's blonde curls.

"Argh, dammit. Cut it out," Pax protested and grabbed at the arm of Travis's pulled taut beneath his chin.

"Say uncle."

"Fuck you!" Pax's face was red again, and Becca's hands went to her face in anxiousness.

"Don't worry," Sky came up and patted Becca's arm then, "they don't really hurt each other. But boys will be boys." Sky shrugged.

"Say uncle," Trav repeated and lightly punched at Paxton's side. "Don't make me choke you out, boy."

Damn, Travis really was the "god of war," holding a surprising advantage over the younger man, who was both taller than him and outweighed him. Travis was indeed choking Pax out with a big arm around Paxton's reddening neck. Becca feared Pax would actually pass out before he finally said, "Uncle," and Trav's hold on him released. He shoved at Pax and stood.

The tension in the room mounted when Pax jumped up and got in Travis's face. "Dude! What the hell was that?"

"Showing you who you're messing with, that's all... *Poseidon*." Travis might not be quite as tall or broad as the formidable line-backer, but he was just as fierce in his demeanor as he and Pax clashed once again.

Becca gulped as Travis's chin went up in challenge, and Pax shoved at his chest, pushing him back a step or two.

Both jaws ticked, eyes narrowing. Becca wasn't sure what to do, but Skyla finally stepped forward, putting a hand on her man's exposed bicep. "Alright, Ares, put your horns away."

"Yeah, if you ass-clowns are done measuring each other's dicks, can we finally bob for apples?" Zeus put his two cents in, stepping between the two and pushing them apart with an arm on each of their chests.

Becca had never seen soft-spoken Paxton so riled up...and over *her* to boot. Pax scowled at Travis and turned away, coming back to Rebecca's side and taking her elbow in his hands. "You okay, sweet-ness?" He pulled her still tingling elbow to his lips and kissed it gingerly, making her heart soar on a cloud of happiness that nothing could dissipate.

She gave him a soft smile and nodded. She realized her woman-hood was humming as he pulled her back against his chest and pecked her lips softly before turning to his guests. Rebecca was turned on by Paxton's protective instincts, seeing him defend her was arousing and swoony, despite that she'd been afraid Travis was actually going to hurt him. That Pax cared enough to take up for her made her feel incredible.

She didn't miss the smirk on Travis Redmond's face as he play-fully slugged at Pax's shoulder. Pax pulled him in for a half-hug, patting his back as he took his outstretched hand; all as right as it was before the tussle. Men!

Becca heard Travis say as she turned to head back into the

kitchen, "You'll thank me later, Pax. That got your lass as wet as a monsoon."

Pax snorted. "What makes you think I need *your* help getting my girl turned on, you crazy fuck?"

"Just trust me... you'll thank me later. Women love when men defend their honor."

Becca couldn't contain the grin on her face; Travis knew the truth. Women were suckers for a hero... *Especially* this *woman*.

CHAPTER ELEVEN

P axton knocked on Becca's door later that night. It was after two in the morning, and he was amazed that he wasn't passed out drunk somewhere like most everyone else seemed to be—save for the pregnant women, of course. Linc and Val had gone home to their boys, and TJ and Brooke had taken an Uber a while ago. He'd heard stories of TJ's stamina and Brooke's relentless rowdiness and was glad he wouldn't be witnessing either firsthand. What he'd seen of them earlier was proof enough. Not that other couples weren't hooking up tonight, but Brooke and TJ would probably be keeping half the house up in their fury to copulate.

"Sorry to interrupt," he stated, opening the door and propping himself in the doorframe. Becca stilled in pulling the dangling earring from her ear and looked up at him with wide green eyes. "I, uh, I wondered if we could talk for a second."

"Sure. Is everything ok?" The apprehension on her beautiful face solidified what he'd been worried about earlier. She wasn't comfortable with him and, deep down, that bothered him...a lot.

"Yeah, uh, wanna sit?" he asked, closing the door as he motioned to the bed. He took the corner closest to the door, waiting for her to follow suit. Finally, when the bed sank in next to him, he began. "Look, I don't want you to worry about me coming on to you."

That sounded bad. Not what he had planned. *Try again, idiot!*

"I mean, I want you, Rebecca. There's no doubting that, but I don't want you to think that I'm going to push myself on you. I'm not that guy. And I know things have been kinda rushed so far, and I'm sorry for that... What I'm saying is—"

"You don't plan on sleeping with me," she finished for him.

He turned to face her, taking the hand that rested across her thigh. She looked dejected, and it tore into his heart. "No, I don't," he confirmed. Her eyes moved up to his, looking fragile, hurt, and clear. "It's not the right thing to do here, Becca. I can't take something from you that isn't mine to steal. You're a beautiful woman. You deserve a beautiful union...with the man who will be your husband one day."

"And that's not you," she stated, her sweet voice free of sarcasm and scorn.

"Exactly. I mean, this is all a show. I don't want you to be hurt by me, emotionally or physically. When this season is over and we go our separate ways, I'd like to think I've gained another friend, not reduced myself to the type of person who would selfishly take advantage of someone in your position. That would be cruel and unkind of me to do so. I may not be the nicest guy in the world, but I won't be the worst either. I have a lot of regret in my life, and I don't want you to be yet another one."

Rebecca's head lowered. She stayed quiet for a long time, her breathing slow and steady. "I understand," she said quietly, almost inaudibly.

"If things were different—"

"But they're not."

"You're amazing, do you know that?" he asked and squeezed her hand softly, rubbing his thumb over her soft skin.

When he looked back up at her face, a single tear fell down her cheek.

"Dammit, Becca, please don't do that."

"What?"

"Cry because of me. I'm trying to save you tears in the long run."

"I know. I'm sorry."

"My little *naia*, you have nothing to be sorry for."

"Don't call me that."

"But you are... my sexy little *naia*."

Becca huffed and her chest heaved. His fingertips sought the gold braid that got to rest on her perfectly round breast and she gasped. "Pax," her groan of protest was music to his ears, for the sound of his name on her lips never failed to excite him.

"Just because I don't mean to take your virginity doesn't mean we can't play, Becca." The eyes that searched his looked hurt and torn but also eager and filled with want. He smiled. "Lay back, sweetness, I want to taste your nectar."

Rebecca's mouth opened in surprise, but she did as he asked and laid flat of her back. His cock was fully erect as he looked her over. "Fuck, Amphitrite, you're gorgeous."

His fingertip moved down her breast to her belly and lower, swirling the fabric that lay where her mound was. Her whimper turned him from hungry to starving in a matter of seconds, and he fought the urge to lift her skirt and shove his engorged cock deep within her. Dammit, he knew he wasn't going to be able to keep doing this... but then he'd come in here and not been able to help himself. He'd tried to be honest, but the honest thing to do was tell her how fucking obsessed he was with taking her virginity. Whether he deserved it or not was beyond the fact. He'd tried to reason with himself and tell her what he knew he had to, but that hadn't stopped the desire he had for this gorgeous seductress...and wouldn't.

So, he squatted to his knees, threw her dress up and began loving her with his mouth instead.

BECCA KNEW she should stop him. Tell him no. Tell him to get out. But she couldn't stop her body from wanting him, no more than she could stop the sun from shining or the moon from waxing. Even as her heart broke, desire flooded through her like a beach overcome in a hurricane. As his tongue assaulted her dripping wet womanhood, she was helpless to the pull of magnetism between them.

"Oh, Poseidon," she groaned as her hands fell into his hair and her orgasm came upon her, wave after wave of spasms hitting her with a force stronger than the last. Her grip on his hair let up as he rose and moved to straddle her chest, ripping her gown in the process as he exposed her breasts and pushed his erection between them. He pulled her arms to her sides and pressed them into her breasts, pushing them together as he began to thrust into the valley between. In three pumps, he was crying out in pleasure as he pushed her chin up and ejaculated all over her neck and into her hair.

"Oh, oh shit," he groaned as he rocked and quaked, stroking her cheek as he did so.

Finally, he stilled and sighed as she looked up at him. She watched his Adam's apple bob as his eyes lowered to the mess he'd made.

"I'm sorry, Becca," he said almost inaudibly.

She turned her head as her entire face quivered in emotion. She felt Pax move off her, then he pulled her up. She attempted to swat him away, but he was much stronger. Soon, she was pressed against his chest and sobbing uncontrollably. She sobbed for herself, for feeling inadequate, for wanting something she knew she would never have, but mostly she sobbed for how unfair life was. How close she'd been to something, someone, she'd always wanted, yet never been able to have. All because he didn't want the same things she did, apparently.

"I'm sorry, baby. Please don't cry. I'm a dick. I'm selfish. Please forgive me." His words filled her heart, for how could she not forgive him.

She looked up, into eyes that seemed so sincere, so genuine. "I forgive you."

"You do?" he asked, shocked.

She nodded and kissed his chin, leaving him bewildered. He continued to stare at her as if she weren't real until he pulled back and looked down. "Damn, I ripped your gown and made a huge mess."

"I don't mind," she answered truthfully even as she felt his seed running down her chest.

"Is that so?" He sounded amused. She nodded again. "My sexy little *naia* likes to be ravaged by her god, huh?"

Becca couldn't hide the smile and blush that followed, getting a chuckle out of Paxton.

"Well, I think we need to clean you up, you wanton little sex kitten, you."

He pulled her to the bathroom where they disrobed, dropping their clothes to the floor, and Becca stood naked before him, feeling both confident and unsure at the same time. His eyes moved over her reverently as if he'd never seen a woman before, and she knew she was blushing as her own eyes fell over his gloriously naked frame. He was so big and broad, his chest, his arms adorned with aquatic tattoos, his torso even…and his thighs. He was a powerful linebacker, a defensive warrior in all his magnificence. Her eyes fell to his penis, growing before her eyes, and she shivered in desire, fear, and anticipation of showering with him.

He walked forward and turned the water on, leaving her to stare at his splendidly plump ass. She could bite it, it was so delicious. He grinned at her knowingly and extended his hand. Becca took it and let him pull her into the water where he kissed her with a passion she'd always dreamed about but never felt until Paxton Guthrie. He was such a force to be reckoned with; like being sucked into a whirlpool, Becca was helpless to escape his grasp.

When this was all over, she would hold onto these memories as tightly as she could, praying they didn't shatter like the shards of a broken glass whose pieces she'd never be able to put back again. Which was why she had to savor every second of this.

She fell to her knees then, pulling from his embrace with such speed that he was reaching for her, but she shoved his hands away and found his member. It was rock-solid and ready when she enveloped the head of him with her mouth.

He sputtered and groaned and grunted as she loved him with instinct and urgency. His hand gripped her hair, and he smiled down at her as she fed off his reactions, letting him guide her to explore something she'd never done before but had always been fascinated by. Soon, he was falling apart again as she rocked his world as best as she knew how for an inexperienced rookie.

He shivered when she pulled her lips from his shaft and continued to lightly stroke him with unhurried fingertips, captivated with his girth, the undeniable draw of his masculine body, a stark contrast to herself. He moaned so sexily, and she loved how he was putty in *her* hands for a change.

She moved to speak, but he was faster. "Becca," he said as he cupped her cheek, letting the water run over their chests, "everything I said before... I can't... I don't... *Fuck*, I want you. And I don't know how to turn it off. Every time I try, I don't succeed. I can't fight it anymore."

"Then don't," she blurted out, getting a confused frown in answer. "Paxton, I want it to be you. I want you to be the one to take my virginity. I know I should want to save it for my future husband, but I don't. I want this experience with you, no matter the cost."

But as he pulled her to her feet and kissed her, she let those words sink into her brain. She wasn't sure she was prepared for the cost, for her heart was at stake now.

She'd gone and fallen in love with him. God help her when this was all over and they had to part ways, her heart would be forever lost.

Pax awoke to the sunlight slanting across his chest. Becca always kept the windows wide open to let in as much sun as possible. He smiled over to the dark brunette hair that shimmered with copper hues where the rays of sun touched it. The blanket of brown spilled over her pillow in ribbons of curls, over her naked porcelain back.

Paxton could have groaned aloud. She was the most beautiful thing he'd ever seen. Those thick lashes of hers rested on her high, rosy cheekbones. Her lips were full and kissable. Her hand was resting on his bare pec, making his already stiffening morning wood even more prominent.

He gulped, looking down to the disrespectful member with both awe and disgust. How could he have let it happen again? After telling her the truth of how he felt, he'd still ended up doing everything but sticking his dick inside her. What was wrong with him? What was this woman doing to him? He'd never been this obsessed over one pussy before. He was only twenty-five years old; he still had many more he wanted to conquer, lots of time to mess around before settling down.

But all he could think of was how amazing being sheathed by Rebecca's heat would be. How sweet she'd been thus far. How beautiful her mouth had been taking his cock down and loving him with such purity that it'd stolen his breath away. It had been the first time she'd done that, he could tell by her hesitations, but she'd done it better than any woman ever had before her. How was that even possible? And why was he so infatuated? Perhaps it was that sweet smile of hers that echoed her innocence, that sexy face she made when her world split apart, the utter trust in her gorgeous green eyes. He couldn't put his finger on it but knew he was going to have to rip the Band-Aid off and get it over with if he ever wanted to overcome this obsession he had.

Taking her would be as easy as stealing candy from a baby, like a thief in the night. All he had to do at this very moment would be to move between her legs and guide his cock in with a slow thrust. He would bet she was still wet from their actions last night. He could imagine how wonderful it would feel, and she wouldn't even be mad; hell, what goddess didn't want to wake up to her god worshipping her? He almost moaned aloud at the thought of it.

But he wouldn't. Despite what she'd said and despite that it would be done and over in a few good pumps. One, because he wasn't that big of an asshole, two, because he wanted her first time to be as close to what she imagined as possible, and three, he knew deep down that he was full of shit. There was no way one time with her would be sufficient—no damn way in hell. The minute he succumbed and took her, he was doomed to an abyss of unwavering want.

He was so enthralled in his own thoughts that he didn't notice she'd awoken beside him until her fingertips began to trace the shape of his pec, and he shivered.

"Mmm, I love that I can get that kinda response from you first thing in the morning."

Ok, she's awake now, lover boy. Do it, his mind screamed.

Again, he quieted it and placed his hand over hers, feeling his dick jerk in response to her stroking.

"As much as I would love to pick up where we left off last night, *naia*, I can't. I gotta go to practice."

"Can you save that for me?" Her eyes moved down to his erection, hidden beneath the thin quilt. He was two seconds away from saying, "Fuck it" and jumping her.

"Only you, Amphitrite." The thoughts of her beautiful lips on his hard cock again got a moan from him.

Becca's giggle made it worse, and Pax took a deep breath in and counted to ten. When he let it out, he got out from under the covers and faced away from her, looking around for his boxer-briefs. He found them and moved to pull them on, giving his mind a barrier even if he didn't really want one. He turned to see Becca grinning again, hand covering her enticing, quilt-covered breasts, facing him. Her hair spilled around her like ribbons and her lips were swollen from all the making out they'd done last night. He gulped, he was in deep shit.

"What do you want for dinner tonight, Pax?"

"Baby, I need nothing aside from you to sustain me." It was halfway true. The temptation of crawling back under those sheets was becoming increasingly difficult. If he didn't get out of that room, and quickly, he wasn't gonna make it to the complex…not today.

"Do I not get a kiss, Poseidon?"

Pax grunted and practically whimpered as he turned. "Becca…"

She sat up and dropped the comforter, and he groaned aloud. She had the single-most exquisite set of tits he'd ever seen, and they beckoned to him like a glowing fire to a freezing man. All he could see in his head was his cock sliding between them last night, and he pouted. Jesus, what was happening to him?

"That's fine. Don't kiss me now. I'll expect many more to make it up to me though."

He licked his lips as her fingertip went to her nipple and tweaked it. He groaned again. "Becca, please stop?"

Her giggle caused him to growl.

"You're a bad girl, *naia*. I'm gonna have to spank you."

"I can't wait." The eyes that stared into his were not those of a virgin but of a naughty vixen hell-bent on sucking him down into the pit of her unending pleasure.

God, it was tempting, so damn tempting, and he was so close to giving in when they both heard the door alarm chime and a loud slamming of the front door.

"Jesus," Pax flinched and came back to reality. "You, stay." His eyes roved her alluring frame for one second more before he was opening the door and going to investigate.

REBECCA CAME DOWN the stairs just minutes after Pax, dressed in nothing but a robe of fine pink silk.

"Paxton?" she asked as she stopped to see him leaning on the counter, looking at her sister. "Veda."

"What you preps got in this house to eat? I'm starved."

"What the hell was that noise? And who'd you piss off?" Becca asked, coming over to her twin and stopping on the other side of the fridge from her, where Veda rifled through it.

"She must've angered the mighty Hades, I take it," Pax smirked at her from the bar.

"Hades? Quil?" Becca's brows drew in consternation. Veda and Quil had seemed to hit it off last night. What on earth had happened in the short span of a few hours?

Veda's eyes burned into hers across the door of the fridge, giving her a, "Don't even ask," look.

"I can't imagine he was disappointed with the way things went *down* last night," Pax teased.

"Can it, merman," Veda mocked the name she'd heard Travis use last night.

Trav walked into the kitchen then, clad only in PJ pants. "Fuck, I need coffee."

"Morning," Pax said and was in the process of making some as they spoke.

"Fuck my life," Veda said under her breath as she began pulling eggs and turkey bacon from the fridge. "How do you get used to seeing so many hard bodies all the time?" she asked Becca.

The men seemed oblivious to their obvious perfect male forms. For a moment she and Veda indulged, until Trav stretched and caught them eyeing him, frowning. "Ladies, I'm an engaged man. I'll thank you to stop ogling me like I'm an ice cream on a hot day. My woman is a redhead and, as you know, they don't call 'em spitfires for no reason."

Veda snorted with laughter, and Becca lowered her head shamefully.

"C'mon, Ares. Any other day, you'd flex and have them drooling all over you." Pax flexed his own beefy bicep for good measure, giving Becca an eye as he puckered his lips at her, and making her bite into her lip to keep from moaning aloud. "Don't stop now."

"Ah, young Padawan, you have much to learn about love."

"Love," Veda snorted. "No such thing."

"Do I detect a cynic in our midst?" Brett's deep voice boomed as he and Madi were next to enter.

"You don't believe in love?" It was Travis who asked.

Veda shrugged and threw some bacon onto a sheet pan, moving to the oven to turn it on. "I know it's over-rated, that's for *damn* sure."

"Those are some interesting tattoos," Brett said, his eyes running up Veda's arm at the sleeve of tats she had there, ranging from namastes to Celtic crosses to skulls.

"Yeah and not easy to cover on the field with you guys, either," Veda answered, moving to the opposite counter to crack eggs into a bowl.

All the guys looked back at Vey, perplexed, save for Brett and Paxton who looked apprehensive.

"Yeah, let's keep your appearance here a secret outside these walls, how about it?" came Madi's authoritative voice.

Uh oh, not good, Becca thought.

"You're a cheerleader?" Trav asked, dumbfounded.

"Guilty," Veda puckered her lips, giving her best cynical expression—the one she was notorious for in the Ryan household.

Skyla came into the kitchen at that time, swearing, "How the hell did you manage to sneak under the radar, you shifty li—?"

"Whoa, Sky, I think—" Pax interrupted.

"Easy, Fireball," Trav cooed and took her hand in his, bringing it to his lips.

"Travis Lamar, don't talk to me in that tone of voice." She huffed and pulled her hand away, coming over to Veda and crossing her arms over her chest. "I'll ask *again*, how did you manage to get your-self invited?"

"She's my sister, Skyla," Becca answered, blushing. She realized when she'd introduced Veda last night that she'd had a mask and costume on and was now free of those this morning. She also realized as she came to stand beside the tattooed and pierced twin of hers that everyone saw just how much they favored one another.

They all looked to Becca with a deer-in-the-headlights look on their faces.

For once, the stunning ADA was at a loss for words. But finally, Sky spoke, "I—I apologize—"

"Not necessary, ADA Larson." Veda gave Skyla a weak smile then looked to Madi. "I know I'm not to fraternize with the players. Although, I'm not one to follow the rules much...apparently."

Dammit Veda, shut up! Becca wanted to scream at her wild, rash, irresponsible sister, but held her tongue as the tension in the room mounted.

"Don't worry ladies, your men are safe...for now."

"You little *bitch*!" Madi was the one who lashed out then, and Brett quickly gripped her shoulders from behind and backed her up. Madi's scorching eyes went to Veda then up to her husband's before she turned on her heel and left the room, followed by Skyla.

"Veda!" Becca scolded. "Do you know who you were speaking to?" Becca's voice lowered.

"Just another rich bitch from what I can gather." Veda was nonplussed as she scrambled the eggs without breaking stride.

"That 'rich bitch' is our CEO," Pax growled at Veda.

"My bad." Again, Veda didn't blink.

"Well... I'm sure it's not a big deal that she was here, so long as no photos leak out of her without her mask or anything," Travis was the first to try and remedy.

"Oops," Veda smirked under her breath, getting a huff out of Brett as he crossed his arms over his chest and stepped forward.

"Are you just *trying* to get fired?" he asked.

"At least getting fired is better than quitting. I'll get unemployment benefits."

Brett scoffed and shook his head, leaving the kitchen as mortification ran through Becca's veins. Her face paled, she felt sick to her stomach. The room was spinning. Her sister was making them both out to look like gold-digging idiots, and there was nothing she could do about it.

Even Travis was at a loss for words as his brows went up in surprise. "Wow! You got a Yeti, Pax? I think I'll take my coffee to go." Travis moved out of the kitchen then, leaving just himself, Becca, and Veda.

Pax frowned as he looked at Veda with growing anger. "I know what you're trying to pull and guess what? It isn't gonna fly. Do you really hate me that much?"

"Hate is a strong word, Paxton."

"Veda, what—?"

Pax interrupted Becca then, stepping in front of her even as he took her outstretched hand in his and squeezed it tight. "You don't get to tell me how to live my life."

"I don't give two *shits* about your life. I just want mine back and ever since *this* happened." Veda turned and pulled Paxton's hand from Becca's. "I haven't had a moment's peace."

"Jealous much, are ya, lass?" Pax mocked, and Veda growled and slapped him across the face, getting a gasp from Becca.

"Veda! Stop it!" Becca pleaded.

"Keep it up and I'll fuckin' marry her just to piss you the fuck off." Pax's eyes narrowed.

"Stop!" Becca shouted to the top of her lungs. Both heads turned to face her then, surprised by her bravado. "I am *not* a bargaining chip, I am not a toy, and I am not going to sit here and allow *either* of ye to treat me like I'm not standing right fecking here. To hell with ye both."

With that, Becca fled upstairs.

CHAPTER TWELVE

"Becca, please call me back. We need to talk." Pax left yet another voicemail on Becca's cell phone, worried about how upset she'd been that morning.

TJ was grinning at him like the Cheshire cat, and Pax scowled over at him.

"You should've tapped that while you had a chance, Poseidon."

"Fuck you," Pax grumbled. "Not all of us just want an ass to hammer, *Hephaestus.*"

TJ shrugged. "I'd tap it again and again. It was so fucking worth every second."

Pax didn't wanna hear it, especially not when it was all he'd thought of for weeks now, making love to Rebecca Christine Ryan. He threw his phone back into his gym bag and shut his locker.

Becca probably wasn't going to call him back. She'd been embarrassed, angry, and had felt used—and she should. Pax had no right to say what he had, but he needed to know what she wanted to do. If she was calling it off, he needed to be prepared with a statement for the media. But that was really the least of his worries; the truth was that he was scared he'd lost her—*really* lost her—and his mind, heart, and soul were torn in two. He wasn't ready to let her go. Not yet. He'd enjoyed having her around, having her to talk to, tease and mess around with. He told himself it was just because he'd not dated in a while, but he knew it was something more. He couldn't put his finger on it, but he knew Rebecca was different. She was special, she was...

"Get out of my fucking face right now before I make you regret it, *ese*," Hades growled at Zeus as they stepped into the locker room from the practice field.

"D'you suddenly forget who the fuck you're talking to, Quil?"

"I didn't forget... *Zeus*."

Uh oh, trouble in paradise.

Brett had a hold of Quil's shirt collar. "Get your head out of the clouds and into this game or you're sitting the bench come tomorrow night."

"Stop talking to me like you're my fucking coach."

Pax looked to TJ, who was ready to step in before Zeus shoved Hades away. Hades held Zeus's eyes for a moment before stepping over to his locker. They were both drenched in sweat from running drills.

Brett stopped in his tracks to look down at Pax, who looked up at him guiltily. Brett whirled away angrily before taking in a deep breath and stepping forward. He crossed his arms over his chest, letting Travis and Linc by before he said, "Alright. Everyone, stop and listen up!"

Trav and Linc moved to the bench to sit, catching their breath as they glanced up at their leader.

"I get it. Alright. We all had a good time last night at Paxton's party. We had a little too much to drink. And *some* of us had more fun than others..." TJ snorted in amusement, and Brett gave him a second to gather himself before he continued—with a look that told TJ to shut the hell up before he got his nose busted. "Now, I don't care who you fuck around with or what you do on your own time. But when you're in *my* house, you play by my fuckin' rules. If that's not kosher then you know where the damn door is. I plan to take this team to the Super Bowl. If that's not on your agenda, and you're willing to let personal matters interfere, then you're in my way. And *if* you're in my way, I will terminate you."

Pax looked up at Brett in surprise as Brett's eyes fell to him and then shot over to Quil. Paxton had never heard Brett as grave as he was now, and despite the threat, the promise of a Super Bowl was as alluring as getting into those tight panties of Becca's; Pax couldn't resist the appeal of glorious victory. He smiled up into Brett's face and nodded.

"Now, who's with me?" Brett's tone lightened as his eyes shot up to Quil's. A moment passed between them—of competition, challenge, then understanding—before Brett put his hand out, palm down in their group huddle formation.

Linc and Travis's hands shot into the mix, followed by Pax and TJ's. Other players joined in before Quillan finally added his hand to the top and looked up to their QB with a respectful nod.

"Gods of the Gridiron," they all chanted and Pax felt a sense of renewal between them all.

They were going to be champions. They were going to the Super Bowl.

"WHAT THE FUCK DO YOU MEAN?" Pax asked, feeling angry.

"She'll be communicating with you through me, buddy," Kenny said.

"But she'll be living under *my* damn roof."

"Pax, just be glad we aren't having to shell out any more money. You'll be seen out in public together, the happy couple under all other pretenses, but let's not make a big deal out of this, ok? It's just until the season is over, then your life can go back to the way it was." Kenny sighed over the phone.

But Pax didn't want things to go back to the way they were. He didn't want Rebecca staying with him if he couldn't talk to her, interact with her, have any type of relationship with her. Sure, his days were busy during this time of year with practice, workouts, meetings, games, events... but he could make time for her.

"It's what she wants, Paxton. Just oblige her, please?"

But how could he? She would be sleeping half a football field away from him.

"Pax, there's more..."

Oh hell, what now?

"Veda was fired." Before Pax could respond, Kenny continued, "A very interesting photo of her and Quillan surfaced on social media this morning, which the team handled swiftly and efficiently, chalking it up to Photoshop and the like before they took it down. I mean, you were there, you probably know more about it than I do. Needless to say, though, after that shit she pulled last game with having the balls to come up and talk to you, this was the final straw."

Well, the sarcastic rebel had finally gotten what she'd asked for. And if Pax knew Veda at all, he'd bet a good chunk of change she'd done it on purpose—to get that unemployment she'd been wanting. But unemployment couldn't be much, and Pax knew they struggled financially. It made him feel worse than he already did; right now, he felt like the biggest jerk in the world.

"So, can we please just let this shit die? I'm begging."

He should. He should pretend that the last several weeks were just a big mistake on his part, chalk it up to a lesson learned, and move on.

But as he walked into his deathly quiet house, up the stairs and past Rebecca's room— where the door was shut and a light was on beneath it—his chest hurt. It hurt with a pain he'd not felt in a long time. A pain he'd been all too familiar with—heartbreak.

He'd give Rebecca a little time to calm down, let her anger and aggravation with him die down some, but this wasn't over. He wasn't gonna give up and just let her shut him out without some closure.

He needed and deserved that at least.

He headed into his room and threw his gym bag down onto the bed, folding himself so that his elbows rested on his knees. He wasn't going to give up on her, on them.

Them? There *was* no them, was there? But there was… As much as he'd never wanted it, it was there. The desire to have something more with her than a fake engagement.

Now, he just had to convince her to give him another chance. And, knowing how stubborn her sister was, that wasn't going to be an easy task.

THE WEEK WENT by painfully slow as Rebecca got into a new routine. That first day was the hardest; going to Paxton's game on Monday night, sitting in the box, socializing with the women who looked at her as if she were a bomb waiting to go off, and cheering for a game that her heart wasn't into. But Tuesday was easier; she dove into her work at the museum and volunteered at the hospital while her mom got her infusion.

By Thursday, Becca had almost forgotten about Paxton…*almost, ha!*

Friday came and still, she ignored the sound of the front door when he entered, the racket in the kitchen when he made his protein shakes, the sound of the basement door as he went down to work-out, the draw of the magnetism when she heard his footfalls on the stairs. Her heart would bleed when he would stop but never knock on her door. He simply hovered, as if waiting for some moment that never came.

And her life continued, the world continued to spin until that following Monday night. She was reading her book, the one she'd been neglecting, and had to find out the next plot twist despite that she'd caught up on the TV series and already knew. The scene didn't fail to shake her and she began to cry—sob was a better word for it; she felt as helpless as the characters in the story she loved so much.

Rebecca let her feelings of helplessness, her anger at Paxton and Veda, her disappointment with her life and the world completely destroy her along with the pages of *The Fiery Cross*.

She was so distraught that she didn't realize the door was opening, and Paxton Guthrie's beautiful face was looking in on her, as if he could somehow cure all her ails.

She swiped at her eyes speedily, not wanting him to see how upset she was, and pulled every ounce of confidence she could muster. "What do you want, Pax?"

"I'm sorry. I heard you crying and..."

"I don't just barge into your room and bother *you*, now do I?"

"No, but..."

"Then why the hell are you in here?"

Consternation marked his handsome features as he entered and closed the door behind him. "Rebecca," he began and looked down, shoving his hands into the pockets of his khaki shorts. "I'm sorry for what I said that day to Veda. I shouldn't have, and I didn't mean it."

Becca looked away. "It doesn't matter." It was true. It didn't matter what was said and what wasn't said; it changed nothing. They weren't meant to be. They were as different as two people could be, night and day, the prince and the peasant girl. She was like Cinderella; she'd gotten a fair glimpse of the elegant ball, but her short clock had struck midnight and her carriage had turned back into a pumpkin.

"But it *does* matter. To me it does."

"Why?"

"Because I hurt you and I never meant to."

That should make her feel better, but it didn't. It didn't take the pain of the truth away.

"Look, I know this whole situation is messed up and I've destroyed yours and Veda's lives, your mom's too, but I never intended for all this to happen like it has. You have to know that."

Of course, he hadn't. It'd just been another date to him, another woman, another day in his *perfect* life. A kiss that was akin to the shot heard round the world. If they'd never kissed, none of this would've happened. Their lives would be just as they were.

"But I don't regret any of it."

She looked up then into his gorgeous blue eyes, eyes that were as bright and cerulean as the blue seas he commanded being Poseidon, the water god of the gridiron. She gulped. He was telling the truth.

"I don't want this to be our lives for the next two to three months, Rebecca. I want to dine with you, take you out, enjoy my time with you while I can. Until…" he trailed off.

He wanted to sleep with her. She knew that to be true. He wanted to conquer her. That's all this was. A way to get her where he really wanted her…into his bed. She stayed quiet as he moved forward and squatted, taking her hand in his.

"I don't know what the future holds, but I know that I can't keep living in this house with you, day after day and not seeing you, not speaking to you…not touching you." His thumb moved over her knuckles, making her shiver. "Please tell me the distance is killing you, too?"

There it was; proof that she was right. He just wanted her flesh, not her heart, not her love. The distance was killing him, only because he couldn't touch her, not because he missed her laugh or her jokes or her company.

She nodded gently, because she *did* miss his touch and realized how much she'd craved it; her heart rate doubled when his fingers moved up her arm to her shoulder, then finally to her face.

He gave her a smile. "You volunteering tomorrow?"

She nodded again.

"Can I join you? I wouldn't mind spending my day off with you."

"Veda will be there," Becca smarted hotly, feeling her cheeks flame.

"That's fine. I'm not worried about your sister."

You should be, she wanted to say but held her tongue.

"I'll meet you downstairs at ten?" he asked and brought her hand to his lips, kissing the palm. She pulled her lips in, attempting to hide how rattled he made her. She nodded again and he beamed, the beauty of it making her chest ache. "Good. It's a date then."

She couldn't help her smile even as her heart broke all over again. She was wishing for something she could never have, postponing the inevitable.

But she could do this, for her family, for her livelihood, for Paxton Guthrie.

She could play her part, until February.

She just prayed she had a heart left before all was said and done.

"Quil!" Pax chuckled in surprise as Quillan turned to him. The tall TE shoved his phone into his pocket and approached Pax then.

"Pax, *qué pasa*, man? What are you doing here?"

"I could ask you the same question, brother." Pax laughed and pumped his hand.

"Oh, just waiting on Quinn to get her transfusions. They take a while." He blushed, and the red painting his face was foreign to Pax.

"She doing ok?" Pax asked, concerned.

"Yeah, she's ok. She..." he trailed off, not eager to answer. Of which, Pax wouldn't press. "What about you? What are you doing here?"

"Becca's mom is getting chemo. We volunteer while we wait. It passes the time."

"Oh, well that's good. I should probably start doing that. It will distract me."

"Yeah, you totally should!" Pax insisted. He frowned as he saw Veda approaching with Quil's little girl in tow. Quinn was jabbering away, talking Veda's ear off as they approached hand-in-hand, Veda's tattooed arm coming into view.

"And then Daddy said I jumped *so* high I could've touched the sky."

Veda laughed, like truly laughed, and Pax's eyebrows shot up. It was as sultry as Rebecca's in its authenticity. For a moment, Veda appeared to be a good soul enjoying the company of a little girl with a chronic illness who'd connected with her on a level that no one else could.

Veda stopped dead in her tracks when she saw Quillan. Her jaw fell, full lips opening as she stared up at the six-foot, six-inch team-mate of Paxton's.

Uh oh, Pax thought. They haven't seen each other since...

"Veda?" Quil asked. "Wh—?"

"Quillan?"

"Daddy!"

Pax stood as still as a statue as the eyes bounced back and forth between the two lovers that obviously still had something hot soaring between them—Pax knew that look all too well.

"Daddy!" Quinn shouted to get her father's attention, and Pax held in the laugh that threatened his throat.

"Yes, *reinita?*" Quil looked down at the adorable mini-Quil with light brown curls.

"I want to have lunch with Veda."

Oh, boy. Pax held his breath, waiting for one of them to protest, but Veda's eyes locked with Quil's again, in a look of challenge. The game was on.

"That's fine, Quinn. Whatever you want, *mi amor.*"

Wow! For a big, strong guy, he was put on a spiked leash where this kid was concerned.

"Pax, would you like to join us?" Quil asked and looked to Pax whose mouth opened in an O.

Becca was his rescue as she came up then, slowly as if waiting for an explosion.

"Quil, what a surprise?" Surprise indeed!

"Becca, uh, Quil and Veda were going to lunch with the little princess here and wondered if we'd like to join them."

Quinn looked up at Becca as if seeing a ghost. "Whoa. Daddy, they look alike."

Veda answered Quinn, who still held her hand in a death grip. "She's my twin sister. Her name is Rebecca."

"Hi." Quinn grinned, an adorable little angel with an agenda no one knew. "I'm Quinn."

"Hi, Quinn." Becca waved and smiled up at Pax. "Sure, we can go to lunch. We're all caught up."

Quil gave a tight smile and nodded to Rebecca, who returned it with one equally as firm.

Well, this will be interesting, Pax thought.

Veda and Quinn took the lead; Quinn picking up exactly where she left off in her story.

Becca gave Pax a grin, and he took her hand.

Perhaps nothing was impossible after all... A little faith, hope, and love never failed.

"THAT WAS INTERESTING, HUH?" Pax asked as they came in the house from volunteering at the hospital for the better part of the day.

They'd had dinner with Becca's mam and seen her off to bed before heading home themselves.

They'd had a noteworthy lunch with Quil, Quinn, and Veda, noticing the hesitance, discomfort, and sexual tension brewing between the two. Becca hadn't had a chance to talk with her sister about what had happened since Halloween night. She'd been working or at Pax's when Veda had their mom and vice versa. Veda had been picking up more shifts at the club she worked at. Becca would get to the bottom of it and find out for sure if Veda had been the one to get herself fired, or if it had been someone else at the party who'd purposefully tagged Veda in the picture. Becca maintained that social media was a bad idea, which was why she didn't bother with it. Becca was the introvert of the two, so there *was* that.

"Interesting is a term that's putting it mildly," she answered.

"They definitely slept together," Pax continued.

Becca laughed and tossed her purse onto the side counter along with her keys. "I'm sure they think that about us."

Pax shrugged. "I doubt it."

"Why?"

Pax gave her a crooked grin and moved to the fridge, getting out his bottle of Kefir. "There's definitely sexual tension between the two of us, that's for sure, but not quite like those two. Halloween night was fruitful for them."

"Again, how do you know?"

"I just do."

Becca's brow went up again, waiting for a legit answer.

"Well, there's a look a man has when he's seen a woman naked."

"You've seen *me* naked."

"Ok, a look a man has when he's taken a woman."

"You sound like a medieval brute."

"You *do* realize that no one talks like you do, right?"

"I'm a historian," Becca defended and crossed her arms over her chest.

"Still. It's not fittin' for ye, *Sassenach*."

Oh, her poor body. It shivered hearing him utter those sexy words. She gulped and let her eyelids flutter closed.

"What would it take for a man to take a woman as fine as yourself, Ms. Ryan?"

Not much if she were being honest, especially after how swoony he'd been today, placing puppies in sick children's arms and feeding their hopes with cuddles.

"Would a kilt be too much to ask?" she teased.

"On the contrary." His blue eyes danced and held hers in a battle of bravado. She knew she would lose, but she held the stare as long as she could until she finally blinked. He smirked, cocky god that he was. "But I am Poseidon, not a Scottish highlander, unfortunately."

"Guess I'll have to settle for a toga instead then."

Pax burst into laughter and moved toward her, making her heart beat faster, and her laughter faded. He stopped within inches of her and reached up to finger the curl in front of her face, the one that had fallen loose from her bun. He then touched her glasses.

"I've had lots of fantasies about you with these on, you know?"

She felt her mouth open in surprise even as his lips fell to hers. She moaned when his tongue invaded, plunging in, and she stepped into his alluring arms. The feel of his solid, hard frame against her own did wonders for her damaged heart. His hand cupped her face as he angled her jaw, deepening the kiss and making the few inhibitions she had left fly right out the window. He pulled back after a moment to murmur her name and nibble her exposed neck as goosebumps broke out on her skin.

"I want you. I don't wanna spend another night without you."

Would she be brave? Would she finally give herself to him? She'd said she wanted to, said she didn't want to save herself. What was she waiting for?

She nodded even as his fingertips touched the portion of her collarbone, bare beneath her silk blouse. "I want you too, Paxton."

He grinned as he looked her over for any reluctance. When he didn't find any, he picked her up fireman style and carried her up the stairs. Her heart galloped and her lungs burned. This was it. She was doing it, for real. As much as it scared her, there was a part of her that was relieved. *And if you do marry*, she told herself, *you'll have this out of the way and not feel as nervous on your wedding night.* If that was supposed to make her feel better, it didn't. Her wedding night was a long way off, and this was the here and now—and here and now she thought she would faint as Pax began unbuttoning her shirt and kissing her again. She followed his lead, letting their mouths tangle and suck and explore as her own hands moved to the buckle of his pants.

He chuckled as he pulled her shirt from her shoulders and moved next to her bra. "You should probably not start with my pants with your inexperience, my little *naia*."

Instead of being offended by his statement, she was grateful. He was right, she needed to pace herself. Shirt first. He chuckled again as her hands moved to the hem of his shirt. "Mmm," he murmured, "your hands feel so good on me, Rebecca."

"Yours too," she agreed as his hand cupped her lace-covered breast and squeezed gently, testing the firmness there. She shivered as a finger dipped into the bra cup and brushed her nipple. His head fell and he kissed the meat of her breast as his hands fell to her jeans, quickly unbuttoning and unzipping her. She moved her focus from him to her bra and unclasped the back, anticipating his mouth on her once more. He grinned as she pulled the material from her shoulders and let it drop, moaning when his mouth returned to her breast. His hand cupped her there and brought the aching peak to his mouth to torture. Becca gasped and moaned as his hands descended her bare back to the lace panties that barely covered her ass cheeks. He gripped her there, pulling her into his massive frame.

"Good lord, sexy lady. I don't know how long I'll last with you like this," he sputtered his words at her nipple.

"Oh Pax," she whimpered. She was ready to open her legs—her body—to him, but realized he was still fully clothed; her hands had stymied their attempts to undress him in order to unburden herself.

He took a step back only long enough to peel the shirt over his head and unbutton his jeans before launching himself back at her, his mouth returning to hers in an overwhelmingly powerful kiss. His hands were greedy, kneading her breasts then moving to her ass and back again, feeling her up then down, as he feasted on her lips. Soon, her hands were tugging at his jeans and sliding into the soft denim to feel his stout thighs. Her hands moved lower to touch the part of him that fascinated her even more than his hulking body and chiseled muscles did. That part of him that jutted out at her, swollen and thick with need. The need she was eliciting within him. The need to take her, own her, and love her like she had never been loved before.

She gulped as she traced the length of him, hearing him groan in desire as his mouth moved to the crook of her neck, his palms gripping her ass cheeks once more and spreading them. She pressed herself to his chest, loving the broadness and heat of his big frame, the protection of his sheltering arms, and the lust that he invoked within her with every touch of his hands.

"Mmm, Paxton," she moaned as his lips came to her face, kissing her jaw. "Will it hurt?" she asked as his eyes came to hers and he paused for a moment.

"I honestly don't know. I've never been with a virgin."

She looked away, chewing on the inside of her cheek, feeling butterflies fill her stomach.

"Hey," he said and cupped her face in his big palm. "We don't have to do this. You can say no, if you want."

But how could she say no? His manhood was primed and ready for loving her, she saw, as her fist gripped and squeezed it; he shivered with desire. She shook her head.

He gave her a reassuring smile and grabbed the hand she was stroking him with, pulling it into his own and interlacing their fingers. "I know what they say about men and their boners. But I *can* stop. You just say the words. No *is* an option, and I'll respect it if this isn't what you want." He was serious. Dead serious.

"No. I want to. I do. With you," she reassured him.

"I'll go slow. And I'll make sure you're ready for me. Don't be intimidated by my size."

How could she not be? How in God's green earth was that gigantic rod going to fit inside her?

He pulled her into his arms again and backed them to the bed, the backs of her knees hitting the edge of the mattress. He laid her down, and she began to panic, realizing how close they were to this sacred act.

Paxton pulled his jeans off and his boxer-briefs. The bed sank in as his knees moved between her legs. Her breathing became ragged as he moved atop her and she felt his big chest hit hers.

"Damn, you're so tiny, Becca. I'm afraid I might break you."

In more ways than one, Becca thought. Paxton's lips came back to hers, and he began to kiss her. She forgot about the pressures of what was about to happen and just enjoyed the melding of their mouths and tongues, the feel of his hands on her naked flesh, cupping, squeezing and stroking. Her body was alive, her sex was tingling and oozing desire, and her legs were opening of their own volition when she felt his fingers pierce her opening.

She grunted, only to realize how tense she was as Pax stroked her thigh with his other hand. "Shh, easy, baby, it's just my fingers. I'm just getting you ready."

What did he mean by that? The wetness? She blushed up at him even as he smiled.

He must have decided she was because he was moving in between her legs, aligning their bodies. She realized he was pulling something down the length of himself. *Oh my God, a condom.* How had she forgotten about using protection? But just as she scolded herself, she felt a widening between her legs, a stretch, and she gasped as she looked up at Pax's focused face then down to see he was guiding himself into her, the head of his cock disappearing inside her.

Her sharp intake of breath had him looking up into her eyes. "Does it hurt, baby?"

Becca shook her head and pulled her lips in to concentrate on what he was doing. He pushed a little more and gauged her reaction. The feeling was that of being filled, a slight pressure and discomfort, but it wasn't painful. Little by little, inch by inch, Pax slid more of himself inside her, until his shaft was filling her completely. She grunted from the strain but was grateful it wasn't as agonizing as she'd read about in romance books.

"Are you ok?" he asked as he looked down into her face, sweat breaking out on his brow. She nodded, but he asserted, "Rebecca, baby, I need to hear you say it. Keep your eyes on me. I can't do this if I don't know how you're feeling."

His tenderness touched her, and she grinned up at him, glad it was him she'd decided to lose her virginity to. "I'm grand, Pax. Now what?" she asked.

She wasn't oblivious to what happened next. There would be

rutting, thrusting, and rocking of his pelvis into hers until he was spent—at least that was what she'd seen and read anyway. But reading it and feeling it were two very different things. As Pax's body lowered, and he withdrew then plunged back into her, something incredible started to happen. Some wanton, primal nymph within her began to awaken, coming alive as her lover drove deeper and deeper inside her, his sex hitting clandestine alcoves within that made her tingle and cry out with the need to feel more and more of the undulating waves of pleasure assaulting her. Like a reverberating echo that audibly split inside a cavern, the stroking of his body within hers created a rippling effect.

"Oh, Jesus, Mary, and Joseph," she swore and moaned. Pax took her lips, and her hands gripped his shoulders and back as his need began to overtake him. He thrust higher and harder, hitting even more spots that made her body shake, shiver, and quake beneath him. His hands moved over her naked torso, exploring her, his index finger and thumb teasing her nipples. His head flew back and he whimpered, attempting to hold himself from the restraints of his natural instincts.

"Oh, God, Becca. You feel so good, my sexy little *naia*, so damn good," he groaned, his breath choppy as he looked down at her.

He was waiting for her, but she wasn't sure if she…

Then it happened; a swirling, pulling, tingling began somewhere deep inside, somewhere she'd never felt as his hard member hit it over and over again. Suddenly, she was sucked into a vortex of intense pleasure—pulled into a rogue wave. Down, down, down she went, to Atlantis where magical sea sprites exploded in thousands of lights, dancing and cascading, before she was crashed back onto shore. Her cries of ecstasy were foreign screams in her ears, and her voice cracked as her entire body spasmed in climax. Her fingernails dug into Paxton's back, and her face buried into his shoulder, biting in as she held on for dear life afraid she would drown in this sea of bliss.

Suddenly, Poseidon roared, his body wracked by the same tumultuous waves she was being hit with, and he shook with fury as the storm engulfed him too. When they were both left in its wake, she looked up into the clear blue eyes of her lover. The man who'd taken her virginity, the man she'd unselfishly chosen to give herself to.

And she didn't feel as if anything had been taken at all. It was the first time in her life she'd ever felt so full and complete—her body *and* her heart.

CHAPTER THIRTEEN

Paxton hadn't been shocked to find that Rebecca's hymen had been broken prior to her first sexual experience. That wasn't unusual, especially since she was twenty-four-years-old and not sixteen. It could've been broken on a bicycle, putting in a tampon, or any kind of injury...or so he'd read in a *Cosmopolitan* magazine article years ago. She seemed more surprised than he'd been, but they were both grateful it hadn't hurt her too much. What had shocked Pax was how incredible he'd felt afterward, how attached he'd felt toward her, how protective. He'd heard about earth-shattering sex but had always assumed it was an exaggeration, not a real concept. Now, he knew for a fact that it was.

After their love-making, for that's precisely what it'd been, he looked her over in awe and wonderment, touching her face to make sure she was really real. Her glasses were still on and her bun was a mess of curly tendrils; she'd never been more beautiful than she was in that moment. Her cheeks reddened from sexual bliss, her eyes filled with the same emotion. He chuckled, getting a deep one from her that jolted his sex like a live wire. He then had to explain to her why his eyes were practically rolling into the back of his head when she did so.

From there, their night consisted of exploring each other in every sense of the word: physically, sexually, and emotionally, telling one another stories of their childhoods, their dreams, and their darkest secrets before pulling the other back into the throes of passion where they sought ecstasy in the arms of the other.

Paxton had never experienced anything like it. Like her. Rebecca Ryan, his sweet *naia*. Whether she was indeed a nymph or a dolphin was debatable, and he didn't care because she was his; his to love, torment, and adore with each stroke and kiss and thrust of his cock inside her. And he apparently did all three well because she kept climaxing over and over again, fascinating him as he tumbled with her and succumbed to her as much as he dominated her. Never had a woman captivated him so. And he knew what the feeling was before he could put words to it—despite that he hadn't been ready, hadn't wanted it, didn't need it, fought to expel it. It was love. Plain and simple.

Their night had been perfect, more than he'd ever hoped for, and the next morning came with the promise of a new day to do it all over again. Leaving his bed was one of the hardest things he ever had to do. Especially when faced with reality, knowing that he'd been abandoned by love before, as a child. What made this any different?

He tried to banish the dark thoughts from his head as he showered and begrudgingly left Rebecca to head to the complex, fighting the urge to run. He tried to tell himself that Becca was genuine, she wouldn't just leave him, but his insecurities surfaced throughout the day. This was the problem with love; it made him vulnerable, made him weak, made him unsure of things he'd been sure of all along, things he'd left in the past.

The guys seemed to notice something was different and called him out, teasing him.

"Leave him be," TJ mused.

"Why? Is it your turn to be badgered?" Trav asked.

"A gentleman never kisses and tells," TJ smarted back.

"Who *ever* said you were a gentleman?" Linc snorted and playfully punched at his middle.

"What about you, Quil? What happened between Hades and Medusa? She add another snake to her pile Halloween night?" Trav teased Quil, who looked undeterred by his comments.

"You'll never know if she did or not."

"Well, we know that Pax finally took the plunge. Kid hasn't been this light since his rookie year." This tease came from Brett, who beamed at him.

It was true, Pax felt like he was soaring on cloud nine. He just grinned back, not needing to say a word.

"Good for you, Pax." Quil patted his back after the others went to the weight room. "It's good to see that look on your face for a change."

Pax wasn't really aware that he had a "look," as much as a different mindset, but he wouldn't argue with his teammates about it. Although, he *was* curious about what happened with Quil and Veda.

"And what about you and Veda?" Pax asked, evaluating his super-secretive TE once he and Quil were alone in the locker room.

For the longest time Pax wasn't sure Quil would answer him, but finally he said, "It's complicated."

"Complicated because you have a daughter?" Pax asked, treading carefully.

"That's one reason."

"You're a widower?"

Quil shrugged. "Veda just— Well, she isn't what I need." Quil looked down at that, as if regretful that she wasn't. What had happened Halloween night? And the connection they had at lunch yesterday seemed genuine enough. Maybe Veda wasn't the cold-hearted bitch Pax thought she was. Maybe she had a softer side. Like Becca. They *were* twins, after all. It was possible that Veda wasn't her "evil" twin, so much as just an altered version of her. Or at least, Pax wished it was so, for Quil's sake. Quillan Layton was an enigma. Broody. Quiet. Mysterious. Reserved. But put him on a football field and he was as passionate as any of the rest of them. Veda was too, when it came to her family. Protective. Ruthless. Maybe she and Quil weren't that different after all.

"Maybe she *can* be, for your sake…and Quinn's."

With that, Quil shrugged and moved off to go workout.

"OH GOOD, YOU'RE HOME."

"Shh," Veda scolded, once again watching her laptop while their mam slept.

"Veda, why are you always so grumpy when you see me?"

"Grumpy isn't the word I would use to describe my feelings toward you right now." Veda's lips puckered, and her dark brow rose. Her nostrils flared and her nose ring sparkled.

"This is why I wanted to talk to you."

"Well, can it wait until this episode is over?" she hissed and held her laptop tighter.

Becca felt her anger rise and moved forward, slamming the lid on Veda's computer and propping her hands on her hips.

"You bitch!" Veda growled. "I was about to find out—"

"I don't care!" Becca's frown deepened as her sister rose to confront her. "We need to talk, and I'm tired of you either ignoring me or pretending like nothing is amiss."

"Fine. Say your peace so you can go back to your mansion, *Queen*."

"That's what this is about, isn't it? You're jealous!"

Veda snorted and rolled her eyes.

"You are!" Becca confirmed. "Why?"

"I'm not jealous. I'm annoyed. I'm bitter about the fact that you aren't here to help me with Mam."

"I'm still helping you."

"No, you aren't. You're never here—"

"I work."

"And so do I!"

"Yeah, well if you didn't get yourself fired—"

"Don't you dare! You invited me to that party, even knowing that I wasn't supposed to be there with the players."

"So now I set you up? As if you were planning to keep the job, anyway. You can't keep *any* job you have."

There. She'd said how she really felt. Veda was irresponsible, unreliable, and immature.

"Kiss my ass. You don't know what it was like, so don't even talk to me about it."

"Well, if you had a *normal* job, but nooo. Little miss model is too good to get her hands dirty, so let's priss around and—"

"I don't need your snide remarks right now, Bec."

"Are you gonna tell me what happened with Quillan on Halloween night or are you just gonna skirt around the truth, like you do everything else in your life?" Becca sighed heavily and sat at the ottoman in front of the chair Veda had occupied. Veda followed, returning to the chair, and crossing her legs. "What happened to us? We're sisters. We used to tell each other everything before Pa left."

"You're keeping secrets, too."

Becca shook her head. "Only because you make me feel worse about myself. This whole Pax situation was originally your idea, remember?"

"I know and I hate it!"

"You hate it because you're jealous," Becca accused again.

"No, I—" Veda huffed out and looked away. Becca could see tears gathering in her eyes. "Yes, ok, a little, maybe. It's just..."

"Just what? Talk to me, Vey."

"I thought it would open doors for me, *too*."

"Well, you kinda acted like a bitch to everyone on All Saints Day, if I remember correctly."

"Aye, but it was because he pissed me off."

"Quillan?"

Veda nodded and lowered her head.

"What happened, Veda? Did you two…?" she trailed off.

Veda nodded again.

"And?"

"And nothing. We were drunk, and he realized what a mistake he'd made the next morning," Vey scowled.

"I'm sure there's more to it than that." Becca's brows went up; she knew her sister well.

Veda looked away, again keeping her secrets to herself.

"And what about lunch that day, with his daughter? You two seem to have—"

"Differences of opinion is what we have. I don't wanna talk about Quil. Please?" Her plea was heart-wrenching. He'd hurt her.

"Fine, but don't get mad at me about what's going on then."

"I just thought our lives would be better, Becca. Not worse."

"Our life isn't *bad*, Vey."

"Isn't it?" Veda's tears shot through Becca's heart like arrows.

"No, it's not."

"Mam's treatments—"

"Are working."

"We're on the verge of eviction."

"Don't worry."

"Don't *worry*? How can I not? You're not here."

"I'm sorry."

"I don't want your apologies. I want us to figure this out together. When that engagement is over, and Pax kicks you out—"

"He's not gonna kick me out!" Becca retorted angrily.

"No? Your perfect prince charming would *never* do that, would he? He's so damn perfect and all. Open your eyes, Bec! You're simply just playing house until the man tires of you. He's a legendary football player with nowhere to go but up. You're beautiful, but don't kid yourself. What would he want with you, when he can have any girl his heart desires? And he's always gonna have girls throwing themselves at him, left and right."

Becca wanted to pretend that Veda's words didn't hold merit, but they did, and stung something fierce. Veda must have sensed it, for she went on, throwing more fuel into her fire.

"You and I know that we have to watch out for ourselves, no one else is gonna do it. And I would hate to look back and say 'I told you so' when he leaves you with nothing but a broken heart. I can already see in your eyes that you care for him. I wouldn't be surprised if you up and screwed him... I love you so much, but dammit, sister, you're so feckin' gullible. What ever happened to saving yourself for the man of your dreams?"

Pax is *the man of my dreams*, Becca wanted to say but her sister's logic was starting to outweigh her romantic thoughts on the matter. Veda had very valid points.

"Becca, I'm not trying to hurt your feelings here, but it's the same reason why I'm not gonna chase Quillan. No matter how handsome he is or how amazing the sex is between us, I have to be real here. Men like them don't fall in love with women like us."

Becca's head shot up, and she saw the pain in her sister's eyes. God, why did Veda always have to be right about everything? Becca had seen the silver lining, but truthfully, there wasn't one. Not in the end. Becca was the collateral damage. Paxton's life would go on, and hers would forever be ruined by one night—one amazingly wonderful night.

Veda pulled her younger—by three minutes—sister's head to her chest, and together, they sobbed until they were spent.

Veda stroked Becca's hair as she came back up to look into her face. "I'm sorry. I didn't think about any of this. I was so wrapped up."

"I know. It's ok. I don't blame you. It was fun while it lasted, but let's be honest for a second. This can't go on forever. Come next year, you and Pax are done. Then where will you, me, and Mam be? Out on the streets."

"I'll get another job, I'll—"

Veda shook her head. "No, you help with Mammy while I continue at *RISE*."

"Veda, I thought you said you were gonna stop working there?"

It was great money, putting a huge amount into the bank when their mom's cancer came back; but a gentlemen's club wasn't where Veda needed to be. *RISE* fed her wild side, and Becca feared for her safety there—in more ways than one. Plus, it wasn't the most moral decision given their strong Catholic upbringing. If their mother ever found out Veda worked there...

"It's only temporary, until I can—"

"Veda..." Suddenly, Becca remembered what Madi had said. "I..." God, how could she even be considering a bribe? It was so unlawful and shameful, but if it saved them from losing everything, she had to consider it. "What if there was another way?"

After all, they needed the money desperately. This would ensure their future, as well as free Rebecca from everything else. The thought made her sick to her stomach, though.

"If you have suggestions, Bec, I'm all ears."

"TELL ME ABOUT YOUR FATHER, PAX," Becca cooed as Pax kissed her neck in the pool that night.

"Mmm, I'd rather tell you about my rock-hard—"

"Pax," Becca giggled even as he leaned in to kiss her. He beamed as he pulled back and looked her over. They'd been talking about their childhoods, languidly lounging in the heated pool that cool November night, following Paxton's hard practice and a light dinner.

"My father left my mother and I when I was just a kid."

Becca's brows went up in surprise, but she said nothing.

"I honestly don't even know my true ethnicity. My dad looked nothing like me, and I think it bothered him more than me, having a son who—simply in his appearance alone—was a constant reminder of his biological failure."

"Oh Pax." Becca cupped his cheek and gave him an understanding smile.

"My uncle was my savior, though. He put me straight. I am who I am because of him."

"My dad left, too. I had a baby sister that had the same cancer Mam does. After she passed and Mam got sick, well, he couldn't handle the heat so he got out of the kitchen."

"So, you know how it feels?" His eyes were sad as he looked down. "It sucks."

"And your mom?"

"My mom is awesome." He smiled then, the sorrow instantly gone. "Sweet, giving, and beautiful. Hawaiian and tough as nails. I'm looking forward to having her here for Thanksgiving. She has a new boyfriend, though." Pax's teeth clenched as he looked away.

"Uh-oh."

"Yeah, I haven't met him yet, but I can hear it in her voice that it's pretty serious."

"And what will she think of me?" Becca couldn't hide the eagerness in her tone. Despite the talk she and her sister had today, she was going to soak up every second that she had with him. If this only lasted until January second, then she would love him until the final stroke of midnight on New Year's Day. This was her dream, after all, to be here, in his arms, feeling his body against hers. If she couldn't have him in every sense of the word, at least she could have him for now.

"Are you kidding? She's gonna adore you! I mean, what's not to love about an innocent, fun-loving historian?" His mouth returned to torment the flesh of her neck, and she was glad she left her hair up in a bun.

His hand moved to cup her breast and she shivered when her eyes fell over his face. "I'm not so innocent anymore."

"You're so beautiful. Have I told you that?"

He could say it a million times a day, and she would never tire of it.

"I think *you're* beautiful, Paxton."

"Even if you don't know where I come from?"

"You mean you weren't dropped straight from Heaven?" she teased and stroked the lines of his chiseled chest and abs. He moaned and closed his eyes, his skin breaking out in goosebumps where the chilly air touched it.

"I've never had a woman's touch do to me what yours does," he murmured, his blue eyes opening to hold her captive.

Her heart fluttered, and hope gripped it tightly on the wings of optimism. Veda could always be wrong about him. What if she was wrong? What if he—? No. She couldn't let herself fall too deeply into this dream world. She had to have the strength to be able to put all the pieces back together when this was over. If she let herself believe that he was falling in love with her, then she'd never be able to get through it; she'd never be able to walk away.

When he kissed her, it was hard, fast, and furious with need. He was Poseidon after all, right?

In a matter of minutes, her bikini bottoms were slung to the side of the pool and Pax was thrusting into her with one smooth movement. Her head flew back with the motion, but her body took him in as if starving for his caress.

"Oh God, Becca. I'm so addicted to you."

"Mmm, Pax."

She threw her arms around his shoulders as he gently pistoned into her, grunting as he pulled back just enough to look into her eyes. He watched her as he loved her with his sex, observing her reaction to him, gripping her hips, and angling her so that he could fill her completely.

She gasped as her body relented to his ministrations, and he brought her closer to climax. His forehead fell to hers as she tumbled beneath his wake, over the crest, and into the abyss of an endless ocean of pleasure where Poseidon captained her safely to the surface. He held her both captive and secure while his release came at the same time as hers. They were breathless as they returned from their voyage on the high seas of love, and when their ship was safely docked, her lover grinned knowingly at her.

"Now I know what Jamie meant in the meadow that day with Claire."

Becca looked at Pax as if he were nuts, and he laughed, his still waning erection jostling her sensitive insides and making her moan.

"When he said he felt like God when he was inside her."

"Oh." Becca blushed brightly.

"I feel like the god, Poseidon."

"Oh?" She couldn't help the giggle that came to her lips.

"Yeah, I possess you, body and soul and captivate you with my 'trident.'"

Becca full out laughed this time, getting a deep groan from her god.

"Lord, maybe I'm wrong. Maybe you're the one who possesses me instead." He moaned into her ear as his mouth returned to the neck of hers that seemed much more sensitive when it had Paxton's lips sucking on it. "Mmm, I wanna go finish season 2," he muttered even as he thrust his hips into her pelvis, his shaft once again fully sheathed inside her.

"Oh, mmm," she groaned in pleasure.

"After I've made love to my sexy goddess, my naughty little *naia*, once more."

And he began to love her again, his mouth moving to her breast to torture it with a slow and lazy tongue, causing her to cry out.

"Mmm," he gasped then looked back into her face, capturing her lips. "What does *a rúnsearc* mean?" he asked softly when he pulled back.

"What?" She couldn't focus; her body was being assaulted by wave upon wave of pleasure, making words and sentences superfluous.

"You called me *a rúnsearc* before. What's it mean, in Irish?" His pumping into her was slow, calculated, and hit the nerve endings of some incredibly sensitive G-spot she hadn't known existed.

She cried out before whispering, "My secret love."

The grin on Paxton's face was naughty, smug, and happy as he sent her spiraling back into that tumultuous sea of Poseidon's.

CHAPTER FOURTEEN

"There's my *keikikāne*," the beautiful, deeply-tanned, dark-haired beauty said as she pulled Paxton to her slender figure.

This woman had raised Paxton? She looked like a model: tall, athletic, lean, with a warm and friendly smile.

"Aloha, you must be Rebecca. I've heard so much about you. I'm Tara Guthrie."

"Mrs. Guthrie, I'm so happy to finally meet you."

The beautiful woman pulled Rebecca in for a tight hug. So, Paxton hadn't told her the truth. Did anyone know the truth beyond Pax, her, Veda, and Madison? It didn't matter. The ploy would be up in little over a month.

Pax and Becca were having Thanksgiving with his mom and her new boyfriend, Lance, now, and later with her mom and sister. They would be having another celebration tomorrow with the team.

"Aloha, *Makuahine*." Pax pulled his mother into his big arms and squeezed.

She returned the embrace, cupped Paxton's big jaw, and kissed it delicately, tears twinkling in her eyes. The love between the two was endearing; despite that Pax's "father" had left him, it was clear that his mother's adoration had not wavered as a result.

"Aloha, *Haole*," came a deep voice. Pax gaped as a tall—even taller than him—broad, dark man that favored Tara stepped across the threshold.

"Uncle Kawai!"

Kawai beamed as he pulled Paxton's handshake into his chest, giving him a half hug. When Kawai pulled back, he and Pax gave each other a fist pump that ended in a shaka sign.

"I can't believe you came. You haven't been to the mainland in years." Pax's laugh was hearty and genuine.

"I know, it's been a while. Let your *'anakala* take a look at you. Such a big, strong *kekoa*. And bigger every time I see you." Kawai patted Paxton's back, obvious pride in his voice. Then the giant man looked over to Becca. "And who's this *nani* lady?"

Becca smiled into a bronze face with pearly white teeth and big brown eyes that sparkled. She took Kawai's massive hand and shook it before he cupped hers and brought it to his lips.

"This is Rebecca. She's my fiancée." The term still sounded so strange coming from Paxton's lips; Becca gulped.

"Aloha. I'm happy to meet you, I'm Kawai Akina, Paxton's uncle."

"Aloha. Rebecca Ryan. Paxton's told me so much about you." Pax had warned her about how frequently Hawaiians used the term 'aloha,' and knew she should say it back out of respect.

"Hopefully it's only the good stuff." Kawai laughed, deep and hearty.

"Oh indeed."

"Only the best stories, uncle." Pax laughed and roughly patted his uncle's shoulder.

Tara stepped forward and smiled brightly at Becca, taking her hand.

"Ms. Guthrie, your son—" Becca began.

"Chose a beautiful bride. Look at you. I can see why Paxton is so taken with you." Becca blushed. How could the woman say that? She'd been through the door just a mere matter of minutes. The smile on Tara Guthrie's face was genuine enough, and it rattled Becca. Pax should have told his family the truth. It was going to hurt them so much when they found out this was all a sham, that he'd lied to them.

Paxton's mom pulled her back in for a hug, and she squeezed her in return, unable to help herself.

Tension seemed to mount as "the boyfriend" stepped through the threshold and squared off with Pax, who was the first to speak.

"Pax Guthrie. Welcome to my home."

"Lance Penrose. It's a pleasure to meet you, Pax."

Pax's smile tightened, of course he couldn't say the same. But he took the man's extended hand and shook it firmly.

Lance wasn't what Becca had been expecting. He was balding and thinner, but his smile seemed genuine enough. He appeared to be as nervous to meet Pax as Becca was to meet the family she would never be a true part of.

"Lance works in real estate on the island," Tara said.

Just as Becca started to ask which island—since there were many in the chain—Pax grinned as if knowing her thoughts. "Oahu."

Lance gave Pax a strange look, and Becca blushed brightly. "I'm sorry. I knew you all lived in Hawaii, but I never asked which island." *Great! Cover blown,* she thought.

"Never been to Hawaii?" Kawai asked.

"No. It's on the bucket list for sure though."

"Becca's originally from Ireland."

"Oh, how neat." Tara seemed surprised by that. "I've always been fascinated by the Celts."

"She's a historian. She can tell you all about them."

Becca felt her cheeks pinken again and hated that all eyes were on her now. "Well, you all must be hungry. Please do come in and make yourselves at home."

"Yes, leave your bags here. I'll get them later. Unless you'd like to freshen up."

Becca had moved her things into Paxton's room, just for the few days his family would be with them. They had been making love on an almost daily basis and, of course, slept in the same bed together, woken up together, and showered together, but not having the seclusion of her own area stressed her out a bit. Knowing this was only temporary was starting to break her heart.

Everyone moved into the open kitchen then where baked brie, jams, various cheeses, olives, and crackers were set up on tiered silver platters along with vegetable crudités. Pax laughed with his uncle while Becca asked his mother if she'd like something to drink. Pax popped the cork on some champagne and poured them all hearty doses. He then toasted to *Ohana* and to his bride-to-be, tearing Becca's heart into even more pieces than it already was.

They spoke about Paxton's upcoming game, his record this year, then Becca's work, her family, and finally, Tara and Lance's upcoming wedding in February. Becca wasn't sure who was more floored, her or Pax, who looked like he'd lost his appetite as he pulled the celery stick from his mouth and set it on a napkin.

His uncle Kawai saved the day by reminiscing about old times and soon, they were moving into the dining room for their mid-day meal.

No one volunteered to say the blessing, but Becca shyly offered up a whispered thanksgiving and crossed herself, blushing when all eyes fell on her. Sonia came out about that time, bless her, bringing dish after dish of food.

Becca knew Pax respected her Catholicism, but he'd never spoken of religion or God around her. He practiced meditation and fasting, but not for religious purposes; he was wholly new age, although she wasn't sure that he would even "identify" as such.

Sonia had prepared a feast of turkey, grilled salmon, cornbread and Irish soda bread stuffing, a fresh cranberry mold, a green bean casserole at Paxton's request, and colcannon at Becca's. She'd also made honeyed sweet potatoes, gravy, and creamed corn along with a beautiful caramel apple pie and a bourbon chocolate pecan pie. Becca wasn't sure how she would possibly eat again at her mother's house but took little bites of everything, praising Sonia for such a delicious spread.

When Pax passed the champagne around for more libations, Lance toasted Paxton, his home, and his happiness. Becca could see Pax was weary of the man's true intentions. Pax was always one to give people the benefit of the doubt, but this was his mother, and Becca couldn't blame him; if it were her mother, she would feel the same way.

They had an amicable meal, despite the slight tension, and soon the men were off to the living room to watch football and the women were in the kitchen, cleaning up.

Tara smiled over at Becca then as she washed dishes and Becca dried, sending Sonia home to enjoy her own Thanksgiving.

"I can see my son cares a great deal for you."

If she was fishing, she was doing a great job; Becca's cheeks flamed in bashfulness. "Pax is wonderful."

"He has a heart of gold and the spirit of the sea, my *makai*." When Becca's brows furrowed in question, Tara laughed. "He was born to the sea, my son. He's always been one with it—from the minute his little feet hit the sand. His father and I got him when he was barely two. So small and afraid. He grew up on the beach, never wanting to part with it. He was all-out surfing by five. I think it was where he felt the most at home. When his father left, I thought I'd lost Pax too." Tara's head bowed. "But he quickly connected with my brother, who wouldn't let him be lost to the world. He was a great father to Paxton."

Becca smiled. "I can see that he loves you both very much. He speaks of you often."

"We aren't the only ones he loves." Tara's eyes twinkled, making Becca gulp.

She wished she could tell Pax's mother the truth, but she didn't have it in her to do so—and it wasn't her place either. She just attempted to smile back, getting lost in the task at hand.

Later, they'd gone to see Becca's mom and sister and had a pleasant enough time, despite Veda's ever-sullen gaze on Paxton. Veda had the chronic chip on her shoulder where Pax was concerned but seemed far away, excusing herself right after their dinner and not coming out of her room for dessert. Becca wondered if they would ever be able to make amends when all this was over; so much had happened in such a short time span. It left her feeling drained and even more broken.

They came back to Pax's and were now preparing for bed. Their nighttime routines were robotic as they both absorbed all that the day had brought them.

Becca felt strange sliding in beside her god of a linebacker who lovingly wrapped his huge arms around her, pulling her into his barrel chest.

"Mmm, this is nice," he murmured in her ear.

Becca couldn't help the giggle at her throat. "Pax," she scolded as his hands moved bravely lower.

"What? How can I have such a tempting little *naia* in my bed and not answer the call of my body?" his voice lowered as his lips brushed her ear, making her shiver, and causing her nipples to harden beneath the thin silk of her shift. "If it feels good, do it, I always say."

His hand moved to her breast and squeezed possessively. She moaned hungrily.

"Fuck, Becca, look at what you do to me, my Amphitrite." He pulled her hand to his prominent erection.

"Pax, I don't want your family to hear us."

When his hand moved down to her belly, she gripped it in her own and looked into his eyes.

"How would you feel if you were to hear your mother doing this?"

"Gross!" he sneered. "Way to kill the mood." He grumbled and rolled back to his back. He huffed out and crossed his arms over his chest, getting a snicker from Rebecca.

"I'm sorry…"

"Gah, I don't like that guy."

"Would you like *any* guy your mom chose?"

Pax shrugged. "Probably not."

Becca smiled and leaned in to kiss her lover's cheek, rubbing her hand over his perfectly chiseled chest. "I'm sorry," she repeated.

He moaned, whether happily or in torture she wasn't sure. "That's fine, sweetness. Just know that when we leave Brett's tomorrow, you're all mine. Even if I have to go out to the barn and take you there in a damn stall in the hay, I *will* have you."

Little did he know, he already had her—every single piece of her: heart, soul, and body.

PAX LEFT practice that Saturday feeling tired; it was probably a combination of his routes and the excessive sex he'd been having. He'd never had as much sex being a single bachelor as he had while being falsely engaged. The thought made him smile as he moved from the garage into the mud room. He removed his sneakers and grinned as he heard Twisted Sister singing to him from the kitchen.

His eyes weren't prepared as they fell on his fake bride to be. She was clad in a jersey—and not just any jersey, his jersey. Number 52 swallowed the entirety of her back, but it was her sexy, creamy legs that drew him in; they were bare. She had a crimson thong on beneath the jersey, and Pax moaned as his eyes took in her plump butt cheeks when she reached up on her tiptoes to grab a platter.

A wave of sudden awareness hit him square in the chest, knocking him backward.

Becca was cooking dinner, humming and hadn't noticed him. She turned then, rocking air guitar as the guitar rift of "I Wanna Rock" belted out to them.

She stilled when she saw him, those cheeks of hers as red as little apples, and he fought the urge to pounce on her. She giggled and reached for the speaker, turning the music down.

"Hi," she said, pushing her glasses back up her nose with her flour-coated index finger. Her dark hair was down, curled in ribbons, and her face was lightly covered in makeup. She looked stunning, and he wanted her with a hunger that wouldn't be squelched.

He lunged and grabbed her around the waist, getting a squeak out of her before he slammed his lips to hers, marking her, then thrusting his tongue in as one hand moved into her dark hair and the other lowered to grip one of those firm ass cheeks.

"Mmm, hell of a way to welcome a man home, lass," he mumbled when he pulled back for a breath.

Rebecca gulped then nodded, licking her lips and making him growl when she pulled at them with her teeth.

A sizzle from the stove drew her attention away, and she turned to attend something in a skillet.

Pax stepped up behind her and wrapped his arms around her tiny waist, oblivious to the delicious smell coming from the pan; he was too entranced with the lilac fragrance in Becca's hair. "I could seriously get used to this, Bec," he whispered into her ear as he moved her hair aside and nibbled at her neck.

"Pax," she giggled as his hand moved up the jersey to cup her breast.

"This jersey has never looked so good, baby. But I'd rather get you out of it."

She gasped as his other hand slid up her side. She swatted it away and scolded him. "Let me at least get the stew finished."

He grumbled then finally looked down to see what she was doing. A large pot was boiling and she was stirring it while a dozen sea scallops browned in some butter. His belly grumbled, but it was his cock that took center stage as he began to run the throbbing shaft across Becca's ample bottom.

"God, I want you."

"I figured you'd had quite enough salmon, and I'd enough turkey, for a few days." Becca continued, as if he wasn't swelled to bursting. "Plus, I wanted to dazzle you with my cooking skills. Irish fish stew." She looked back at him shyly, and he grinned.

"Sweetness, you constantly dazzle me. But your first mistake was wearing my jersey with nothing underneath it." He squeezed her breast firmly, confirming his suspicions.

She tried to hold her composure as she lifted the skillet and poured the scallops into the pot then turned the stove eye to low, plopping the lid back onto the simmering stew. She whipped around, a mischievous grin on her beautiful face.

"Oh, just wait 'til you see this," she tittered again as she lifted the jersey that was tied at one corner to reveal the thong. It read, "Release the Kraken."

Pax was torn between amusement and arousal as he groaned and pulled her back against him. "You naughty little *naia*. Whatever am I going to do with you?" His lips claimed hers again as he lifted her. Her legs wrapped around his hips and he backed them into the wall.

Becca's passion was burning as hot as his as he began to lift the jersey over her head and tossed it to the floor.

"How *dare* you disrespect Poseidon's property!" She gaped, even as she ran her hands through his locks, still damp from his shower.

"This is Poseidon's property right here." He buried his head in her bosom and began loving her breasts, getting little mewing sounds from her that stroked his desire to a roiling peak. He was peeling the thong down when Rebecca protested. "What is it, angel?" he asked and pulled back to look into her glowing green eyes.

"I want you naked, too."

He smirked. "Anything my Amphitrite desires." He jerked his tank top off in one fell swoop.

"Mmm," the moan that came from her lips nearly had him reeling. "God, Paxton, I love your muscles. They're so sexy." She roved her hands over his naked torso, loving his hard flesh with adoring caresses; fingertips danced over his shoulders, down his pecs, across his abs.

"Nothing is sexier than you are, sweetness." He kissed her creamy mounds to prove it, then kissed her lips hard once more as he jerked the thong aside and wiggled his shorts down his hips. When he entered her, he nearly came undone. "Shit, baby... Damn! How are you even sweeter than last night?"

He focused his attentions fully on pleasuring his sea goddess, watching her face as he made love to her against the wall, loving her gasps, her moans, and her body taking him in with such ease. He soon moved them from the wall to the low, island countertop, afraid he would hurt her back in his fury to make her his. And she was his, wholly and completely, as she split apart, wave after wave lapping her, enfolding him, beckoning him closer and closer to capsizing.

"Pax," she gasped when she came up to the surface from the abyss he'd thrust her into.

"Yes, my sweetness," he gritted his teeth, so close to surrender as his hand moved up her thigh to grip her tighter to him, even as her legs wrapped tighter around his hips. He groaned.

"I-I want to... to captain the ship."

If he hadn't been so close to an orgasm, he would have full out laughed. But he could do nothing but yield to his little dolphin, the mermaid of Poseidon's sea, the siren that had sank her claws so deep into him that he knew there was nothing that could disconnect her from him.

He guided them to the floor, positioning her atop him where she mounted him like a seahorse. She was the goddess of the sea, after all. Her hands moved over his chest and she gasped and groaned and climbed, her bottom bouncing on him with a rhythm as old as the sea itself. And he succumbed, overcome by the tides she commanded in him.

As he came back to shore, he grinned as he looked up at his queen, feeling love seep from every pore of his skin. He loved her, her fickleness, her sweetness, her nerdiness. All of her. And when this phony engagement was over, he was going to ask her out on a real date and court her, win her heart. Historical romance book boyfriends eat your hearts out!

"WHAT IS *THIS*?" Pax growled, slamming his phone down onto the table with an angry fist, the fury on his face unlike anything Rebecca had seen before.

She took one look at the text message, and her stomach sank. The eyes that looked down on her were furious. "Pax, I—"

"You let Madison *bribe* you?"

"No, I—"

"I don't know what makes me madder: the fact that you accepted a bribe or that you find money more valuable than what we have between us!"

"Paxton, I—" she began again, only to be cut off.

"How *could* you?"

He was hurt. She was surprised but not completely. After all, this was a shot to his pride and nothing more...right?

"I mean, I understand you need the money, Rebecca, for your mom and all. But all you had to do was ask me. I would have given you anything you needed. This... this is a low blow."

"Paxton, I didn't..." But she didn't have the heart to tell him that it had been *Veda* not her that had done this. She'd told Veda about what Madi had said, and Veda, without her knowledge, had taken it upon herself to go to Madison and accept a bargain. It wasn't the first time Rebecca's twin sister had pretended to be her. Hell, all she had to do was cover her tattoos with that expensive makeup she had, take out her nose ring, throw her hair up, don a pair of glasses, and steal some of Becca's clothes, and they were identical. As much as it upset her that Veda had done such a sneaky thing, the look on Paxton's face hurt more. But she simply couldn't tell him that it had been Veda; he hated her sister enough already. "I'm sorry." She lowered her head.

"Sorry! Were we gonna talk about this or were you just gonna up and split when the money transfer was complete?"

Becca didn't know all the details about what had taken place. Although she planned to tear her sister up one side and down another. She shook her head.

"Do I have any say on the matter at all?" His blue eyes tore into her so deep that she winced, but then she remembered how he'd taken her by storm at the hospital that day.

"I didn't have a say when you first took control of the situation, now did I?" she retorted; he wasn't blameless about all this either.

"I was trying to save us both. I reacted as quickly as I could. The media are blood-thirsty hounds. We were very lucky things worked out like they did." Pax huffed and turned, running his hands through his long curls. "After all I did, this is the thanks I get. Back-stabbed? I should've known better."

Becca's heart tore at that. Fresh blood seeped out and poured down her body, all the way to her toes; it hurt. "What do you mean?"

"Madi warned me, and I should've listened, but I was too blinded by your purity to think you'd do something so devious."

Becca gulped. "Pax, I—"

"Go pack up your things. I'll have you driven home. The jig is up; I don't wanna see you again."

PAXTON'S MOOD was toxic at practice that next day. He couldn't focus on anything except the rage building inside him. How could Becca throw away everything? All for money. His love, his charity, his sacrifices, and for what? A measly three million dollars. Brooke had been the one to send the message to him, and he'd not questioned it at the time.

Brooke: I thought you might find this interesting. The text message had said.

It was a screenshot of a check made out to Rebecca Ryan. And his heart had broken in two. But he'd not really talked to Rebecca about it. Not gotten her side of the story. Although, he had no desire at the time to hear it, he did now. Now that he'd had time to think about what it meant, and why she'd done it. He wasn't as angry now so much as hurt. Why did everyone he cared for have to up and disappoint him? And she hadn't fought to stay. She'd simply up and left as he'd asked. Was he not worth fighting for?

That was why he was so angry. Because if she'd loved him in return, she wouldn't have been able to leave so easily.

Just like your father, the thought reverberated through his head.

Pax smashed into the dummy on the two-man sled and shoved with all his might, thrusting his anger, pain, and fury into the equipment. His blood pressure shot up, and he roared as it moved easily across the turf.

He ran his drills robotically, his mind searching for answers that he probably would never get.

It was all a big mistake, he told himself. To trust anyone else. To let her into his heart like he had. She'd seemed sweet and innocent, but perhaps she'd never been. It had all been a game. Madi had been right; Rebecca was just another gold-digger.

Paxton shuffled into the locker room to shower, seeing Brett, Quil, Josh, and TJ looking forlorn.

"What's wrong?" he grumbled, not understanding why their faces were as tight as his own.

"It's Sky. There's been an accident," Brett answered.

"Is she ok?" he looked around for Trav but knew that he'd probably already left to go meet her—wherever she was or was headed to.

"We don't know anything beyond the fact that her Navigator was hit head-on. Totaled."

"Is she alive?" Concern pulled at his heart for his friend, his team-mate, and the woman Travis Redmond held higher than anyone, even his brothers.

"She's alive... but it doesn't sound good, man," Josh stated, looking down.

"Fuck." Pax fell to the bench; his body overcome with adrenaline and worry.

"Look, I know we aren't all Christians here." Brett's eyes fell to Paxton's then. "But I think we should have a quick team prayer for Skyla. Would you guys be alright with that?"

Every man stepped forward, all fifty-three Gladiators, and bowed as Brett began to speak softly, asking for Skyla's safety and protection. Not a dry eye was left when he finally said, "Amen," and they all rose.

Just when Paxton thought his day couldn't get any worse, the unthinkable had happened; his family was in danger and the shock vibrated through him like a gun blast.

"TRAVIS!" Becca was shocked to see Travis Redmond sitting in the waiting area of the hospital as she moved through the corridor.

His handsome face looked up, covered in tears and redness, and a jolt went through her heart.

"What happened?"

"Becca." Travis bounded up from his seat and clasped her shoulders. "It's Sky. She... she's been in an accident. They think she's got a concussion and she..." he trailed off and looked down, a man in turmoil.

"Oh, my goodness. I'm so sorry. Is she going to be ok?"

Travis nodded, but his lip quivered as if he were holding something back. Her eyes held his as he wiped at his tears. She'd never seen him so distraught, and it tugged at her heart. It was like a needle pulling a thread through her body as she moved forward to embrace him. She felt his big frame shudder as he expelled his emotions.

Where were the others? Where was Paxton? Then it occurred to her. It was Saturday, they would be heading off to Kansas City for their away game. No one was coming.

Travis was having to bear the burden of this alone.

"Trav," came a familiar female voice, and Becca turned to see Madison glowering at her.

Becca released him as Travis saw Madi. He moved toward her, pulling her into his embrace.

"Oh, Madi, I can't believe it. I—"

"Oh God, I'm so sorry. I don't even know what to say." Madi's own emotions took hold of her, and she and Travis mourned together, holding each other tightly.

That's when Becca realized what had happened.

She took one last look at their sorrowful hold on one another, hugged her middle, and wordlessly stepped back out into the lonely hallway to go retrieve her mother.

"How the hell are we supposed to win this game without Ares?" Pax grumbled at halftime, fiddling with his shoulder pads as Brett's lips tightened.

They were down by two touchdowns and getting killed. All of them were worn out, sore, and not up for another hour and a half of getting their asses handed to them like they'd been the first half.

"Have a little faith, Pax," Josh stated and patted Paxton's back as he passed by.

"We're a team. One man isn't going to make or break us," their stoic captain answered.

"Bullshit. We're getting slaughtered out there, in case you haven't noticed, *Zeus*. You can't score, and Linc and I can't stop them. What do you suggest? We need our running back, among other things," Pax smarted.

Brett wiped the sweat from his brow and stepped forward. "In case *you* haven't noticed, Poseidon, we're *all* on edge tonight. Not just you!"

"At least Skyla's still *with* us," Pax sassed and moved to turn.

He didn't get far before Brett's hand came to his throat and shoved his back hard against the locker. Despite that Pax weighed more and was just as tall, Brett's dominance overcame him—strength born from authority not size or power. Pax was helpless under the intense eyes of the mighty Zeus. "Ow, dude."

"Shut the fuck up, and quit acting like a little brat who lost his damn toy." Brett's fist slammed hard against the side of his head, and Paxton swore he'd never seen his QB that angry—alright maybe that one other time when Langley had attacked Madi. "You're so self-absorbed sometimes, Paxton. I swear to God. You don't even know what's going on right under your nose."

"What are you talking about?" Pax choked out.

"You don't know, do you?"

"Know *what*?" Pax gripped the wrist that captured his neck tightly.

"Skyla lost the baby, Pax."

Realization dawned on him. *Holy shit!* He'd forgotten that Skyla was pregnant. His breath whooshed out as Brett released him.

"No, you've been too busy in your own damn grief to see anyone else's. Of course you wouldn't know how that felt though, would you? You've never loved anyone aside from yourself! Love isn't something you want. It's a joke, right? Well, tell that to Travis, who could give a shit less about this game right now! Now, you get your ass out there and do what you were trained to do; you stop the rush, you stop the pass. Play defense like your damn life depends on it."

Pax couldn't even come up with a response as he stared blankly back into the face of a man he admired as much as he did his uncle Kawai.

"Quil, let's go show these Chiefs that the Gods of the Gridiron aren't backing down without a fight. Let's go win this game, for Ares."

"For Ares!" Quil's fist hit Brett's.

And just like that, Pax's head was back in the game.

CHAPTER FIFTEEN

"How are you holding up, buddy?" Zeus asked Travis as he shook his hand and pulled him in for a half hug.

They'd all met up after practice three nights later at Brett's favorite pub, Trenches, not far from their houses in Morgan Falls—Pax, Brett, Josh, Travis, TJ, Berkley, Linc and Quillan.

Skyla had come home from the hospital just the day prior, following a D&C and observation after the head-on collision. The girls were all hanging out with Sky tonight, so the guys had decided to pull Trav out and see if they could cheer him up and surround him with a little team spirit. He'd not come back to practice today. He was returning to work on Thursday, so it'd been Zeus's idea to bring him out for a round of drinks; he'd reluctantly obliged.

"As good as can be expected," Trav answered and returned Pax's grin with a mock-slug to his jaw, getting a laugh out of Pax.

"Well, we're glad she's home and resting now," Pax stated, simply because he wasn't sure what to say.

"Sorry for your loss, *amigo*," Quil patted Travis's shoulder with eyes that reflected his sorrow.

"Thanks, Hades." Trav nodded. He greeted the others, and Brett motioned for a round of the Bud in his hand as they all sat around a table he'd reserved in the back.

"So, do we know who did this?" It was TJ who asked the question.

"I have my suspicions, seeing as she got one of the biggest crime bosses in Atlanta arrested and he's looking to serve the remainder of his life in a maximum-security prison."

"Oh, jeez," Pax whistled.

"I thought she was safe," Brett said with a frown.

"Yeah, she and I did too, for a time. I had a feeling this wasn't over. Don't you sometimes hate when you're right?" Travis sighed with a humorless laugh and thanked the server who sat his beer down before him.

"But you said the judge didn't grant bail so how can he—?" Linc began.

"I said he was *one* of the biggest crime bosses. He's not the only one. Geraci's part of a crime family. He was one of several."

"There's more bosses?" Serious Zeus asked, brows drawn.

"Sky said she thought there were two more, four in total. One died many years back in a fire at his club."

"His name was Perelli, right?" Berkley asked, and Trav nodded, taking a sip of his beer.

"So, if he's havin' people follow her and attack her then what—?" Josh asked.

"She'll have a police escort now when I'm not around. When she's at work and when she's out and about. I was going to hire a body-guard, but her boss was quicker on the draw than I was, insisting she be protected at all times so now she will be."

"Well, that's gotta give you *some* peace of mind," Quil stated, and Travis nodded.

"I hate it for you though, brother. I know how excited you were for this baby." Lincoln patted his friend's shoulder. He'd known Trav longer than the rest of them had. They'd played in San Antonio together before getting traded to the Gladiators as a package deal from the Stallions.

Ares nodded solemnly and looked down. "Good thing is that she's able to have more children, and she only ended up with a mild concussion, a few cracked ribs, and some bruises and cuts. It could have been so much worse. Thank God for airbags."

"Well, here's to the small things then," Brett agreed and raised his beer.

"And here's to family, guys." Travis held up his own beer and gave them all a warm smile. "Thanks for always being here for me."

"Sláinte," Pax responded automatically, and his heart froze. He suddenly realized just how much he missed Rebecca: her laugh, her sweetness, her energetic spirit...and how much he loved that sexy, dark-haired Irish lass of his.

He loved her with a desperation that frightened him.

He'd not fully breathed in her absence. He'd just gone through the motions of his life without her this last week, and God, how empty it'd been since he told her to leave.

Pax had seen how quickly and fleeting life could be when Hunter had passed—and how devastating loss was. Now, with what had happened to Sky and Travis, it was like a clearing had opened up in his mind and heart.

He'd always kept himself distant, always prided himself on being aloof to love because of what happened with his father, always enjoyed being untied, untethered, free. But he'd not been truly free until he'd been in the presence of perfection and that perfection was Rebecca Christine Ryan.

He'd been an absolute and total fool. He needed his sweet naia, his Amphitrite—for what kind of sea god was he if he couldn't make waves? She was the tide to his surf, the sand to his beach, and the wind in his sails. She completed him in every sense of the word.

Now, it was time he manned up and told her.

THE WIND WAS cold as it hit Rebecca's back on her way into the apartment complex. She stopped dead in her tracks to see Paxton Guthrie standing outside her door, curly locks touching his shoulders, his hands shoved into his pockets. She almost dropped the bags in her hands as she looked up into his solemn, handsome face, into those blue eyes she'd literally lost herself to. He looked as beautiful as always, square jaw covered in a short, trim beard of blond with a red tint where the rays of sun caught it.

Becca gulped as she took in his tan sweater and jean clad frame. He looked downright edible, even if her heart split at his words the last time they'd seen one another.

"Here, let me grab those for you." Pax moved for the bags literally falling from her arms, and she shivered as his warm palm brushed her flesh.

"Th—thank you," she mumbled as she continued to stare at him like he was a ghost.

It had been almost two weeks since she'd seen him. Two long weeks. Two weeks of torment. Two weeks of regret. Two weeks of feeling like the lowest scum on earth. Two weeks of feeling like he hated her, and he should, for she'd not said anything back to him. Nothing to defend herself. Nothing to excuse the why of what had happened.

"I—uh. Mind if I come in?"

"Sure…I mean, no. Of course! Please, come in."

He nodded and followed her as her shaky hands fumbled with the keys. Finally, the lock gave way, and she entered first, knowing he wouldn't go inside before her.

They moved silently to the kitchen counter. When Veda saw Pax, she growled before retreating to her room, laptop in tow.

Veda's attitude had only worsened in the last couple weeks, and Becca knew it had everything to do with Quillan—or, better yet, the absence of Quillan. She and Veda, despite living together, hadn't spoken to one another, aside from the shouting match that had ensued the day Becca came home from Paxton's, tail set firmly between her legs.

"HOW COULD YOU?" *Becca asked, throwing her bag down dramatically into the empty recliner next to her sister.*

"One day you'll thank me for getting you out of this mess."

"I don't need you to rescue me, Veda."

"Obviously you do!"

"I didn't tell you to go to Madison. I was going to—"

"No, you weren't. You would have chickened out like you do everything else. We need that money and now this BS is over and done with."

And my heart along with it, *Becca thought.*

"You could have given me a heads up. You made me look like a fool."

"Oh, you got to be the bad guy for a change? So sorry, little nun. Doesn't feel so good, does it? But someone has to do the dirty deeds around here."

"Not every man is evil, Veda." Tears came to her eyes then.

"I just brought you to reality before he had a chance to break your heart in two, like he would've if you'd a'let him."

"I can stand up for myself."

"No, you can't! You're soft, just like Mam."

Nothing Becca had ever said was going to convince Veda that their father wasn't a malicious man for leaving them or that all men weren't their father. It was just gonna take time...and love. Which was something Veda had never had from a man. Thus, her hate for them all.

"I want you to stay out of my business, from now on. I mean it."

"Oh, did you grow a set of balls, little sis? Well grand. Since you don't need me anymore, I'll be in my room!" With that, Veda had stalked off, slammed her door and had not else to say since.

NOW, Becca remembered the conversation all too well and how Pax had told her he didn't want to see her again. She felt tears sting her eyes and pulled her chin up, praying she had the strength to have this conversation in the first place.

"I had no right to say the things I said to you," Pax said softly, slowly as he looked into her face. "I was angry and hurt, mostly hurt."

She pulled a breath in and attempted to rein her heart in, but it hammered away at the closeness of his body to hers.

"I didn't mean what I said about not wanting to see you again. I mean, I did at the time, but... Dammit Becca, why did you do it?"

"I didn't," Becca stated truthfully.

Pax rolled his eyes and threw a shaky hand through his messy locks.

"It was Veda," Becca finished. "She went to Madi behind my back, pretending to be me."

"Ha," Pax laughed humorlessly, "of course she did," he muttered. "No surprise that she hates me. I get it, though. I'm not to be trusted. I'm an outlander, right?"

"Pax," Becca rebuked.

"No, just hear me out, okay? Then I'll leave, but I need to apologize. I overreacted. I'm not good with relationships. Women. I don't even know that I've had a real relationship with a woman. Ever. I've been with many over the years. Took them out on dates, to bed, but I haven't had a steady girlfriend. So, I'm a little clueless as to how the whole give and take thing works. And I'm sorry that I let you down. But as I understand, that's what people do. They take out their frustrations on those they love most."

Becca's heart had stopped in her chest. She was frozen. What was he saying?

"I'm sorry, Rebecca. I'm sorry that I was a dick. I'm sorry that I hurt you, but I've come to realize that life is really short, too short to let something like money stand in the way of who I love. I don't care that you took the bribe...or Veda for that matter. I don't care that you chose the money instead of me. All I care about is that I love you, and I couldn't wait another minute to tell you that. I messed up, and I want a second chance to prove myself to you."

Tears flowed down her cheeks at the genuine look on his handsome face. She was two steps from walking into his arms and telling him how much she reciprocated his feelings when Veda's voice intervened from the hallway.

"Why?"

Pax frowned as he looked her over with surprise and unease. "*Why?*" He seemed dumbfounded.

"Yes, *why* do you want another chance?" Veda's voice rose as she came to stand next to Becca, between Becca and Paxton.

"Because I love your sister, Veda. I don't want to live without her in my life."

"And you don't care that she chose to take the money?" Veda's eyes were unbelieving. Of course she would assume he had an ulterior motive for coming here—didn't *all* men?

"It wasn't her who chose that, was it?"

Veda snorted. "She still walked away from you."

"Because I told her to."

"And what makes you think she didn't choose that?"

"Because she loves me."

"Oh?" Veda turned to look at Becca. "Is that true?"

Becca nodded and smiled into her sister's stunned face. "I do."

"So all is forgiven, then?" Veda smirked.

"That's what love is, sis. Forgiving someone, even when they make the wrong choices. Even when they think they're doing the right thing for your sake." Becca reached out and took Veda's hand. "I can love you both, Veda. I have enough to go around without sacrificing one or the other."

Veda's lips quivered. "And what if he hurts you again?" Her green eyes bore into Pax's face with fury.

"Then I'll forgive him again. Until he sees that my love for him is unshakeable, that nothing can destroy what I feel for him. Love is stronger than any other force on earth. It can overcome even the biggest obstacles in our paths."

Veda covered her hand over her mouth and turned to look at Becca, then she reached out and grabbed Pax's arm. "And you? Will you take care of her? Keep her safe?"

"I swear on my life."

"Take this and repeat after me." Veda pulled a Claddagh ring from her hoodie pocket. It had been their mother's. Becca gasped as Pax took it and smiled down at Becca. "I pledge my hands that I may be your friend, my crown that I may always remain loyal, and my heart that I may love you as best I can."

Paxton stepped forward and placed the ring, heart inwards on the third finger of her right hand, as Veda instructed. He then winked at Veda, as if to say, "I can take it from here." Veda smirked playfully and stepped back to give them some privacy—what privacy she afforded anyway, protective big sister that she was.

"Rebecca Christine Ryan. I know we aren't really engaged and this whole time it's been 'fake,' but my sweetness, *nothing* has been fake about how I feel for you. Somewhere along the line, I gave you my heart, and I would willingly do it all over again, despite the many hurdles we've faced along the way. I don't know what our future holds or that you even want to be my wife one day, but I do know that I want you in my life. I want you to be there when I've had a rough day, I want to hold you, laugh with you, enjoy all the time I have with you. I want to share my dreams with you, my hopes, and my fears. I pledge my hands in friendship, my crown in loyalty, and my heart in love eternal to you. Do you accept this token of my affections?"

Becca beamed into his equally as happy face and nodded. He pushed the ring onto her finger. A perfect fit, if she did say so herself, and peered up into the handsome face that held her future.

He pulled her into his arms then and kissed her soundly, pulling back only for a breath.

"Veda? Where are you going?" Becca asked as Veda began to shove her shoes on and gather her keys.

"I think you two need a little alone time, don't you?" she smirked. "Besides, now that you got your man, I think it's time I went and got mine."

Becca laughed, and so did Pax, his forehead hitting hers softly as he admired the ring on her finger.

"I love you, sweetness."

"And I love you, Poseidon. Even if you are a jealous god."

"Only jealous when it comes to you."

He leaned down and kissed her again; softly, sweetly. She kissed him back with force, and soon, his lips were hungry and his passions needy as his hands roved her back.

"Mmm," he moaned, "where's your mom?"

"Hospital. I have an hour before I have to go get her."

"I might need more than that," he teased as he backed her down the hallway toward her bedroom.

"Well, that's all you get, hippie boy."

"Your tongue is bound to get you spanked, Amphitrite."

Becca giggled as his hands went to the hem of her shirt, then moaned as his palms touched her bare flesh. "Mmm." She kissed him back as his body pinned hers against the wall. "You've promised that before and not delivered."

"Well, my naughty little *naia*, I think it's time your god kept his word, don't you?" His voice deepened as he raised her hands above her head with one hand and feasted on her neck. All the while, her body quivered as his other hand teased her flesh, moving his fingertips over her as if he had all the time in the world. Her pants were down around her ankles and her shirt was tugged up above her bra, her nipples hard and aching, when he finally spun her around. She heard his zipper give and felt the velvety soft tip of him touch her ass cheek. She moaned as he began to rub it across her plump flesh, then felt his shaft smacking her left and right across her butt cheeks. It might've been funny if she hadn't been so aroused that her wetness oozed down her legs, shamelessly. Her cheeks pinkened, and she felt dizzy with need for him.

"Mmm, Pax. I want you inside me, please?"

"Are you begging me, sweetness?"

"Yes, I'm begging. I need you. I want you."

He chuckled even as he spun her back around and kissed her hard, grabbing her breast and kneading it in his huge palm.

She was scooped up into his massive arms as if she weighed no more than a feather, and settled onto her bed, where her god smiled down on her, touching her face as if she were a precious piece of glass he feared he would break.

"I love you," he said again. God would she ever tire of hearing his deep voice say such a wonderful phrase?

"I love you," she answered back and grabbed for his hard manhood, anticipating the feel of him inside her. "Please, make me yours, Paxton."

"How can I say no to my sweet goddess?" His hand peeled the lace down from her bra. "You always wear the sexiest damn lingerie to be such a bashful little historian." His mouth took her nipple in as his hand moved in between her legs.

She spread them easily, wanton as a slag, but she didn't care. He was the only answer to the ache that resided there, the only cure for the ailment throbbing within her.

They both gasped and moaned as their sexes met. Pax kissed her passionately as he began to slide smoothly into her, shivering when he reached the hilt.

"My god, Becca, it feels like it's been an eternity without you, my love. How did I ever survive?"

"Never again." She punished him with her mouth, kissing him hard and passionately, letting her tongue torture his as she wrapped her legs tighter around his waist.

"Oh shit, baby," he whimpered as she rocked with him, higher and higher, arching her hips with his. "So good, Becca, so damn good."

He cupped her bottom and gripped it hard, pumping into her while her soul-rending release came. Pax was climbing with her, over the wall of bliss, and skating down it with her as she surfaced. He then dipped into her slowly, achingly slowly, as his body loved hers.

She'd barely had a chance to breathe before he was pulling out and flipping her over.

"Now what did you say about that spanking, little *naia?*"

Becca gasped in surprise as his big palm lightly smacked her bottom with a thwack. "Paxton Andrew Guthrie, how dare you!" her cheeks reddened as he did it again.

"Ms. Ryan, you know you shouldn't tempt a god."

But she moaned and forgot his words as she felt his hard shaft filling her again. "Oh, God," she whimpered.

"That's Poseidon to you, sweetness, you keep forgetting. Do you need another spanking to help jar your memory?"

But she gripped his muscular thigh and dug her nails in as she pushed her bottom into his thrust, and he took her from behind, grunting as the pleasure became too much for him. She quickly saw who owned who as his moans became thicker, breathier. His hands gripped her waist with a possessiveness that touched her even deeper than where his cock was lodged.

Soon, they were spiraling together as they crashed into one another, not unlike the waves of the sea he was the god of. Their releases were perfectly timed and assaulted them with such force that it took their very breaths.

They came down from their highs slowly as Pax stroked her back and hair, groaning his love for her as her inner walls continued to milk every last ounce from his rigid member.

"Oh, my love. I missed you," he confessed when he flipped her over and pulled her to his sweaty frame.

"Hopefully you missed more than my body," she smarted even as he chuckled and his lips touched her forehead.

"Oh, aye, lass. I missed all of ye."

"Don't you dare…" she giggled and grunted when he grabbed her breast.

"I still have to make love to you in my kilt."

"You did *not* buy a kilt."

"I swear I did." He gave her a crooked grin as she looked back into his face, astonished. "Just because Halloween's over, doesn't mean I can't dress up for my lady."

"You are full of surprises. You know that, Pax Guthrie?"

He kissed her again, and she lingered there when he finally pulled back. "We do stupid things for love, you know?" He grinned again, and she melted for the tenth time in a half hour.

Suddenly, he sat up, his brows hitting his forehead.

"Holy shit, Becca! That's ridiculous."

Becca felt her cheeks flame as she looked to the wall of her room Paxton was focused on. She gulped as he took in the numerous photos, posters, and Fatheads of the man she adored, in various forms of dress and football poses. Her entire wall was dedicated to the celebrity crush that had become her real life one; the one who was now her lover and love of her life.

When Pax looked back to her, she shrugged.

"My, my…" he stroked his chin. "I think I need to bend you back over for a spanking, little *naia*."

"Oh, is that so?" Her hand moved beneath his sweater and over his big chest, loving the feel of the muscles that moved beneath her palms.

"Oh yes, I need to punish you for your sins while I look at the wall you've dedicated to your idol."

Becca laughed. "The bible does say, 'Put no other gods before me.'" Becca frowned. "I've been a bad girl, Poseidon."

"Yes, you have indeed." He smirked as he looked the wall over again.

"Take your sweater off, though, before you do so that I can admire your chest," she cooed, even as she began tugging at his shirt.

He grinned knowingly, aware of how sexy he was, how sexy she thought he was.

"Perhaps you were named for the wrong Greek, though?"

"Oh?" he asked, peeling the sweater over his head and tossing it aside.

"Yup, you should have been Narcissus."

Paxton laughed and pulled her back to him. He began loving her all over again, loving her like she'd never imagined she could be loved.

PAXTON SMILED as he watched Becca put her mother to bed and come out the door to greet him.

"She gonna be ok?" he asked.

Becca nodded. "She has three rounds left. Then they'll do another PET scan, and we'll go from there."

"Well, I handled the medical bills. You and Veda no longer have to worry about losing the apartment."

"Pax, you didn't have to—"

He held his finger to her lips, shaking his head as he smiled big. "I wanted to. I'm your fiancé, remember? I can't have my bride losing her home."

Becca looked down, her lip trembled but she didn't cry. "That was very generous of you."

"Becca, I would do anything for you. You know that, right? Move any mountain. Give you the shirt off my back if it meant keeping you warm, keeping you safe."

She gave him a sweet smile and pulled his hand to her face, nuzzling it lovingly.

"I know you gave the money back to Madi. She called to talk some sense into me, even after I'd already decided what I was going to do." He held her gaze, wondering why he'd ever doubted her trustworthiness. He knew she'd told Veda about the bribe, and Veda had been the one who'd "officially" taken it. They were sisters. Sisters told each other everything… or so Madi said, anyway.

"So, I haven't seen Jeremiah lately. Was that you?" Becca's dark brow rose, her lovely lips puckering.

Pax shuffled his feet, looking down. "Let's just say, I had someone go talk to him. They were *very* persuasive about the distance he needed to keep from you." He would say no more on the matter, for the thought of another man touching his beautiful Irish goddess was infuriating, bringing out Poseidon's fury.

Becca looked up, her emerald eyes as green as the island she reigned from sparkling back at him in the light from the hallway. "I love you, Paxton Guthrie." The words, once more, stole his heart and had him a puddle of goo on the floor.

"And I you, Sass—"

"Don't." She shivered, and he smirked. "My mother's home now. I don't want to wake her raving like a banshee while my lover does unspeakable things to me."

"Mmm, what unspeakable things did you have in mind, my little *naia*?"

The giggle that came from her throat excited him beyond words.

"Later, Pax. I gotta have you anticipating our next union, lover."

Pax practically growled as he pulled her to him and savored her sweet, honey lips with a deep kiss. "I'm always anticipating that, my love."

Becca giggled again when he pulled back. "So, I did something." She pulled her lips in, looking mischievous, and his arousal began to throb uncomfortably between them.

"Oh? And what did you do? Were you a naughty little goddess?"

Becca put her fingers up "measuring" an inch, and Pax tried to quiet his laugh so as not to wake Kathleen. Becca then pulled him back to the kitchen where she moved to the table and grabbed up an envelope.

She looked apprehensive as she bit into her lip and her cheeks flushed. "I took it upon myself to have your mother pull your adoption records. I know you've always wondered about your origins and who you are, so I wanted to find out for you. I'm a historian, after all, so I couldn't just let the past be the past."

Paxton's heart hammered in his chest, anticipation, dread and excitement racing through his veins. He gulped audibly.

"I wanted to give it to you for Christmas, but I've never been very patient."

She started to hand the envelope to him, but he shook his head.

"You...you read it to me." His hands were too shaky; he wouldn't be able to hold it steady.

She smiled softly and looked down at the papers before her. "Your birth name is Alexander Miller. You were born in Burbank, California. Your mom was—"

"Annie Miller, father was a trucker from Alaska who went by the nickname of Bear because he was such a big dude." He knew all that. Tara had actually given him those records years ago.

"Yes. Well, I dug deeper than that. I found your family tree and did the DNA ancestry for you. Your roots are half Australian, a quarter German, and a quarter Scandinavian. Now you know who you are."

She looked apprehensively up at him—fearful she'd overstepped, he was sure. But Pax was overjoyed. That she cared enough to do something so significantly sentimental touched a place deep within him, and he grinned big.

"Becca, this is... Wow! Thank you. This means so much." He reached for her hand, then pulled her into his arms, grateful to have a woman so beautiful both inside and out. A woman who genuinely cared for him and listened to him. A woman who had given him the gift of a past... a woman who he couldn't wait to share his future with.

EPILOGUE

"Veda?" Becca knocked lightly on Veda's door, hearing her cries echoing through the quiet hallway.

She'd decided not to stay the night with Paxton. She hadn't known when, or if, Veda would be home, and she'd left her mother alone far too many nights as it was—despite that Mam said she was fine and for them to stop worrying about her.

She looked fine. In fact, Becca's mam was starting to look healthier than she had in years. The glow and color was returning to her cheeks, and there was a pep in her step she hadn't had before. The treatments seemed to be working, her illness appeared to be diminishing; Becca knew it to be true.

She felt her heart break a little when she opened her sister's door to see Vey sitting there on her bed, sobbing into her hands.

So, the reunion Veda had spoken of must not have gone so well.

Once Pax had come to confess his love, it appeared to light a fire under Veda's ass to go talk to Quillan, and Becca had been glad. Her sister hadn't seemed happy in a long while, but that Halloween night Becca had seen a sparkle in Veda's eyes that signified hope when she'd been dancing in Quillan's arms. It'd been subtle, and Veda wouldn't admit to it to save her life from damnation—for she really *was* that stubborn—but Becca knew she cared for Quil, even if he didn't return those feelings.

Becca prepared for the worst as she came to sit next to her sister, pulling Veda's hands from her face and coaxing her twin to her chest. Becca stroked Veda's thick hair and let her sob for the longest time. No words were needed between them. They were twins; she felt her sister's pain as acutely as if it were her own.

"I take it you didn't get your man tonight?"

"I chickened out because I'm a feckin' coward," Veda choked out and wiped at her nose, angrily.

"You are the bravest person I know."

"It's all an act," Veda retorted heatedly and pulled her head from Becca's chest. "I didn't go to him."

"Why?"

"Well, first off, I don't even know where he lives."

"You have his number, you could've called him." Veda just glared at Becca, as if she was so far beyond that. Becca added, "You could've had me ask Paxton." No, that wouldn't have been an option for her prideful sister, either. "Ok, what's second?"

Veda furrowed her brows.

"You said, 'first off.' That leads me to believe you had other reasons, too."

Veda huffed and looked away before finally saying, "What do I even say to him? 'Hi. Remember me? I was Medusa. We fucked at the Halloween party.' Besides, I'm pretty sure he thinks I'm the one who sold him out on social media. Hell, I'm no better than a traitor—look at what I did to you. I just fuck people's lives up, apparently."

"No, Veda, you don't. You were trying to protect me. And furthermore, how could he *ever* forget you? I saw some serious sparks flying at that hospital cafeteria, so he *obviously* didn't forget you. And you're not a sellout, you would never jeopardize his career. He just doesn't know you."

"He thinks I'm a bad-news slut."

"Were those his words?" Becca felt a flash of anger at the thoughts of Quillan speaking so ill of her twin, no matter that Veda hadn't made the best impression where the Gladiators were concerned.

"I know that's what he thinks of me." She left it at that, but Becca knew there was more to that statement with the edge in her sharp tone.

"Wait, what aren't you saying?"

"I saw him again, at *RISE* a couple weeks after Halloween."

"Oh." Becca blushed. So, they'd been seeing each other; that answered a few questions she'd had on the matter of Quil.

"I'll be quitting soon, by the way, as soon as I can get a steady thing going with modeling."

"I'm glad to hear that." Although Becca wasn't sure if this whole modeling thing was the right thing for Veda either.

"I got a few promising gigs from Brooke," Veda said as if trying to ease Becca's mind.

"Well that's good."

Veda gave her a withered smile. "She said I have a lot of potential."

"See, our lives don't suck as bad as you thought, lassie."

"Don't say that," Veda practically cringed, looking down, and Becca felt a jolt go through her—a chill down her spine that signified Veda's rolling confessions weren't over just yet.

"What is it, Vey? Please tell me. You know you can talk to me about anything."

"I know and I'm so grateful you're my sister. But I feel so ashamed."

"Why? There's nothing for you to be ashamed about."

"But there is... Becca, Quil and I didn't use protection at the Halloween party." Veda blew out, like her lungs had held the weight of the world and she could fully breathe now after expelling the secrets there in. "I didn't even think about it at the time. I mean, we were in the moment and it was so unexpected... I just took a test, and Becca, it's positive."

A ringing began in Becca's ears, as if she were falling. What kind of test? An STD test? What was her sister saying? That she had some horrible disease, and now Becca was at risk of losing her best friend? "Vey, what—?" Her panicked eyes must have alerted her sister, for Veda's next words stilled her heart completely.

"And I can't keep it. God knows I should, but I can't have a child born out of wedlock. Mam has enough to worry about... but it's eating me up inside." Veda's sobs returned as her lips quivered.

"Wait!" Becca almost shouted. But her heart was up in her throat, making the words come out in a croak. "Veda, *what* are you saying?"

She squeezed her sister's hands, and the look in Veda's eyes was hauntingly desperate and sorrowful. "Becca, I'm pregnant."

THE END

SNEAK PEEK AT ILLEGAL FORMATION
PROLOGUE

Q uillan "Hades" Layton looked back over to the intriguingly petite figure of Medusa. Dark ribbons of hair flowed out from under a crown of plastic snakes, some hissing, some striking, others tangled into the strands that turned mahogany where the light touched it. A black mask concealed the woman's face. Alabaster skin, as fine as any piece of china he'd ever seen, stood out beneath a sleeveless, midnight-black dress, covered in various colors of ink that weaved a pattern of endless stories over slim arms and an ample chest. Plump, milky breasts spilled forth beneath the plunging neckline. A trim waist and curvy hips greeted him, but it was the bright green eyes, as piercing as emeralds, that sparkled beneath the kitchen lights that drew him in.

Quil hadn't originally been that thrilled to join the party. Although he wasn't the *only* single guy present, he was one of the few. It had been a long time since he'd had the company of a woman in his bed and even longer since he'd been on a date. His wife, Rian, had died of a cocaine overdose over a year ago. Quillan had blamed himself, blamed his career, blamed God and anyone else whom he could, but ultimately Ri had loved her drug more than him or their little angel, Quinn, which had led to her snorting far more than she ever should have and ultimately, the action had stopped her heart.

Quil had been the one to find her, cold, blue-lipped, face covered in white powder, nose and forehead bloody where her head had dropped heavily onto the glass coffee table of her hotel room in death. Remnants of that scene bounced through his head like a metal ball in a pinball machine, hitting the nerves with rapid succession.

Which is why you need to avoid this woman, his brain screamed.

She turned from speaking to Brooke Taylor and a little diamond caught the light, twinkling in her nose. Piercings, tattoos, a come-hither glance in his direction--she was trouble; trouble with a capital T. She had to be by the sheer look of her alone. Becca had introduced her as Veda, such an enigmatic name for such an enigma of a woman.

Quil's eyes roved her once more, his fingertips itching to explore those tattoos of hers, the lines and curves of her body. Aside from those markings, she favored her twin in practically every way. Same height, same build, same enticing lips... But the mask reminded him so much of someone he'd met before.

Much to his delight--and dismay--the woman moved closer. It wouldn't do for him to allow her the opportunity to invade his private bubble of brood, but hell, it was Halloween after all and when was the last time Quil had enjoyed himself? Quinn was home safe for the night, with the nanny he'd known since her birth, a woman he trusted with her life. And he had nowhere else to be, nothing else to do.

"You make a fine Hades, I must say," the voice was as sultry as the body and rolled into his ears like a soothing melody.

"And you, a fine Medusa." Quil gripped one of the snakes laconically, watching her eyes follow his movements. "You look so familiar to me. Have we met before tonight?"

Something about a mask had always intrigued him. Elusive, mysterious, sexual. And this woman was all three things simultaneously.

"Oh, aye, we have, Quillan." He detected a slight accent. He, himself, had a slight Spanish one. His maternal grandmother was from Spain and never spoke a word of English to him. "A confusing language", she'd told him, so she'd taught him Spanish instead. His abuela had raised him while Quil's father worked two jobs to keep a roof over their heads.

Quil's brows rose, waiting for the stranger to elaborate. When she didn't, he grinned and brought his drink up. "Call me Quil."

"Oh, you don't prefer *Hades*?" The playful smirk that pulled at the beauty's lip made his belly flutter.

"One and the same. I figured that was assumed."

Veda laughed, sexy and husky. *Damn!* "I go by several names myself."

"Oh? Pray tell what the others are." It hadn't taken her more than sixty seconds to reel him in; he was a goner.

"In certain circles I've been called *Obsidian*." A long, pink tongue snaked out of her mouth akin to the serpents in her hair, slow and calculating, until it was fully unsheathed and licking her lips provocatively, a silver barbell tongue ring showcased.

Quil's sharp intake of breath seem to please Veda and he felt his cheeks flame in both surprise and familiarity. "Holy shit," he hissed under his breath.

She was the masked dancer who'd sat on his lap at *RISE*; the one who'd brought his entire body to life with the French kiss to end all French kisses. He could still feel the dancing metal flicking across his teeth and over his tongue while his body had been engulfed in flames of scorching desire.

"You remember me, dark god?"

Remember her? How in God's holy name could he ever forget her? Pushing her off his lap to tend to Paxton's bruised ego that night had been one of the hardest things he'd ever done in his life. He'd wanted to continue to feel her tongue on his own, on his body, on his cock.

Obsidian/Medusa/Veda's smile said she knew exactly what he

was thinking, and Quil felt his body heat rise as she took a step closer. Her hand pressed lightly to his bare pec and he stifled a growl, loving her delicate touch on his hungry flesh.

Just then, Brooke and TJ squared off in a surprising conversation that promised sexual gratification and an invitation for everyone to move outdoors to watch the women dance around the bonfire Pax and Becca had made out back.

Quil's body sizzled all over as Veda took his hand in hers and began to pull him outside. She playfully invited him to watch as he stood next to Pax and she and Becca lead the women around the bonfire, swirling and swaying, imitating the flames that consumed the crackling wood inside the fire pit.

Veda's movements were smooth and sexual, like she'd been on stage, so alluring and inviting, her focus solely on Quillan. He watched with bated breath, knowing that before the night was out she was gonna be his.

He couldn't wait!

***

Find out *exactly* what happens between Quil and Veda at Paxton's Halloween party.

(This book is set simultaneously as—and following the conclusion of —book 3)

PRE-ORDER IT HERE

AFTERWORD

Thank you *so* much for reading *PASS INTERFERENCE*.
I hope you enjoyed this fun, sweet, and tear-jerking third book of
the series. If so, please be sure to leave a review.

This book was fun to write, light-hearted and sweet, but of course
had to have some twists and a few dramatic moments—in typical
Shanna fashion.

***

The conclusion to the Gods of the Gridiron series is Book 4,
ILLEGAL FORMATION. Quillan—Hades—and Veda's story, is the
darkest book of the quartet. Hades has a lot of baggage, as you well
know, and Veda, too. So be warned, not all fairy tales are without
their traumatic moments. These two are tangled in a forbidden web
and one of them is bound to get burned.

It's set for a November 20th release date.

Pre-order your copy now.

BLURB:

Hell hath no fury... especially if you're *Hades*—the god of death.

TE, **Quillan Layton**, is settling into his role as the newest player for the Gladiators. He's embracing his brooding and dark character's namesake. Hell, it's easy to be such when your life is as skewed as his is. After all, he's a single dad and the widower of a former drug addict who's not looking for love—not in the slightest.

Though when he sees bad girl, **Veda Ryan**, at Paxton's Halloween party, he might just be eating crow. This tattooed, pierced, and cynical Irish "snake-charmer" has more up her sleeve than ink, and one scorching hot night with her isn't quite enough to satisfy the ravenous god within just dying to be unleashed.

Veda, the sharp-tongued twin of Becca's, is an unhappy cheerleader, reluctant stripper, and passionate model-wannabe with a determination as strong as her colorfully art-clad skin. She sees the tall, dark, and *delicious* half-Spanish sex god, Quillan, and knows immediately that she has to sink her teeth into him, come Hell or highwater, and does so that fateful Samhain night in an ***ILLEGAL FORMATION*** of epic proportions.

But Quil and Veda are in for a rude awakening. The old saying goes that if one plays with fire, one is bound to get burned and *burned* these two lovers will be as they fight their sizzling attraction for one another tooth and nail.

Will a devastating secret be enough to bring them colliding together or will it doom Hades and his Persephone to a fiery pit of never-ending regret?

This book is a forbidden/single dad bad girl romance that deals with abortion, a secret baby, violent sexual acts, and addiction.

READER DISCRETION IS ADVISED.

HEA GUARANTEED

ACKNOWLEDGMENTS

I just want to drop a quick thank you to all my new (and continued!) readers, supporters, and fans. I love that you are loving my football team, the Gladiators. Thanks for all your love, your collages, your awesome reviews, and taking the time out of your day to message me, tag me, and make me feel special. It means so so much!!!

—Kisses, Shanna

ALSO BY SHANNA SWENSON

~THE ABUNDANCE SERIES~

Abundance

Return to Abundance

Escape from Abundance

Stars over Abundance

Abundance Legacy

Starlight Valley: The prequel to Abundance (FREE ebook)

~THE GODS OF THE GRIDIRON SERIES~

PERSONAL FOUL: Prequel novella

UNSPORTSMANLIKE CONDUCT

FALSE START

PASS INTERFERENCE

ILLEGAL FORMATION
(COMING IN NOVEMBER)

~THE SIN AND SECRETS COLLECTION~

RISE: A Prequel Novella (Sin and Secrets)

(Coming November 13, 2020)

~Aurora Rose Reynold's HEA WORLD~

Until Kingston

(Coming 2021)

LEARN MORE AT WWW.SHANNASWENSON.COM

ABOUT SHANNA SWENSON

Shanna Swenson is a cardiac sonographer by day and a weaver of various fictional tales by night.

She's been an avid reader all her life and began writing at the age of fourteen. She finally published her first novel, *Abundance*, after it sat patiently on her laptop for well over fifteen years and she hasn't stopped writing since.

Shanna fits her zodiac sign of Cancer with a capital C and enjoys life's simplest things—sunsets, rain, and coffee—to name a few.

When Shanna's not supporting her fellow indies with her face buried in a book or writing her next novel/novella, she enjoys action and horror movies, pro football, hiking, working out, and traveling with her own "knight in shining armor".

You can find her on the following social media platforms.

Her website is www.shannaswenson.com

facebook.com/shannaswen

twitter.com/shanna_swenson

instagram.com/shannaswen_author

goodreads.com/Shannaswen

amazon.com/author/shannaswenson

pinterest.com/shannaswen

bookbub.com/profile/shanna-swenson

www.ingramcontent.com/pod-product-compliance
Lightning Source LLC
Chambersburg PA
CBHW020729210626
46807CB00016B/509